I0770779

GOTHIC GROVE

JA GEORGE

CONTENTS

GOTHIC GROVE

Gothic Grove
A Dark Paranormal Romance

By JA George

Original Formatting by: Mads at Breathless Lit (@breathlesslitpa)
Updated Kindle Formatting: JA George
Original Edits by: Paisley Prophit
Revisional Edits: Kendra at Spice Me Up Editing
Proof Reading: Bri (M
Cover Design By: Sam (damnfinesam.com)

Content Warnings and Triggers Warnings
This is a dark paranormal romance containing multiple POVs, and sexually explicit content featuring MF and MFM pairings. If you are at all disturbed or triggered by spice, dark content, or the paranormal - do not read this book. For real, turn back now – this book isn't for you. This book contains adult content and is intended for readers 18+. Many of my characters suffer from a variety of mental health issues. As you read, please keep in mind that everyone has their own perspectives and experiences with mental health issues. Everyone heals from trauma differently, particularly assault. I worked hard to be authentic in how my characters dealt with their traumas and life in general.

General TW's: dub-con, torture, kidnapping, possession, familial abuse, house fires, biting (vampires, duh), voyeurism, blood/blood magic during spice, edging, dom/sub relationships, going down, violence/mild-ish gore, revenge plots, abuse (including physical and emotion), SA (off page and very vague on page), drugging for purposes of torture, drug abuse and misuse, alcohol use, self-harming behaviors (cutting), suicidal ideation/attempts (off page attempts referenced), PTSD, trauma triggers w/flashbacks, anxiety/panic attacks, depression, and death of mythical creatures (but I promise everything is okay with them in the end so please don't DNF it because of that).

If you encounter errors in the book OR have other triggers you feel should be added, please reach out to me and not the 'Zon. Author email: authorjageorge@gmail.com
Author IG: PNWwritingWitch
Author TikTok: @authorJA_George
Author Facebook Page/Readers Group: JA George/Gothic Grove Readers Group
Discord Group: https://discord.gg/UxQXZkrmuF

It is important to note I use some language that is not translated until the very end of the story - this is purposeful.

This is a dark romance; if you do not like darkness, do not proceed. This is the last warning.

To everyone entering their Reputation Era.

To my husband for always giving me good material.

To my wonderful postpartum doula, Jordan, who allowed me
to write this book.

To Jenna, I will always have a paperback on my shelf for you.
We miss you greatly.

And to my dear, sweet Shadow baby, thank you for allowing
me to heal with you.

CHARACTER AND CREATURE GUIDE

Character and Creature Guide

Five Founding Witch Families:
Mori Family (Head witch family):
Arthur Mori
Katherine Mori
Hansley Mori (eldest; seer)
Reem Mori (middle; glamor)
Astrea Mori (youngest; no magic)

Carmine Family:
Kara Carmine (now Helvig)

Cosark Family:
Andrew Cosark
Mary Cosark
Anita Cosark (eldest; telekinetic)
Justine Cosark (youngest; conjurer)

Fairemore Family

Cordelia Fairemore
Robert Fairemore
Florence Fairemore (eldest; grower)
Annabell Fairemore (youngest; glamor)

<u>Hoar Family:</u>
Marianna Hoar
Francis Hoar
Katlyn Hoar (eldest; water worker)
Feather Hoar (middle; healer)
Patricia Hoar (youngest; conjurer)

Other Families:
<u>Helvig Family:</u>
Alexi Helvig (Vampire Lord)
Ciaran Helvig (Son of Kara and Alexi)

Other Characters and Creatures:
Ava (owner of The Playground)
Poppy: Astrea's familiar, fox
Shadow (best friends to Ciaran)
Samhain: Ava's familiar, raven
Drago (dealer of Eufori; owner of Club Eufori)
Hellbeast: half bear; half wolf creature
Kallen (historic witch)

PLAYLIST

AVAILABLE ON APPLE MUSIC AND SPOTIFY

Blood//Water- Grandson
The Lighthouse- Halsey
Thousand Eyes- Of Monsters and Men
The Devils Backbone- The Civil Wars
The World We Made- Ruelle
You Put a Spell on Me- Austin Giorgio
So Cold- Finger Eleven
No Light, No Light- Florence + The Machine
Lights- Ellie Goulding (Bassnectar Version)
Lilith- Halsey
This Is Me Trying- Taylor Swift
Walk Through The Fire- Zayde Wolf and Ruelle
Revolution- Ruelle
Ease My Pain- Solr and Cece Mix
I'm Seeing Red- Tommee Profit
Revenant- Izzy Reign
Deep End- Ruelle
Snakes- Halflives
Playground- Bae Miller
Purple Lamborgine- Skrillex, Rick Ross

Bad Dream- Ruelle
Seven Devils- Florence + The Machine
Tourniquet- Evanescence
Haunting- Halsey
Cry Me a River- Tommee Profit and Nicole Serreno
Lying From You- Linkin Park
Control- Halsey
Tragic Endings- Eminem feat Skylar Grey
Go To War- Nothing More
Page break*
Darkside- Neoni
Carry on Wayward Son- Neoni
Machine- Neoni
I'm not a woman, I'm a god- Halsey
Gods and Monsters- Lana Del Rey
Madness- Ruelle
Bones- MR MS

READING ORDER

Venomous Love: A Gothic Grove Prequel Novella*
Gothic Grove
Heavy Is The Crown
The Demons They Forged: A Gothic Grove Novella
Ruined Kingdom (coming early 2025)

*not required to read the rest of the series, however they do
enhance the reading experience

AUTHOR NOTE

Welcome to Gothic Grove my spooky and spicy humans. If you are new here enjoy the ride. If you are a friend from the past you'll notice some changes in this newly updated story. Ciaran and Astrea deserved some extra attention. After all, they were my very first publication. So I hope you enjoy the changes I've made!

Long ago . . .
I feel the bond break, my chest heaving and splintering. The wine glass slips from my hands and shatters beneath me. I gasp out, clutching the kitchen counter as lightning flashes and thunder shakes the house violently. Screams of agony rip out of my throat as my knees buckle, dropping me to the old tile floor. *Crack.* My chest heaves again, taking my breath with it.

No, no, no, no. The mantra plays in my mind. Maybe I'm screaming it, because I can see Agnes' blurred feet come into view, her long skirts soaking up the wine now staining the tile. She's saying something, but all I can think is, *He's gone. My mate is gone. My mate is gone.*

ONE WEEK LATER. . .
Agnes' lifeless body lies at the base of the altar, and her blood coats my hands as I say the final incantation for the

ritual. I use the blood on my fingers to paint runes across my body. The coven was foolish to think killing my mate would weaken me. That I wouldn't seek retribution from the families. Agnes was the first step, paying a steep price for involvement. They feared me before, but now, I'll be their reckoning. Now, I'll be their Harbinger of Death. A wicked smile spreads over my face as the power slams into me.

THREE YEARS LATER . . .

I whirl around, looking to all the deceivers who have tried to trap me. Their spell can't hold my power or soul, it can only kill this body. I laugh wickedly. My long black hair hangs down in my face as I crouch low to the ground like the feral animal I have become. The twin snakes pulse on my skin, aching to be released.

They are all hypocrites, each coveting the power I hold but all saying they are containing me for the greater good. My eyes search out the only one who is not a witch – the vampire. He looks at me with hunger, and I know he'll serve my purpose just fine when I return.

Arthur Mori comes forward holding a ceremonial blade, followed by two of the youngest daughters, one of his own coven and one of the Fairmore coven. "We offer these bodies: one to hold the soul, one to hold the power. Neither shall be aware what resides within, passed through the generations. They will be the keepers."

One by one, the people in the circle begin to chant, and soon magic swirls around the circle I'm caged in. After a few moments, I can feel it. My soul. My power. Both being tugged in opposite directions. I scream out in pain and rage at their audacity. They believe they can contain me, believe this will save their futures. My last thought as I'm pulled from my body is, *I will burn these covens to the ground someday.*

PART 1

A WITCH'S CURSE

(The Lighthouse- Halsey)

I stand in the shadows atop the prison and watch the new batch of witches being dragged in. Most already have a vacancy about them, their mind clearly some place their body isn't. Except for one girl. Her wild hair is a flash of both red and white wine. My father's men are having a hard time handling her, despite there likely being a collar containing her magic. I sneer at the thought of the contraption. My father is a power-hungry asshole, and his recent mission to collect all the young female witches has resulted in a full-out genocide of the witch community. The Mori family was the last of the four founding families he attacked.

"I thought there were three daughters," Shadow says to my left. His name fits him well. I didn't hear him approach. He moves with ease via his magic.

"The other two didn't make it," I reply, pushing my hands down the shaved sides of my head. I feel him tense next to me before letting out a breath. We share the same view of my piece-of-shit father, but this is more personal to my friend, having been forced into service to him long ago. We've been working tirelessly to get witches out when we can, but overall it's slow work. The vampires fear losing their food source if they move against Alexi. We have needed someone more powerful to join us, and if the rumors are true, this witch is the one who can help us.

I draw my attention back to the girl as she is processed into the facility. I watch as they rip her clothing off before shoving her into the large cage with the other girls. She sneers at them and yells obscenities.

"She doesn't smell like magic, just a faint whiff of *some-thing*," he murmurs. We watch as she snaps her teeth at the closest guard like a feral beast. "Whatever it is, she is still coming down off it."

The wind shifts again and I continue to track her with my gaze. "She could have a collar on, it's hard to tell from here."

"She won't last long if she's as powerful as rumors say." As someone who was held for a long time due to his power, Shadow is all too aware what happens once my father has you, once one of those collars goes on you.

"Are you sure about what the men said?" I ask. The scent of Eufori rushes into my nose and I don't have to turn around to know he's got the red cigarette in his mouth.

"Positive. There was a video. All the more reason she won't last long here," Shadow replies.

"No. Everyone will want a piece." I scowl at the thought of anyone else touching her, my skin suddenly feeling too tight and my canines descending. "We'll need to move quickly to make sure she is safe."

He only nods before stepping back into the dark and

vanishing through a portal. I stuff my hands in my pockets as the wind picks up. It brings her scent to where I stand, and in that moment, I know I'm in deep shit.

My head is pounding as I lie in the dim, cold cell; the floor is tile and stained with blood and grime. The smell that permeates the air is nothing short of what I imagine death smells like. My first night here, I threw up from the scent. The vomit is still in the corner of the room, a new crusted-over stain on the tile. That was three weeks ago. Or...I think it was. I have lost count of the days I've been here; left alone for hours at a time, only seeing other people when they bring me food and water. The timing of which does not appear to be consistent. My tiny room has no windows, and the only light allowed in is what escapes under the door.

When I first arrived, I assumed I would be placed with the others. But after they stripped us all, they began to sort us. The ones with collars, like me, ended up in this place. Each with our own cell. I've come to realize if you have a collar, you are prized. While the others are used as feeders for the vampires, we're used in experiments. At first, I could hear crying and screaming at all hours, but those sounds slowly died out and now all I ever hear is the drip of water.

Otherwise, the silence is deafening. I assume no one else is alive.

The mattress I'm currently curled up on smells almost as bad as the room, my sweat seeping into it nightly as my body tries to work out the most recent drug in my system. Eufori. It's Alexi's favorite brand of drug. It makes the user compliant, easy to gain control of. Use it often enough on someone, they'll do whatever you want just to get another fix.

The collar around my throat has rubbed the skin raw and I've stopped feeling my magic altogether. The one burst I used to try to escape is no longer pulsing under my skin. It's as if my magic has decided it's not worth the effort to continue trying to push out and has gone back to that place it has always been.

The jingle of keys has me cracking open my eyes in the dark, but it's the heavy footsteps that have me shooting up to a sitting position. The bright lights of the hallway burn my eyes as the guards open the door and push into the cramped space. I'm not sure when I last saw another person. My stomach is hollow and my throat so dry that I can't even swallow. They sneer at me, arguing amongst themselves as to who will have to touch the "filthy witch." I almost snort because I wouldn't be so filthy if they would allow me to shower or use the bathroom instead of living in my own filth. Eventually, one of the guards grabs me and yanks me to my feet, ripping me from my cell and into the hallway.

They push me along the corridor and into a room that is covered in the same yellowing tile that lines my cell. On the right, there appears to be an open bay of showers. The left side appears to be a medical station, the cold metal table stained with what looks to be blood. The lights over my head flicker and the frigid air bites into my exposed flesh. It's a living nightmare straight out of a horror movie.

The guard shoves me under one of the showerheads before turning on the freezing water. Shivers wrack my body, making it difficult to remain standing but I open my mouth and let some of the water flow in before they throw me an old bar of soap and demand I wash myself. My hands shake so bad that I barely get it worked through my tangled hair. The impatient guard finally yanks me out from the deluge of cold water and starts shoving me toward the medical area. Soap still coats half my body. My limbs start to freeze up ---from fear or the cold, I'm not sure---but either way, I want nothing to do with what is about to happen.

"Please," I whimper, my voice a cracking rasp, but the plea only inspires the guards to laugh. They grab me and shove me onto the table before strapping me down, my arms banded to my sides and my legs pulled open. I try to fight but my body is weak from the lack of food, dehydration, and inactivity. Before coming here, I ran miles each day; now, my legs feel as though they've begun to atrophy.

My eyes dart around frantically in a blind panic, until they meet a direct, midnight-blue gaze that looks disgusted. My nostrils flare at the scent of magic and shock courses through my system—a witch? Our eyes remain locked on each other as he steps out of the shadows. No, not a witch. His movements are inhuman, and the light that comes in contact with him seems to choke.

"What are you doing?" His voice is like honey dripping over me, and something in my chest loosens before it pulses with warmth.

The guards freeze when they look at my potential savior, true fear bleeding into their features. "Your father . . . he . . ." one stammers.

The midnight-eyed man steps closer, a true predator stalking his prey. His huge body dwarfs the men who dragged me here. His face somehow holds both boredom and contempt before there's a brief blur of movement, and then warm blood sprays my face. The guard's lifeless body drops in front of me and I strain against my bonds to see his head, no longer attached, roll across the room. I glance back at the cause of his beheading. No, this man is not a witch. He isn't human.

"Leave," he growls. The other guard flees. He turns his full gaze on me, and the force of it is overwhelming.

"Hello, Astrea Mori. My name is Ciaran Helvig, and I would like to help you."

Helvig. Alexi's son. *Fucking hell.*

Two green eyes, full of fear, illuminate the witch's face as she watches me approach. Her limbs are frozen to the table they strapped her to, yet when I'm within arm's reach she thrashes in the bindings. Under the dirt and vomit and blood her scent drifts out slowly, an intoxicating blend of lavender and vetiver. She smells like *mine*.

"Hold still, I'll get you out." She freezes at the command and something primal pulses through me, a curiosity at whether she is always good at taking orders. She flinches as I snap each binding, and I do my best not to stare at her naked body.

"Thank you," she offers hesitantly, curling in on herself to cover as much as her naked form as she can.

I clear my throat and turn over my shoulder, uttering, "Shadow." She cocks her head in confusion until my friend walks through a portal. Her eyes flare and the fear pours off her once again. He approaches her cautiously, slowly handing her the bag of clothing.

"They're clean," he says in a low, soothing voice. "For now, you can at least be comfortable." She glances between us before slowly grabbing them. Shadow and I both turn our backs, giving her the privacy she's been denied for the last three weeks she's been here.

When finished, she says, "You can turn around," in that quiet voice. She slowly spools her long hair into a bun atop her head before crossing her arms around her stomach again. Her neck is now exposed, showing the bite marks from my father's vampires. Shadow's quiet rage simmers next to me as we take in the marks and abrasions marring her body.

I drag my eyes to him and offer a slight nod of my head. He takes a deep breath before leaving through a portal again.

Her eyes snap to mine. "He's a realm walker?"

I nod. "Among other things, yes."

She cocks her head to the side, assessing me. "What do you want?"

"For now? I want you to live."

These rooms always remind one of a waiting room in a doctor's office. Fake plants and all. The only thing missing is the ambiance of nature sounds. The first time I walked into this specific one, Ciaran Helvig was waiting for me, just as he is now. I was tense the whole time, my body on a hair trigger. It was the first time I had seen him since he instructed me to live. And while I was still alive physically, I wondered if emotionally I died every time Alexi cut into me or allowed others to feed from me.

I know these rooms were designed for the vampires to feed from the witches they keep here, but thus far, Ciaran hasn't fed from me. He's clothed and fed me, but never fed *from* me. He's kept me as healthy as he could without alerting anyone to his interference. Sometimes that means coming here and other times it means sending Shadow to me. I know vampires need both blood and magic; after all, magic is what keeps them immortal. So, sometime soon, I know he'll ask to feed or demand it. *Unless he's feeding from someone else.* For some reason that thought bothers me more than I want to admit.

"Astrea. Welcome back." His voice elicits dangerously tempting feelings in my body. He nods to Shadow behind me, who promptly vanishes, before he motions for me to sit down on the couch opposite him.

I don't say anything as I sit.

"I hope I've built enough trust in three weeks for my request to not scare you."

I simply shrug in a noncommittal way. He has, but I don't give him that.

His mouth shifts into a small smile, as if he knows the truth I'm withholding. "I need to feed. I don't want to take a random witch who doesn't know me, nor use one of my father's prisoners, so my options are limited."

Called it. My body tenses as I listen to him. Those feelings I'm pretending don't exist are getting harder to ignore as I think of his fangs slipping into my neck. Arousal starts to pepper my body, and I see his eyes flare slightly, but he says nothing of it.

"And if I say no?" I won't, and we both know it. This is a game for us, and the only way I can gain some of my autonomy back.

He crosses one leg over the other, arms braced over the couch, showing the veins running through his tattoos. "I'll send you on your way. No harm done."

Sitting quietly for a moment, I take Ciaran in, truly look at him. Despite the past few weeks, this is the first time I've noticed his body in all its glory. He looks otherworldly with his thick blond hair pulled back in an intricate braid, runes decorating his scalp on either side where the hair is shaved. It's intricate spell work. "Who did those?"

He shrugs. "I don't remember."

I frown at him, a small snort of disbelief echoing into

the room. "That's a decent amount of spell work to not remember."

"I've had them since I was a kid; I really don't know where they came from." He shifts in his seat, and his shirt pulls tight over his broad chest. "What do you say, Astrea?" I've never mentioned the scent of magic he has coming off him, and now I'm curious if he even knows it's there.

Something pulses deep within me, an ache that's demanding to be relieved. A hunger needing to be sated. My heart skips a beat, and I know this is the moment my path will change. The moment I start refusing to be a victim. The moment I begin to choose how my story is written.

"Yes."

His massive body seems to relax, tension that I didn't know existed leaving him. His eyes shift to a deep red and he beckons me over with two fingers. Two fingers that I know would feel so damn good plunging deep into me. I walk over to him, and his hands shoot out and pull me so I'm standing between his legs. Those powerful fingers dig into my hips in a dark, possessive way. I resist the urge to put my hands over his shoulders, but I can't help the image of gripping his hair hard as I sink onto his cock flashing through my mind.

He continues pulling until I'm forced to put my legs on either side of him. It lines me up directly on top of his cock, which I can feel harden and twitch, no doubt feeling how hot I am through the surgical scrubs I was put in. *Remind me to thank Shadow for the shower before coming here.*

"This won't hurt," he says. I bite my lip, trying hard to hold still against him, and nod. A growl rumbles low in his chest in response, vibrating my core, and suddenly his teeth are in the crook of my neck, drawing deep.

An embarrassing amount of liquid pools in my pants; there is no way I won't leave a mess on his lap. A wanton whimper escapes my lips, and I involuntarily shift against him to gain friction.

Ciaran pulls out of my neck and looks me in the eyes, that midnight blue now hidden behind red. "*Kamerat*," he breathes before claiming my mouth with a devastating kiss. The world around me seems to shatter; my only focus is the feel of him against my mouth. I can't breathe. My heart stops and then jump starts, beating hard against my chest and demanding something I refuse to hear. It's the type of kiss that sets the world aflame and you don't care if you burn with it, as long as you burn together.

When he finally rips away from my mouth, I can barely see straight. I think he curses, but I can't focus. I feel Shadow pull me off him, and my body screams to go back to him. But he doesn't allow it, and I'm taken back to my cage.

CIARAN

The hallways smell like mold and human excrement. My boots click on the old, stained floors as I move through the prison to my father's office. My anger and anxiety are barely contained within my body, my jaw clenched tight as I try to ignore the various sounds assaulting my ears. The cries of those being tortured. And the intrusive visions that Astrea is one of them. Two days after I was tasting her blood, she vanished without a trace. Her usual cell left bare with no indication of where they took her.

That was a week ago now; a week of agonizing worry of what they are doing to her. My hands clench at my sides, and it takes an effort to shake them out into a relaxed state. Shadow and I have a plan in place, but we need to put it into action quickly or I am going to rip this place apart to get her free. *Now you know how he felt.*

My father deciding to wage war on the witches was idiotic. He has never been one to be this shortsighted; we need the witches, and we need the relationship. By destroying the head families, he has started us down a path that will only end in mutual destruction. And it opened the doors for the shifters to move in on our territory. It makes no sense to me. I've always been part of my father's plans, despite his fear of me. He thinks keeping me close allows him to make sure I'm not attempting anything behind his back. Up until this instance, he's been right.

I pass through the metal double doors, ignoring the guards on either side. The difference is stark. These hallways are pristine. Cool white walls line either side of the immaculate marble floors. No screams or cries fill the air. Instead, sounds of pleasure can be heard. While half the facility is used for nefarious deeds, aka my father's experiments, the other half is open to members of the community. Vampires who need to feed and fuck. They pay a pretty penny to have access to witches who are high as a kite on Eufori, the drug that keeps them compliant and happy while the vampire feeds on their blood and magic. All in all, my father is a piece of shit.

Shadow appears suddenly at my side, matching my pace. "We have a problem." His deep voice is barely above a whisper. "They moved her to level four. She's been in an exam room for the past week. I overheard a few of the guards talking about her and what they've been doing. It's not good, Ciaran." Shadow is bleeding tension, and I know he'll wear this as another badge of failure.

I curse under my breath. Level four is where my father does his experiments, and most victims never make it off that level. She's been held on level three for the past month; not the best but certainly not the worst. It meant she was harassed and fed on, but aside from that, she wasn't used, to my knowledge, for any of my father's experiments. Now that he's moved her to the fourth, we need to act faster.

She's already been here longer than I wanted; I had hoped it would only be a few weeks, but it's been a few months since my father brought her in. Unfortunately, he made it exceedingly difficult to get her out by placing one of those collars on her. Thankfully, I think I have finally found a way to get past that.

I rub my chest, that spot in me aching. The spot that always aches when I think of her. "Get her out, bring her to my room," I snarl to Shadow.

"Your father will know." He doesn't say it to argue but more as an acknowledgement that we are about to cross a line we can't come back from.

A growl rumbles from me. "I don't give a fuck. Kill anyone who touched her in that room."

Shadow simply nods at me and peels off, doubling back before stepping through the portal he's created. Up until now, when I've seen her, it's been down in a feeder room. Having her in my own personal room would have been difficult to hide. In the feeder rooms, we were able to use Shadow's magic to glamor her into looking like another witch. The guards typically posted around were told to leave, and none of them were ever willing to risk their lives by arguing with me or Shadow.

My feet come to a halt in front of the two opulent golden doors that close my father's office off from the rest of the facility. He sees himself as a god and demands others look at him the same. He disgusts me. I don't bother knocking and instead stroll in like I own the place, shoving my hands in my pants pockets so I avoid smashing one through my father's chest to crush his heart.

Alexi Helvig is a portly man now, with a large belly and pasty skin. He's currently sitting in a chair with a girl sucking on his cock, holding her stringy and greasy black hair as he forces her up and down. "Don't mind me," I call with an air of indifference. I watch as he rips the girl's head back by her hair, pulling his cock out of her mouth, and shoots his cum all over her with a pig-like grunt.

"Go clean up," he tells the girl, who slowly stands as he puts his flaccid cock away. She doesn't leave right away, which is a bold move for one of my father's whores. Instead, she levels me with an assessing gaze. "I said go," my father snarls. This time she listens, but her dark and unnerving eyes continue to track me as she walks out.

"I see you still need to pay someone to suck you off, Father. That must be embarrassing." I smile as his face turns red.

"You will learn respect someday," he spits. "And if you don't, you'll end up the same way your whore of a mother did."

I shrug, not allowing him to see how the rage flows through my veins any time he mentions my mother. "You keep saying that, but I think if you could, you would have already. We both know that's not the case." I sit down and prop my feet up on his desk. "Now, why don't we get to the reason you called me here?"

He moves by me and slaps my feet off before sitting in the chair on the opposite side. He fills a glass with a thick red substance out of the decanter on his desk—blood. Taking a gulp of it, he narrows his eyes. "My men have told me you've suddenly stopped bringing fresh witches in. What's going on?"

Suspicious bastard. I avoid rolling my eyes at him. "Witches don't trust us now that the families are gone. They don't go out much now. So, it shouldn't be shocking to you that we need to slow down snatching them off the street. You created this system after you slaughtered the founding families." I stand from the chair and start walking back to the door. "If that's all, I am hungry."

"Boy," Father calls. I cringe at the name. "I'm not done talking with you."

I turn back around and level him with a glare. "But I'm done speaking with you. I answered your questions."

"I want you out hunting, bringing in more witches."

I narrow my eyes at him. "Why? You have your little minions to do that."

"You're going to earn your keep. Or have you forgotten our deal?" I watch him slurp the rest of the blood out of the glass. I flash back for a moment to all those years ago, signing my soul away to be this man's puppet, to free Shadow. I will never regret rescuing him, but I do regret the corner my father backed me into with it. At the time I didn't have anyone helping me, whereas my father had everyone in his pocket.

Things would be very fucking different now.

I don't let any emotion bleed into my face despite the rage simmering under me. "How could I forget that, father?" I take a steadying breath. "I don't understand why you need more witches anyway. What are you doing with them?"

He snorts, ignoring my question, and it makes him seem even more pig-like. "Tell Shadow I need to see him later."

I grind my molars. "He doesn't work for you anymore. That was the point of this deal. I play the devoted lap dog, and you leave him out of this."

"Then I suggest you hurry to get me more witches, or I'll have to forget we made that deal, *son.*"

Hell will freeze over before Shadow is ever forced to do that again.

I mock-bow to him, the sarcasm dripping from me. "I'll get right on it." I turn on my heel and walk back toward the door but pause before exiting. "I'll be feeding in my room. Anyone bothers me, and I'll gut them." He simply waves his hand, dismissing me.

I'm not sure what day or what time it is. The days have blended into a whirl of pain and nothingness. My last true memory was feeding Ciaran, and Shadow placing me back in my cell. Not long after that Alexi came with a female. They dragged me from that hell, only to put me in something worse. Days of being worked over by his father, and someone else . . . . I could sense their magic, but any time I tried to focus on it, I was drawn back into the pain of my torture. At some point, I was completely lost in the agony, only to come out of it hearing a female voice, one that sounded strangely familiar.

"This one is different. We need this one to survive. She smells like what I need." But before I heard a response, my mind pulled me back under.

I curl in on myself more, wishing I could erase everything they've done. I send prayers to the gods that no longer listen that Ciaran and Shadow won't come tonight; that they won't try and drag me back to keep me living. I don't want him to. I don't want him to see me like this.

My body is exhausted, and my mind is still hazy. They

started using drugs on me again. Though, these ones, I don't beg for like I did with the Eufori. These burn me from the inside out, make me scream and beg for relief. They keep me awake and alert for all the horrors. I don't know if I've actually slept at all. Reality has no meaning at this point, and I've never wished for death more.

I can barely keep my eyes open as someone shifts my body around, cruel hands grappling for me. I don't make a sound; I just let them manipulate me the way they seem to need. As though from far away, I hear a scrambling sound before that of someone begging, and then nothing. Silence. No hands, no movement. Nothing. I blink lazily, the haze clearing enough to reveal Shadow standing over me, unstrapping me from the cold examination table. I wonder if he can see the fiery path the drugs took through my body. Or the places those men touched. I should feel something, anything, but I'm too tired to care.

"Motherfucker," I hear him curse. I think he pushes a jacket over me before pulling my naked body up into his arms, but I can't be positive. All I know is I'm tired. My eyes stay closed as my body is jostled while Shadow moves through one of his portals. *Things must look bad if he's using his magic to move us.* I can hear talking, and my body is passed to another. I inhale deeply—I can smell Ciaran. He must say something to Shadow because I hear him move away, and suddenly, we are alone.

(Thousand Eyes- Of Monsters and Men)

"Oh, *kamerat,* I'm going to kill them all." He nuzzles my hair, though I think dimly that it must smell atrocious. It's strange, what I choose to focus on after so much horror. No one in their right mind would care about the state of my hair at this moment, but the normalcy helps keep me tethered.

I hear water turn on, and the sound jolts me out of

whatever stupor the days of torture have put me in. I thrash around briefly, but Ciaran holds my arms and body to him.

"Shhh, you're safe right now. It's just us." Slowly, he places us both under the water. I feel him shift, feel my body being placed on soft wood, his scent all around me. *He's washing me in his soap.* The action feels so domestic. He's gentle as he moves over my body, methodically cleaning me. When he gets to the apex of my thighs I tense briefly, but he only washes, all the while making soothing sounds like I'm some frightened animal. And maybe after days of torture, I am nothing more than a beast.

The water turns off and I blink my eyes open just as he lifts me again and sets me on a countertop., Grabbing a fluffy dark towel, Ciaran wraps it around me with care. The bathroom holds opulent countertops made of black marble; the shower that we were just occupying takes up half the room, a rainfall showerhead and a wooden bench within it. The room is steamy, but through it I can see golden light fixtures on the wall. They throw a warm glow around us.

I bring my eyes to Ciaran, who is stripping his wet clothing off. I can admire his body at this moment. It's honed; a fighter's body, with thick cords of muscle underneath tanned skin that has seen more sunshine than most vampires can claim to. He has various tattoos in a never-ending loop over his body, only breaking where scars pop up. His blond hair is held in a bun on top of his head, until he unloops the band holding it up, allowing it to cascade down to his shoulders. When he finally turns and looks at me, his blue eyes are glowing like icy fire.

He doesn't bother hiding his naked body, but I don't let my eyes dip. He moves toward me and grabs a matching towel off the counter, wrapping it around his waist. He takes a deep breath, his eyes fluttering closed momentarily, and when he opens them again he looks at me. *Really* looks at me. The kind of look that goes deep into your soul. The kind that doesn't allow you to keep any secrets. It makes me incredibly uncomfortable.

Without saying a word, he scoops me up off the countertop and brings me into a bedroom. The fire crackles in the room as he carries me over to plush velvet chairs. He sits me down in one, and I watch as he disappears into his closet before returning with an oversized sweatshirt.

"I don't have anything that will fit you, but this will keep you warm and covered," he says as he offers it to me. Of all the times I have interacted with Ciaran, I've never seen this side. He's been cocky, self-assured, and kind, but never gentle, almost as if he were afraid he could break me with one wrong move.

I don't like it, this version of him. But I take the sweatshirt anyway and slip it on over the towel before letting it drop out.

He sits down opposite me, the flames dancing over his features. "I don't want to send you back to him, Astrea. I *can't* send you back to him." I'm not sure if he means to say it out loud but when his eyes cut back to me, I know things are about to change. "What would you do to escape this place?"

I don't answer right away. It's a question that has been bouncing around in my brain for a while. And when it comes down to it, after today, I'm willing to do anything. "Whatever it takes."

(The Devils Backbone- The Civil Wars)

He nods before standing and walking to his bed. I hear the drawer open before he walks back over and bends down in front of me, looking me directly in the eyes. "I have a spell. If we use it, it would mean the collar around your neck comes off. But it would also mean you are in a bargain with me."

I frown at him. "How does it work, and what type of bargain are we talking about?"

Ciaran stands up, his muscles rippling as he moves back and sits in the chair again.

"The spell is a potion, really. It would lock us together. For a short time, no one would be able to sense you; they would only sense me. It would allow Shadow to move us out of this compound without anyone knowing. The bargain? You would use your magic and help me take this city from my father."

I sit up straighter, wincing at the ache in my bruised body. "Where did you find a spell like that?"

"It was left to me in a letter from my mother." I desperately want to ask how his mother gained magic such as that. But grief and I are long time lovers, and the way his eyes flash with it makes me hold my tongue. His tone is firm as he continues, "If you make this choice, you are agreeing to bind yourself to me until we take my father's empire down."

Bind myself to this man or keep being used by his father with no means of escape? It only takes a moment before I nod my head and exhale, "Yes."

I release a heavy pent-up breath as soon as she says yes. It was a risk asking, but one I hope pays off in the long run. Once we are gone, I'll release her from the deal, but I need her to trust me before I do that. Not manufactured trust, either. I'm a better devil than my father.

"How do we do it?" Astrea asks. She looks exhausted, but her emerald eyes glow a little brighter at the thought of escape.

"I'll feed off you, and you'll take some of my blood."

She scoffs. "It can't be that easy."

Taking a deep breath, I shake my head. "It's not. The other part is more complex. We'll both drink a potion prior to that. The potion and the exchange can bring up urges, according to the spell, and I don't want you feeling uncomfortable after everything my father has done."

She doesn't look right at me. Instead, she looks at the flames. She's so still and stays quiet for so long, I begin to worry. When she finally starts to talk, her voice is low and sad. "Did you know my sister, Hansley, was a Seer?" She's never spoken of her sisters, who died the night my father took her. "She would stare into the flames for hours, and I can't help but wonder if she saw this." Her long hair has dried in soft waves since the shower, the white and red mixing-like blood splattered across snow. Her beauty is haunting.

(The World We Made- Ruelle)

Astrea finally turns and looks at me. "I'll do it. But I have one condition." Her green eyes are flaming, and her face is set. "I want you to promise me we'll burn this prison to the ground. And when the time comes, I want to rip your father's throat out."

A sinister smile spreads across my face. "Deal."

"So, what do we do now?"

Ciaran sets about getting the potion together, leaving me alone in his room with instructions to rest. Shadow brought me a pair of leggings and boots, along with a sports bra. At one time, my breasts wouldn't have fit into it, but given the weight loss I've suffered here, they fit just fine in the tiny band. Even the leggings are barely hanging onto my body. Thankfully, Ciaran's sweatshirt covers up how skinny I've become. I feel as though I'm caving in on myself now, an emptiness taking up residency that I worry will swallow me whole when I finally escape this place.

Shadow doesn't say much as he waits with me. We've formed an unlikely friendship through this trauma, a bond that gets stronger every time he scoops me up off this floor, body tensing. And every time I don't comment on his triggers. We pretend, sometimes, to be normal, talking in hushed tones before reality sets back in.

He's never one to waste words, which I can appreciate in a time like this. Once Ciaran returns, they exchange a few words in a hushed whisper before Shadow vanishes through a portal of his own creation. Guilt slices through me momentarily—they're both putting their trust in me to help them, and my only thought is getting free once Ciaran has me out.

When I was first brought here, I heard rumors of Ciaran. The prodigal son Alexi Helvig was allegedly terrified of. The demon in the shadows to the guards. The first time I saw him, he was indeed just that. Those piercing, storm-blue eyes looking out from the darkness. But unlike Alexi, I've never feared him. At least not in the sense of being scared for my life. No; the fear I feel is for what might happen if I allow myself to fall into those eyes.

"Astrea?" His voice breaks through my thoughts. He's changed into a pair of jeans and a black shirt. "Are you ready?"

"As ready as I will be." I stand and move over to him.

He almost looks as nervous as I feel holding the potion. "Once we drink the potion, it won't take long to activate. We'll exchange blood, and that will be that."

"Unless, you know, we suddenly can't keep our hands off each other, right?" I let the sarcasm drip from my voice, my only defense against the shivers wracking my body. Shivers of both excitement and fear. *Something has truly broken inside of me if I'm excited at a time like this.*

"I'll hold back. I won't do anything against your will, *kamerat.*" Someday, I'll ask him what that word means. It started the first time he took my blood. My mouth is too dry to allow me to form words today.

I nod and take the vial he's offering up. The liquid is clear and has no scent. I take another breath, then we both down the contents of the matching vials, his eyes never leaving mine.

(You Put a Spell on Me- Austin G.)

The liquid isn't even fully down my throat before my

body is burning with need. My veins are on fire, my skin is too tight, and a pool of arousal floods my leggings. The magic is a drug as it slips through my veins, seeking whom it needs to bind me to. The empty container slips from my hands, clattering to the floor as I fling myself at Ciaran. He catches me with ease and I slam my mouth into his. I can't help but let out a whimper as he shoves me into the wall behind us. All the feelings I've kept locked away from him are now overwhelming me.

"Please," I beg as he kisses down my neck. I grind myself into him, shamelessly begging for him to give me what I want. "Please, Ciaran."

"Fuck," he groans before he sinks his teeth into me, just below that metal collar. I scream out, the orgasm shredding my body within moments. He keeps pulling from me, the feeling electric in my veins. "You taste so fucking sweet, *kamerat*," he growls as he pulls us off the wall and slides us down to the floor, dragging me on top so I'm straddling him. In a motion too quick to anticipate he pulls a blade out and slices his neck open, then pulls my head down to the blood beading up. "Drink."

With that single command, I latch my mouth onto his neck and pull deeply.

Drinking from Astrea is perfect. Feeling her cum as I pull from her vein is heaven. But feeling her drink from me? That is something that I will never be able to describe. Her body continues to grind into mine as she hungrily takes from my neck, her moans making my cock so hard it's painful. The potion coursing through my veins has awakened something in me, something that is demanding me to take her, something I've tried very hard to ignore since that first feeding. *Mate*.

Fuck. Mate. The word burns into me, the need to claim her pushing me. But I was serious when I told her I wouldn't force anything on her, and a completed mating that she didn't ask for? That would be forcing her. After everything my father has done, that's the last thing I want to do.

I can feel the moment the binding spell works. The moment it all locks into place. Astrea pulls back, my blood dripping down her chin. The haze of the potion slowly fades from her eyes, but the arousal is still prominent. Her green eyes are blown wide as she looks down at me. She looks beautiful like this. Even with the weight she's lost, seeing her on top of me with my blood on her mouth makes me wild.

I grab that cursed metal collar around her neck and snap it off, the pieces splintering in my hands. I brush my fingertips against the raw skin that was under it, anger at my father flooding my veins. She lets out a small whimper. "What do you need, *kamerat*?" I murmur, reaching up and wiping some blood off her bottom lip with my thumb.

She squirms on my lap, making me bite back a groan. "I need more," she whines.

"More what? Use your words."

"You. I need more of you. Please." I question for a moment whether she means my blood or my body, but Astrea answers it for me when she grinds down hard on my aching cock. "I need you. . . inside me."

"Are you sure?" I hate that I have to ask, but a promise is a promise.

She grinds down again, no hesitation in her face. "Fuck. Yes. Please, Ciaran. Erase everything they've done."

A feral groan escapes my mouth. That was all I needed to hear. Flipping Astrea over so I'm on top, I sit back and pull her leggings off, exposing her glistening pussy to the firelight.

"You're dripping already, Strea. Look at how needy you are." Pushing my thumb through her folds to gather moisture, I move back up and circle her clit. She arches her back and I grin at the response her body gives me. I watch as she claws at my sweatshirt to get it off. Seeing her in my clothing pulls on the need to possess her. To show the whole world she's *mine* and *only mine*. She pulls the sweatshirt up and over her head in one motion before she latches onto her small breasts, kneading them through her bra.

"Please, Ciaran. I need to feel you." The sound of her begging almost has me cuming in my tight jeans.

I pull my hand back and push up on my knees, unbuttoning my pants as I stand so I can tug them off, and I see her eyes devour my cock as it springs free. I kneel between her legs again, but instead of lining myself up to her, I drop my head down and lick from her tight hole to her clit. She screams, and I can feel her gush as I push a finger into her while slowly circling that bud of nerves with my tongue.

"Oh, fuck. Yes, that feels so good. Oh, god."

I pull back, earning a whimper from her. "You don't pray to a god. You pray to me. You understand?"

She nods frantically and moans, "Yes, Ciaran." My name on her lips sounds sweeter than any music I've ever heard. I add another finger, pumping in and out of her tight channel. I can feel her pussy pulsing around them.

"Oh, Ciaran, please. Fuck, I'm so close. Please don't stop."

I let out a huff of a laugh and circle my tongue over her clit one more time before pulling up and away. "You aren't cuming on my tongue today. I want to be buried deep inside that pussy when I finally allow you your release."

She nods, watching me with heavy-lidded eyes, and lets out a breathy moan when I breach her with the tip of my cock. I push in slowly, disappearing into her inch by inch.

"You are squeezing me so good, Astrea. Oh, fuck." I can barely focus on anything but not filling her up right away. "Gods, you're tight," I groan as she drags her nails down my back. I start to pump into her faster, and time somehow slows around us. A tiny voice at the back of my brain tells me I need to stop. I need to be careful. But a louder voice in me screams that she is mine, and that is the voice I listen to. Her head is thrown back like an invitation, eyes closed and mouth open in a silent moan. I sink my fangs back into her neck, drinking her deep, and her wetness gushes over me as she screams my name, cuming on my cock. I'm not far behind her—one, two, three pumps and I'm filling her up.

And in that shared moment, I realize two things: I started a mating bond, one she didn't ask for. And that magic I taste on my tongue? That magic is ancient and *dark*.

We lay panting in the aftermath for a moment before he's pulling free of me and standing up. Ciaran gets dressed rapidly, his eyes shifting back to blue but staying wide. I rub at my chest, the feeling of that binding spell pulsing beneath my fingers. It is a need burning through me that I can't name, but the further he gets from my body, the more intense it feels. Like ants crawling over my body. I want to squirm and itch. I don't like that it gets better when he is close. I see him pull his phone out and shoot off a text, and I hastily pull my clothing back on, feeling suddenly vulnerable.

"Shadow will be here in a moment. We'll leave after that," Ciaran says, his voice sounding distant.

I fold in on myself, wrapping my arms around my body. "Right now?" The events are starting to slowly catch up to me. Everything is closing in on me like a snake constricting its prey.

"Yes." I watch his fist clench and unclench rapidly, as if he is avoiding hitting something.

His shift in demeanor is throwing me off. "Did I do something wrong?" I ask hesitantly.

He runs his hands through his long blond hair. "Fuck. No, you didn't, Astrea. Everything is fine."

Before I can question anything, Shadow steps through the door. He looks between us, something passing over his face before he shoots a look of surprise to Ciaran, who gives a slight shake of his head. The movement was so small I could have missed it, but it was a clear sign not to ask questions. Nerves rattle against my rib cage and that place in my chest starts to clench in panic. Something isn't right.

"We need to leave," Shadow says, his low voice breaking my thought process apart. Ciaran reaches his hand out to me, and I hesitantly grab on. Relief floods my body now that we are touching again. *So stupid, Astrea, not to get more information about this spell.* If his touch is the only thing that makes it better, how the fuck am I going to run?

I watch Shadow open a portal and take a deep breath before we all step through.

CIARAN

The deep unease I feel is riding me hard. Knowing Astrea is my mate is making me twitchy. I knew the moment Shadow walked in he could smell it on us. But it's clear Astrea has no idea, and truth be told, that might be for the best. My father did a lot to her and telling her about the mate bond now could be a foolish mistake. Letting her heal for a while, allowing her to adjust, would be the smart move. Even if it makes my skin crawl.

Shadow drops us out into an old motel deep in the city. It's the one we always use as our halfway jump point. The owner is a witch who has no love for my father and what he does in that prison. Normally from here we would get the person to Ava or Drago, depending on what mental state they were in. But Astrea is different; we've always known she wasn't going to either of those places. The problem is, now I can't imagine her going anywhere but my own home.

Grabbing the keys from the owner, I let us into the room she'll be staying in, for now. The motel is old, the carpets a reddish-orange spattered with black stains. The bedspread is a paisley print that looks like it was only in style during the seventies, and the walls are covered in wallpaper that has long since faded and is peeling off the walls. I move through the room, double-checking that no one is in here and earning an eyebrow raise from Shadow.

"Fuck off," I mumble, which earns me a small smile and his hands held up in a gesture of surrender. Astrea stands off to the side, her arms still wrapped around her middle and eyes wide as she takes in the room. She's closing in on herself, her emerald, green eyes starting to dull and disassociate.

"You'll stay here for a while until we figure out our next move. It's safe. No one will find you." I move over to her but stop short of reaching out to pull her to my body. "You can't leave, though, Astrea. Once they know you're gone, they'll be looking for you. It won't be safe."

She nods but doesn't say anything. The movement of her rubbing her chest doesn't escape my notice.

"Shadow and I will be in and out to check on you, and to bring you food. I'll try to find you some clothing as well."

"You aren't staying?" Her voice sounds so small but the panic is unmistakable. Panic that matches what I feel but refuse to show.

"No, not yet. It'll be a dead giveaway if we all disappear together." She flinches slightly, and I finally give in to pulling her to me. Immediately her body relaxes, and my own nerves smooth out. "You'll be okay, Astrea."

She doesn't say anything in response. Shadow moves in behind us and heads toward the bathroom, flipping on the light. The yellow light bouncing off the yellowing tile is less than welcoming. "There is shampoo and soap in here. It might look bad, but it's clean," he says.

She pulls away enough to nod at him, again remaining

silent. I want to growl at him for suggesting washing my scent off her.

"We need to leave," Shadow continues to me, barely containing the eye roll I know he wants to give me. "We've already been gone too long."

My body riots at the idea of separating from her, but I know he's right. I slowly pull away and see her eyes are shining with tears. This is the most vulnerable I've seen her, and it's killing me to leave her like this.

"We'll be back tomorrow, *kamerat*. I promise. One of us will check back in, okay? Just try to rest tonight," I tell her, desperately trying to ignore the pain in my chest. Shadow opens another portal, and I step away from her, each movement somehow feeling like marching toward a death sentence. Like it's the last time I'll see her. "Wait for me," I beg before I step through, and she vanishes from sight.

(So Cold- First to Eleven)

The pain of watching Ciarán move away from me is otherworldly. My chest heaves, feeling like it might actually crack. The old motel room AC is the only sound aside from my own heavy breathing as I clutch my chest. The damn spell is splintering my insides. *You sure this is a spell?* I shake my head, ignoring my own voice. Ignoring what that might mean. Instead, I focus on my next steps. I count to ten, grounding myself for a moment, before I move to the small mini fridge and grab as many of the drinks and food items as I can shove in the pocket of the oversized hoodie I'm wearing. Again, my chest feels like it's cracking a little more and I nearly double over. I take deep breaths until it eases, then straighten up. A tear slips from my eye as I rush toward the door.

My hands shake as I quickly open the door to the old room and peek out. The breezeway is empty. Pulling the hood over my hair, I step out and shut the door behind myself quietly, sending a prayer to whatever gods might still be listening to ensure I'll survive this. Survive leaving *him.*

Because I know I'll survive running; I know that now that I'm free, I will claw tooth and nail if someone tries to take me back. I refuse to be held captive. But leaving him is something I'm not sure I'll make it through.

The sounds of the city echo in my ears as I quickly move toward the street; it's overstimulating after so long in that prison. I walk a few blocks before I see a black Ducati parked on the side of the empty street. Sending up a thank-you to Reem for teaching me how to jumpstart a motorcycle and ride, I make my way over to it, keeping a careful watch to make sure that no one is around. As a ten-year-old, I had no reason to think I would need this skill, but right now? Right now, I've never been more thankful.

As soon as the bike comes to life, I throw myself over the seat and shift into gear, speeding off into the night. The further I go, the more pain I feel in my chest, but I can't go back. I refuse to be a pawn for anyone anymore.

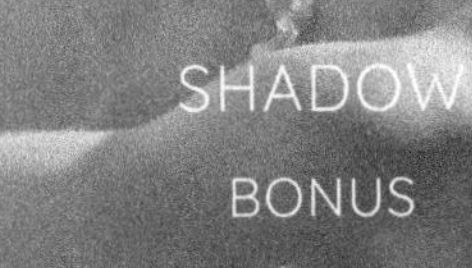

Finding Astrea on level four shook loose too many memories from my own past. My hands trembled for some type of release, whether by blade or joint, I didn't fucking care. I just needed something. In the end, I let my beast out briefly to play with the guards who held her, and the room was awash in their blood and body parts. My beast is happily sated for now. This won't go unnoticed, that's for sure. My brand of killing isn't something you can hide.

When I picked her up, the scent of drugs still moving through her was strong. But more than that, I could see the vacancy that's entered her eyes. It's one I'm all too familiar with. It's the look of someone who has left the building, so to speak, despite their body still being here. Dissociation is a blessing and a curse.

Ciaran's voice shakes as he instructs, "Go check on her." It's only been twelve hours since we left her, but he's barely managed to contain himself.

I let out a long sigh that earns me a growl. I throw my hands up. "I'll go check but you know it won't help." He mutters something like 'fuck you' as I open a portal to the motel.

Making my way down the breeze way, I knock on the door, listening for any movement, "Astrea?" I ask cautiously. Anxiety pelts my chest as the silence grows and I have visions of my own 'rescue' from Alexi. The blood and depression. The anguish. "Fuck it," I snarl.

Opening a portal, I step into the room—the very empty room. "Fuck."

The gas on the bike ran out on the outskirts of the woods. Sixteen hours of ride time, and my ass is numb as I climb off with stiff limbs. Part of me—a huge part—is deeply regretting running. Particularly given the roundabout way I took to my destination. Hansley's voice echoes through my head for a moment,

"*Remember the cabin will always be safe for you. No matter what.*"

She had to have known what was going to happen. Otherwise, why would she say that?

A soft chittering pulls my attention to the brush. A small, fluffy red head pops out of the dense shrubs, her dark eyes blinking at me as if startled by my presence.

"What are you doing here alone?" I ask the baby fox, bending down slowly. The creature approaches cautiously, sniffing my outstretched hand. "There's a good girl," I coo. Slowly she allows me to touch her soft fur. "Oh!" The feeling radiates through me, a familiar. As if the fox knows, too, that we belong together, she jumps up into my arms.

Burrowing deep into the stolen sweatshirt, there's a deep surge of warmth instantly flowing through my chest.

"Come on girl, let's go home." I snuggle her in, walking carefully until I hit the wards of our property. The feeling of Hansley instantly makes me weep. Warm tears fall down my face as my feet step over the wards and my knees drop to the ground.

Safe.

I'm finally safe after all this time.

PART 2
WELCOME TO THE GROVE

ONE

A witch is only as good as her coven. Power should always be shared in order to ensure the coven's survival. Any witch found to be keeping power to herself that could benefit the whole will be punished to the fullest extent of the law.

– Mori Family Grimoire

One Year Later

Astrea

I wake dripping with sweat. My nightmare is still so vivid, I can taste the magic on my tongue. Feel the rage simmering under my skin. Feel the agony of the one I love being ripped from me. The dreams are always a rotation between nightmares that aren't my own, the death of my family, and my time spent in captivity. It makes sleeping less than enjoyable most nights.

I kick the sweat-drenched covers off my body and pad

into the bathroom, where I turn on the shower before stripping off my shorts and T-shirt. I don't bother looking in the mirror. I don't need to see the haunted look that has taken residence in my emerald eyes. Stepping under the cool mist, I let the vision of the nightmare wash away; it was something my middle sister, Reem, taught me before she was killed. *Imagine they are drifting out of you, Astrea. Let the water take them away.* The singsong melody of her voice is still clear as day. The thought of her sours my stomach, grief edging in like a sharpened blade.

The intrusive images of their dead bodies in our home invade my brain, and the smell of my parents' burning flesh comes back in a rush. I lean my head against the shower tiles, shaking, as I try to keep the guilt from eating me alive. Guilt that I couldn't save them. Guilt that I was, and still am, useless.

Breathing in through my nose and out through my mouth in a poor attempt not to vomit, I turn the water off, jump out, and wrap myself in the threadbare towel from the rack. I wring out the excess water from my long, deep-red and blonde hair before pushing it up into a bun. *Please don't puke, please don't puke.* I brace myself over the sink until I feel my stomach settle. When I finally look up and catch my reflection in the mirror, I wince at how sickly pale I am. The dark circles that have sunken under my eyes are a stark contrast. It's not a good look on me.

Once dressed, I walk to the front door and step out onto the porch, clutching my favorite coffee mug. This time of year, the forest looks desolate. The trees are old skeletons and when the wind blows through them, you can hear their bones clicking. My sister and I would come here in the summer when the trees were full of leaves and the grass was lush. The greens were so vibrant, it had to be magic. I would lie in the fields while Hansley reinforced the wards around the property that kept this place invisible. I never asked her why she only took me here, why Reem was never invited. Looking back, Hansley spent a lot of time with me one-on-one after I turned sixteen. I never thought to ask why.

And now I'll never know.

Anxiety and regret press at my chest, a heavy weight trying to drag me down. I take a deep breath, the cold air practically freezing my lungs, and know without a doubt that the wards will fail soon. I try to reach for my magic but I come up empty. It won't be long before I'm exposed to those who might be hunting me. Won't be long before I'll need to run again. I make a mental note to check the protection jars. They lie tucked away along the property line, a last measure of defense once the magical ones fail. While my magic is nowhere to be found, at least I can still make those.

Another breath is dragged from my chest as I attempt to control the panic that is hedging its way into my thoughts. It's difficult knowing you have magic you can't access. I can feel it trapped in the hole in my chest. It's behind that occasional burning that ripples through me, through my heart center, and that deafening silence. I feel as though I have a vast pit of emptiness residing within me, begging to be filled again.

I assumed it would come back once that damn collar that kept my power contained was off. But it's still *silent.* My hand strokes the light scars left by that collar, an action I barely register doing anymore.

Maybe my mistake was binding myself to *him* to get the cursed thing off me, but what choice did I have? I needed out. If I had known this is where I would end up, I wouldn't have made the deal. But I was desperate, and he seemed so confident that the bargain would just be a way to get me out of his father's prison, so I trusted him. And I was a fool to do so.

The cool wind blows through the trees, snow floating down around the cabin like I'm in a snow globe. I move off the old porch, the worn wood pulling on my socks, and back into the warm cabin. Moving to the moth-eaten couch in front of the fireplace, I curl up and slowly continue to sip, staring into the flames and praying they'll provide some answers . . . they don't. My older sister, Hansley, was the Seer in the family; strongest in a generation, yet even she hadn't seen it coming. Or maybe it was my family assuming they were untouchable, like so many of the families during that time. Only one was truly untouchable, and they decimated the rest of us.

When I fled captivity, I was the last of the founding families still alive. One by one, the daughters they had kept died from the experiments they were doing on us, searching for an ancient power. I only escaped because I made a deal with the devil.

My brain involuntarily flashes to Ciaran Helvig, the devil himself, and my body shivers with both fear and need. The Helvig family took everything from me, but it hasn't escaped me that I'm alive because of him. I let out a long breath, the familiar panic trying to crawl up my chest as I think back to my life before this. Before my soul was sold off to *him*.

For centuries, we had been at war with the vampire community and had formed an uneasy peace only after far too many casualties on both sides: the Helvigs and our own founding families decided joining would be ideal. And so, a witch was married to Alexi Helvig, with the guarantee that his vampires would be able to feed and the promise that they wouldn't kill any of our own by overfeeding. It was a pathetic deal, and we should have known the piper would eventually call and it would all come crashing down. One by one, they stole us, torturing the daughters and slaughtering the rest.

As I set my mug down, wisps of hair escape the bun atop my head and fall in front of my face. I hastily shove them back up and tuck them into the elastic, as though pushing the hair out of my face will push the memories away, but the red and blonde locks only dredge up other memories.

Something of an oddity, my hair is a perfect split of my two sisters': Hansley with her deep burgundy and Reem with her white hair. While both my sisters were tall and willowy, I used to be soft and curvy, much to my mother's dismay. "If you only looked more like your sisters, Astrea, we could find you a suitable match that wouldn't care that you have no magical potential," she would say in her high-pitched, nasally voice. Since my time in that prison, however, I can't seem to keep weight on. *You must be so happy, Mother, to see your daughter wasting away.* Okay, that was dramatic, but compared to my previous body, I feel like I have been shrinking. I have done everything to get my figure back, but my appetite just isn't there. No matter how many hours a day I run or train, I'm very rarely hungry.

"Poppy," I call out into my house as I get up. I move into the small kitchen, if you can call it that, and open up the yellowing fridge. Pulling out some cold chicken, I hear the chittering of the tiny fox before she comes into view.

"Hello, beautiful girl," I coo and bend down to scratch her soft red fur before putting the chicken on a plate for her. Her fur sends a jolt of comfort through me, a sense of calm that pushes against the memories of the past that are threatening to drown me right now. That *always* seem to want to drag me under. "I'm off to work. I'll see you later."

I pull my old coat over my loose sweater and jeans before slipping on my snow boots. I see Poppy curl up next to the fire, her belly full of chicken, and I wish I was staying in with her. It always feels harder to leave her when the tidal wave of my past is trying to crush me.

The air nips at the exposed skin of my face as I step out into the snow and move quickly to the Jeep parked in my driveway. The car is the nicest thing I own at this point, its white paint almost camouflaged in the snow. I saved and bought this one from an older woman whose son had died. She wanted it gone and was willing to take cash. The car rumbles to life and I let the engine warm up, waiting for heat to blast out of the vents and warm the dark interior before I pull on my seatbelt and begin the drive to Jody's.

I got the job when I escaped Gothic Grove to this small, outlying city; the tiny bar a haven for someone like me. It's one of the few not run by shifter packs or the vampires. Jody's an older witch who doesn't ask questions so long as I don't make trouble, and her dive bar has been a lifeline this past year. Truly the only human connection I have these days. Even if I don't speak much.

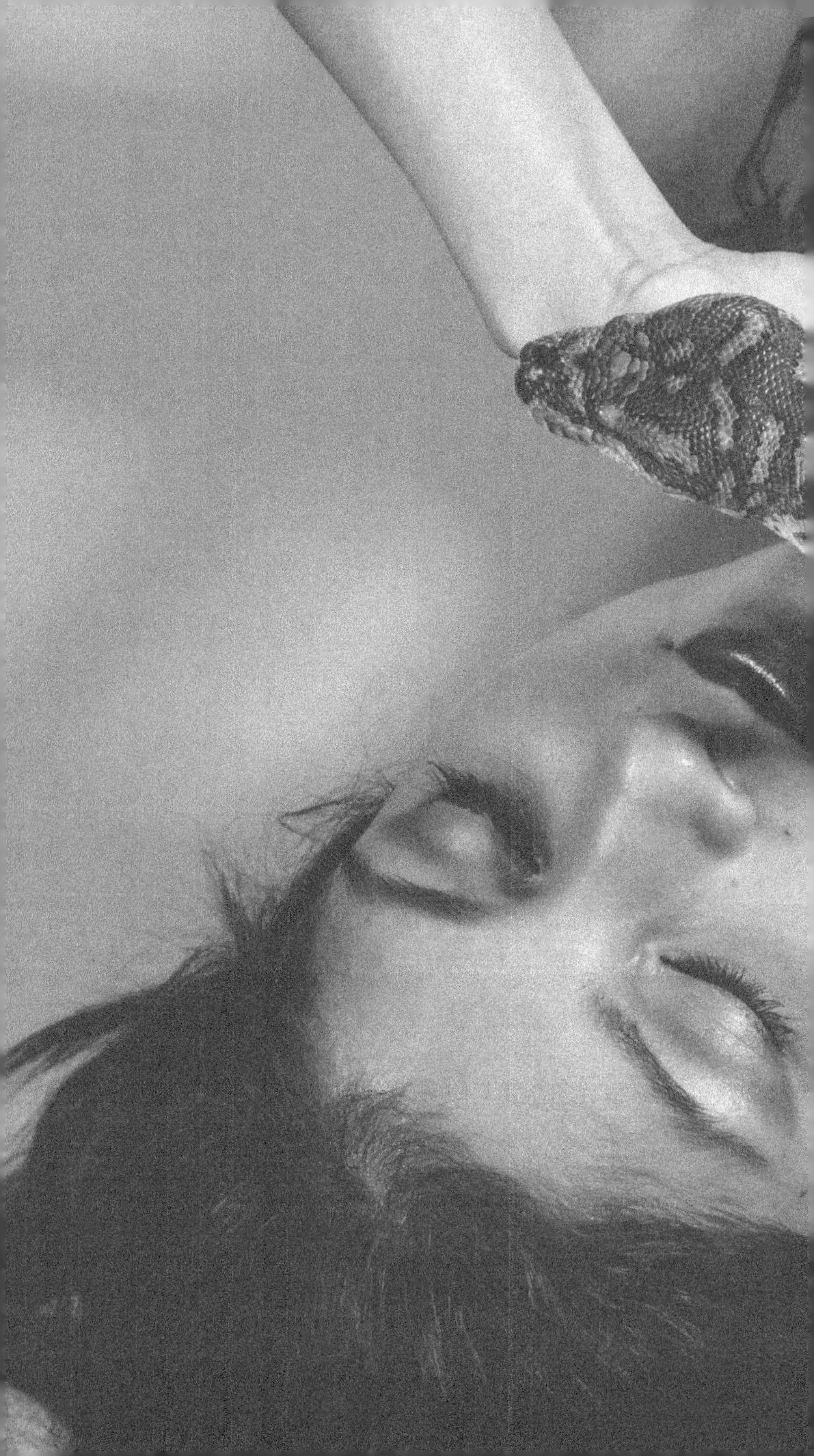

TWO

If a mate is discovered, they should be brought to
the coven. Mates should be bound to the coven or
removed immediately.
Power stripped and used for the coven.

— Mori Family Grimoire

Astrea

The days pass, and I feel the wards dwindle to nothing until they are finally gone. I wasn't supposed to be out here this long, that much is clear. When the last of the magic washes away in the snow-blown landscape, I realize it's the last feeling I'll ever have of Hansley. My heart breaks a little more knowing what I've lost. What I'll keep losing. I've kept myself at a distance from everyone around me out of need, but it still hurts to know I'll need to pack the Jeep up and run from the little normalcy I've found. Deep down, I know this will have to be my last shift at Jody's. My heart cracks open wider with the thought, and I add that grief to the growing pile in the corner of my mind.

When I pull my Jeep up, parking it in my familiar spot, I take a deep breath and shove the tears away. It may be my last shift but I refuse to spend it crying.

"Hi, Jody," I yell into the kitchen, stomping the snow off my boots at the door and hanging my coat up on the old coat rack. She only peeks her head out and grunts, her version of a hello. I don't take offense to it; if she doesn't like you, she won't say anything, so I take it as a win now. The shift moves quickly, and I lose myself in pouring drinks and serving food. It's busy for a Wednesday night, so I don't notice the tingle of someone watching me again until I'm close to the end of my shift. I feel the hairs on the back of my neck rise and take a cautious glance around, but I can't see anyone other than the usual customers. I feel a tug deep in my chest that makes me rub at it absently, my nerves fraying slightly at the sensation. I take a deep breath and chalk it up to the nightmares that shook open that box I've kept locked for so long.

I continue with my shift until it's closing time, and Jody is pulling on her old puffy jacket, the down feathers long ago matted into chunks and the black faded to a gray. "You got it, girl?" she asks gruffly. It's the same every night; she always asks if I can manage it, and my answering her in kind.

I nod. "Yeah, Jody, I got it, head home. I'll see you tomorrow."

She moves out the door without a backward glance, locking it behind her. My breath comes out in a whoosh, the release of tension evident and I pour myself a beer before moving to the radio. I pull off my sweatshirt, exposing my thin tank top and the scars that adorn my arms and back.

After taking a swig of the beer, I move to wiping down the countertops. The old bar always smells like a combination of beer, fried foods, and poor choices. The bar itself is a dive; a hole in the wall that collects all manner of people but if asked, no one will describe who's been there. The fluorescent beer signs flicker and buzz alongside a TV that only gets three channels on the best of days. No matter how much cleaner you use, the floors will always be slightly sticky, and the bar tops can only get so clean. But Jody runs a tight ship, and she knows exactly what sticky spot on the floor is never coming clean versus which one is due to laziness. I learned early on that the bar might be a dive, but it's Jody's pride and joy.

(Blood//water grandson)

An hour passes as I'm cleaning and mopping the old bar. Once I'm finished, I set the mop aside and take the last swig of my beer, the sip lukewarm in my mouth. It's as the music switches songs that I hear it. The scuff of claws and the huff of a breath. I freeze, realizing something is in the bar with me. I move my hand toward the knife on the cutting board next to me, hating myself for not having my twin blades on me. The ones that are always strapped to me, save for when I come to work. The curiosity and questions from the patrons they would garner are not worth the risk. Magic blades are even noticeable by the average witch.

The air stills completely as I shift my gaze to the darkest corner of the bar. I come face-to-face with a beast from Hell—literally. The Hellbeast looks like a wolf yet it's the size of a bear, dripping poisonous saliva out of its mouth, which is currently pulled back in a snarl. This one looks rabid; its brown hair matted down with what appears to be blood and a foul-smelling substance that permeates the air.

They terrorized the prison where I was held. In my lifetime, I have seen Hellbeasts four times, and each of those times, Alexi Helvig wasn't far behind.

Fuck, fuck, fuck. I won't let him take me again. The thought moves across my mind rapidly as I hold the beast's gaze. *Nothing like playing a game of chicken with a Hellbeast.*

I grip the knife harder and count to three before I bolt. The creature follows me, and I can hear it crashing through the bar as I try to make it to the kitchen. I don't—with one swipe, it manages to shove me to the side with a massive paw, its claws ripping through my skin as easily as my clothing. Warm blood flows down my side but I don't drop. I roll the best I can and come up swinging with the knife. I manage to slash it across the face, earning me a vicious howl and a body slam. I barely hold onto the blade, my whole-body vibrating. I let out a low growl at it, my own behavior almost feral as I try to fight back. My body reaches for the magic within me, but again, I'm met only with that hole in my chest.

I throw the knife at it, and the blade embeds in its chest as it leaps for me. It lands on top of me, already rearing back, and I know I'm going to die. Despite how much I struggle, despite the knife sticking out of it, I know that it is about to snap my neck with its massive jaws. *Alexi will be pissed his beast killed me before he got me back.* That thought alone makes me okay with dying.

I close my eyes, bracing for death. But instead, I feel the weight lifted off me and hear a cry before the snapping of bone and the loud thud of a body hitting the floor. I slowly open my eyes to see a blonde, tattooed man kneeling over the beast's body. When he meets my stare, his red eyes shift back to that deep, ocean blue I will never forget. I'm staring at the devil. *My devil.*

"Hello, 'Strea...it's been a long time."

THREE

Ciaran

I have been watching her for a while. The bar is a dive and has no scent of magic. Only a few protection jars are tucked around the edges. It's a stupid risk for her to take, not to use her magic to protect herself when she's determined to work. The building looks like it's in danger of collapse, and the smell of sex lingers in the alley. I planned on going in after she was alone. I knew she felt me; I saw the moment her body tensed. She had the aura of someone understanding they were being hunted. However, I didn't plan on having to dispatch one of my father's beasts. I look down at her as I wipe the blood off my hands, her body in a crumpled mess and her eyes wide.

"Ciaran?" she whispers.

I step closer and my nostrils flare as the scent of her blood hits me full force. I feel my canines drop down and my mouth begin to salivate. I kneel next to her and take a deep breath, cursing not having eaten before seeing her.

"God, you smell just as sweet as you used to." I move to help her up, but she bats my hands away, and with that movement I smell something else under her blood: poison. I grab her, ignoring her shouted protest, and roll her onto one side to expose the other for inspection. The whole thing is a bloody mess of claw marks with poison seeping out of them. The acidic smell burns my nostrils and the green color of it reminds me of bile.

"I guess you came too late, huh?" It's the last thing she says before she passes out cold.

Astrea

I wake up to a fire burning in my side. I let out a long whimper and attempt to move, but my body feels too heavy. I try to open my eyes but they refuse to obey me. Nothing is listening. I'm aware of hands on me, and I wonder if I ever escaped that prison or if it was just a cruel dream I'm finally waking up from.

"You need to stay with me." His voice breaks through the haze. *Ciaran*. I can smell him. Pine and fire. I feel my body being lifted and something shoved into my mouth. "Drink, gods damn it."

I think I try to open my mouth, but nothing is working. I can't get my body to obey me. The last thought I have is that Poppy will be alone.

Ciaran

"Shadow, I need an evac now," I yell into my phone. It

takes less than a minute before my best friend materializes in the bar.

"Jesus, what the fuck happened, Ciaran?" He moves rapidly over to us, looking at the Hellbeast I ripped apart before taking in the sight of Astrea's limp body in my arms as I force my blood down her throat.

"My father," I reply simply, and the growl he lets out rattles the bar. "We need to get her out of here." I glance towards the beast. "And I'm not sure how long that thing will stay down. I would rather not have to kill it again."

He nods. "Where are we going?"

"Her house." I see his eyes close, and after a moment, he nods. A portal opens behind us. The shimmering tear in space shows a small living room on the other side. I lift Astrea's limp body into my arms and follow Shadow. Stepping through, we enter—for lack of a better term—a small shack, and a screeching hiss hits my ears.

"Gods! She's got a rabid animal in here." Shadow steps back as an angry ball of fluff launches itself off the couch. The fox glares at all of us, and I see flames lick out of her tail as her size begins to grow. Then her eyes land on Astrea and the flames snuff out instantly. She quickly runs over to her.

"It's not rabid. It's her familiar." The fox sits back and looks at me as if I have correctly analyzed the situation. Its dark eyes look deep into my soul before focusing back on the witch in my arms. I know most witches grow up with their familiars, and I wonder when Astrea found hers. Has she always been around?

Shadow grumbles low, "I hate familiars. They never like me."

I roll my eyes. "Gee, I wonder why?"

He simply glares at me.

Astrea lets out a long moan, bringing us back to the

current situation, and Shadow starts searching for blankets. He finds a few and lays them out on the ground in front of the fireplace. I watch as he bends over and lets his magic flow into the empty hearth, allowing it to erupt in flames that bathe the entire cabin in warmth.

He straightens his lanky body back up. The difference between the two of us is stark. His muscles are lean, mine big; his hair is jet black, mine blonde. His body is decorated head to toe in tattoos that portray a darker story. If his father had known how powerful he would become, there is no way he would have sold him to our family. I still wish it had been me to kill the bastard.

"You need to get out of here," I say as I move her to the blankets, her body already burning up as my blood counteracts the venom from the Hellbeast. Shadow doesn't move, his body frozen, eyes glued to her body.

"I'll take care of her, but you know as well as I do that you won't want to be here for what comes next." I can see his struggle in leaving us, but he nods grimly. His relationship with her has always been complicated. Aside from also being held by my father, Astrea reminds him of someone *else*. Someone important that he lost. His protective nature comes out strong around her. "We need to know if more Hellbeasts are around," I add, trying to push him.

"If she dies, I'm coming for you, Helvig." Another shimmering portal opens, and Shadow casts one last look at her before walking through.

"Christ," I mutter. I push the loose hair that's fallen out of my top knot out of my eyes and look back down at Astrea. Cursing the circumstances, I carefully remove her clothing before wrapping her tightly in the blankets and hunkering down for a long night.

Astrea

"Admit what you've done!" I bang my fists against the tall oak door of the Mori household in blind fury. I can feel Agnes at my back, nervously fiddling with her skirts. "Come out here, you cowards!" The words come out broken through my tears, my voice catching in a throat that's already raw from all my screaming.

No one comes to the door. None of the other families have so much as tried to pretend they are sad my mate is gone. That our bond has been broken. A car crash, they said. So tragic, they cooed. Attempting to placate my grief, the families held a service with all the covens, a memorial for my mate. It was a joke.

A young witch, Lucy Carmine, pulled me aside after the service and shared that Arthur Mori had been bragging to her about the crash. Men are fools when it comes to a pretty woman and tight pussy. Arthur assumed Lucy wouldn't talk because she was too busy sucking him off. She also admitted that Agnes, my own coven sister, had helped him cast the spell. She will be the catalyst for my spell; her blood will give me what I need. Lucy gave me everything else I'll need to gain the power that will allow me to ruin them.

I bang on the door one last time before I back off the porch onto the rain-soaked driveway, my heart aching in the deep chasm that held my mate-bond. This was their last chance to make amends. Now, I will come for them all.

"Mark my words: I will have my vengeance. Your family will never know peace! I will use your daughters and their daughters to bring these covens down for all eternity. You will never rest!" I fling the curse out like venom, knowing this to be the last time they will hide from me.

I wake from the nightmare, from the surge of memories that aren't my own, for barely a moment before I'm pulled back into the darkness.

FOUR

Some witch families are more dangerous than others.
They covet power and if we follow their lead, we will be met with a violent demise.

-Carmine Family Grimoire

Ciaran

It's close to noon the next day when I finally hear Astrea starting to stir. She screamed and thrashed for hours last night, forcing me to hold her tightly as she cried. She screamed for her mate and my body tensed at that, that deep bond pulsing and reaching for her. As the sun rose, her body finally gave out and she slept. The venom of a Hell-beast causes extreme hallucinations and nightmares. While my blood kept it from killing her, I could do nothing for whatever tortured visions she was seeing. It was gut wrenching to watch, and seeing the white scars that litter her thin body made me see red. She'll now have yet another that I couldn't prevent.

"Strea?" I approach her as calmly as I can, so I don't spook her.

Her emerald eyes flutter open. "Ciaran?" She attempts to sit up, and I move quickly to help ease her into that position. The fox wastes no time hopping into her lap and snuggling her. The creature hasn't left her side since our arrival. "What happened?" Her voice has the same raw sound that it often had at my father's prison. Hours of screaming will do that. I hand her the cup of water I had sitting on the ground next to her.

She takes a sip as I start talking. "You were attacked at work. I just happened to stumble in and save you. You know how much I love a good dive bar."

She snorts. "Yeah, sure." She takes another long sip of the water, letting the blankets drop. As soon as the air hits her chest, she realizes the mistake.

My mouth waters at the sight of her full, bare breasts, her nipples pebbling in the chilled air. She snatches the blanket back up around herself, causing the tiny fox to fly out of her lap. It issues a hissing grumble at her.

"Why are you here?" Astrea asks as she motions for the fox to come back.

"Go get cleaned up. We have a lot to talk about."

"I see nothing has changed. Still just as demanding." She keeps the blanket tucked around her, the fox held tightly to her chest, as she stands and moves into her bedroom. Even covered in gore, she's fucking beautiful.

Astrea

Fucking Ciaran Helvig. I curse as I start the bath. It's been a long time since I last saw him, but my body still reacts like it did the very first time. Guilt gnaws at me for running from him. After all, he and Shadow put their lives on the line to get me out of that place. To get me away from his father. We had an agreement, and I backed out on it. My chest pulses, our binding spell pulling taut. When I left it felt like my body was on fire, like my chest was going to crack in two and I would die. Whatever spell he used to tie me to him is no joke, but I refuse to move from one prison to another, so I have fought it every step of the way.

My body is spent, the tension radiating off me in waves. It's not just the healing injury, it's the emotions that man makes me feel. The trauma of my past being shoved in my face and the idea that my time is up. I can't run anymore. I slip into the bath, letting out a long moan as the warm water laps over my tired body.

So much of my time at the hands of the Helvigs is blocked out. *Thank you, trauma response.* But the parts with Ciaran blaze bright in the dark haze. My time spent with him were the only moments in that prison when I didn't fear for my life. He and Shadow protected me the best they could. Despite running from them, from *him*, I will forever be grateful for what they did. And now, a year later, he's back.

I bring my body out of the bath and wrap a towel around myself before pushing my wet hair into a messy braid. I walk back out into the room and see Ciaran sitting on the dingy couch, his eyes watching me intently. He looks so out of place in my tiny cabin. His Viking frame takes up so much space as he moves to stand with his arms crossed in front of the window. I still have the distinct urge to climb him. I see his nostrils flare, his eyes flashing red briefly before they go back to that stormy blue.

"Go put some clothes on, Astrea." His voice is still like honey, settling deep in my core.

"You're hungry," I say matter-of-factly.

He simply shrugs. "You had to take a lot of my blood. I'll be fine until we can get out of here. I'll have Shadow bring me some when he brings your car back." The idea of someone else feeding him settles like lead in my stomach.

"You should eat." My voice comes out as a whisper in the quiet room.

"You volunteering, *kamerat?*"

I shrug, hoping the towel hides the fact that my nipples have perked up at the thought of feeding him.

But he shakes his head. "No. You aren't in a position to feed me right now. Christ, I can't even feel your magic."

"I wonder why that is," I snap. The rejection stings—he fed off me in the facility. The only difference between then and now is my magic being gone. It makes me wonder if that was all he ever wanted. The guilt I had over running from him wavers a bit at the thought, replaced quickly by anger.

I turn around and move to the tiny closet of a bedroom, throwing on yoga pants and a sports bra under a loose sweater before coming back out. Then, not quite cooled off yet, I go to the fridge and pour a glass of wine before sitting cross-legged on the floor next to the fire. Poppy curls back up on me, and I'm grateful for the contact. Petting her red fur calms me down. It reminds me I'm here, not in that prison. "Okay, let's talk. Why are you here?"

"You know why I'm here, *kamerat*. I would have been here sooner, but you are very good at hiding." He looks me over, head to toe. "But you didn't protect yourself at the bar, and the wards surrounding this place are all gone." He looks like he wants to take a step toward me but is stopping himself. "What would you have done had I not gotten to you? Died?"

I shrug. Death will always be better than returning to his father.

Ciaran's eyes flash to red before going back to the stormy blue, his anger palpable. "I didn't pull you out so you could get yourself killed."

"I'm telling you right now, Ciaran, I would rather die than go back to your father. So if the choice is death or that, I will make sure I'm never taken alive. That's a promise."

Ciaran moves faster than I can track and is suddenly in my face, his eyes blazing red and his teeth gleaming. "I will not allow that. If for some gods forsaken reason my father gets his hands on you again, you will fight. Because that's what we do, Astrea. We fight. And if you die, I will find someone to bring you back." As quickly as he was in my face, he's back across the room next to the window. "You are not allowed to die."

I don't say anything.

He lets out a long sigh. "We need your help. We need to bring my father down; this has gone on long enough. So, I'm calling in our bargain. I need you to help me figure out what he is searching for."

I search his face, noting the tension and exhaustion lining it. Taking a long, deep breath, I finally speak again. "I already know what he's looking for."

FIVE

To contain that power, we split the soul from the
body and the power from the soul.
Each goes into a different family.
As long as the power stays asleep, so shall the soul.

— Mori Family Grimoire

Ciaran

I can see Astrea is uncomfortable the moment she admits to knowing something. I don't reply, just motion for her to continue while I watch the light of the fire dance over her pale face. Since escaping, I had assumed she would put on weight, get healthy. But she's lost the few curves she gained once I started feeding her, and her freckles stand out starkly against skin that matches the snow outside. She doesn't look any better. She just looks exhausted.

She lets out a heavy sigh, as though her very breath is being pulled out of her by force. "He's looking for a very specific kind of magic. One that no one has seen for a very,

very long time." She pauses for another moment. "And he's looking for a way to bind that magic to him. To use it."

"What type of magic?" I ask her.

She doesn't answer and instead asks, "Do you know why it's so rare for a witch to mate?"

"No." While my mother had been a witch, I know very little of her people, aside from knowing we need that magic to sustain our immortality.

She nods, unsurprised. "One reason is only a few have the blood to mate. And if we do in fact find our mate, it creates a powerful magic. More powerful than a coven. So, you can imagine that could pose a threat—one coven gets a mated pair and suddenly the power shifts to them. Well, according to my mother, there was a mated pair of witches, except they weren't part of any of the founding families. Yet, they were more powerful than all of them."

I let out a harsh laugh. "That must have pissed them off."

"Oh, absolutely. But even the most powerful can't escape death. Her mate was on his way home from a meeting with the founding families—they wanted to tap into their power, use it to replenish the coven magic. He'd refused; they had never trusted the families. According to my mother, on his way home he was killed in a car crash. They say the grief drove his mate mad and she became what is now known as The Harbinger. She sought retribution against the families, convinced they were behind his death."

I stop her. "Why would they have killed him?"

She cocks her head to the side, the movement letting the loose sweater slip off her shoulder, exposing her bare neck. I shiver slightly, hunger and need clawing at me.

"Kill a mate and it weakens the survivor, extinguishing the threat. They were the most powerful mated pair to have existed. They had no other match. It's the whole 'if we can't have it, no one can' idea, but they didn't realize what they would awaken by killing her mate. It took all the family heads to cast the spell to stop her. Rumor has it they even went to Hell asking for help from the King. And even then, all they could do was kill her physical body, locking away her soul in one place and that destructive magic in another."

Rubbing my chest absentmindedly, I begin to pace back and forth. "Where did they lock the soul and power away?"

Astrea doesn't continue for a moment, simply petting her fox and staring into the fire. The firelight dances over her thin face, illuminating her cheekbones and causing her freckles to pop out more. Finally, she turns and looks at me.

"I'm not sure. My family grimoire would have the information, but I have no idea if we can even find it – if it's even still in the wreckage of the house. But I think that magic is what your father is looking for."

"How would he even know about this? It feels like an urban legend."

"A soul like hers would want out, would want the magic back. She's missing her mate, who waits for her. She's never been allowed to move on. Just holding onto that fury . . . if it were me, I would do everything I could to be found. Even betray my kind." For a brief moment, I see rage that's not her own move across her face. But just as quickly, it's gone.

"So, how does he find this magic? Or this soul?"

"I wouldn't know. I know your father was trying to force bonds, on the off chance one of us had it. Linking himself to that witch would give him unlimited power."

I go still at the statement, and I see a vacancy entering her gaze that almost brings me to my knees.

"How do you force a mating, Astrea?" I know I don't

want to hear what she has to say. My blood is running cold thinking of what my monster of a father would do.

"The details are what you would assume. Blood. Sex. Magic. The makings of a good album title, you know?" The vacancy still holds residency in her face, despite the quirk of an attempted smile.

"Strea, this isn't funny," I growl.

"I know it's not funny, Ciaran, but it's my way to cope while having to share the shit your father fucking did to me and all the other witches he had at that prison."

I watch her take a shaky breath and run my hand through my hair as a way to hide my own slight tremor. I growl again, "Fuck."

She cocks an eyebrow when I look over at her. "You're much more growly than you used to be. You know that?" She pushes away a stray lock of hair that's fallen out of her braid. "Look, if your father hasn't found it yet, I don't think it exists anymore. He can keep trying to force bonds, but if it wasn't in one of the founding families, it's not going to be in a common witch."

But she doesn't know what I've felt. That ancient magic she talked about; I tasted that deep in her veins, in the bond we started. And given how long my father held Astrea, there is no way he doesn't know. *Fuck.*

"You said he was looking for a way to bond that magic to himself...if he couldn't do it through a mate-bond, how was he planning on doing it?" I ask.

"There were rumors of a spell, a very powerful one, that would allow the wielder of it to link themselves to the source. It's what the covens continued to look for after binding The Harbinger. They wanted to be able to use the magic without the risk of the soul taking control." She pauses again, exhaustion pressing into her. "I think that is what he was trying to experiment with. He was searching for the magic in us while using other witches in an attempt to figure out the spell."

The fire crackles in the space between us. "Any idea if it actually exists?"

A sheepish look crosses her face, "I think. . . I think it was in my family's grimoire."

Shit.

The wind outside starts to blow and I can feel the old house shake slightly, groaning under the pressure. Snow has begun falling in earnest since she woke. I watch as Astrea yawns, and I curse at myself for forgetting she is still healing. The timing of my father's beast weakening her and her lack of magic is making this mission far more difficult. I don't understand what's happened to her magic; the spell I used should never have done that.

And if she hadn't run, you could have helped her sooner.

"Why did you run from me, Strea?" The question is out before I can think. Even knowing that we are on borrowed time, understanding that I need more information on what my father knows, this is still the only question burning in my soul. Her eyes seem to lose focus briefly as if she is thinking of the time we last saw each other. I can almost smell the motel room I left her in, and for a brief moment I can see how she looked when I left her. Broken and utterly terrified, but with a fight in her that seems to be missing now. A flame that's been extinguished over this last year she's spent hiding from me.

Shadow enters the room, appearing as quietly and quickly as only a Realm Walker can. From where she's still curled in front of the fire, I hear the small gasp that escapes Astrea. A strange look passes over her face but vanishes just as quickly as it appears.

"We need to leave. Now." Shadow's voice cuts through the silence as the portal closes behind him. His eyes are hard as he looks around the room but soften when he sees Astrea upright. The whiskey color of his gaze swims briefly with emotion before he's back to business. "We have company coming in less than five minutes."

"Who? Or what?"

"Two more Hellbeasts."

"Fuck," I curse. I look back over at my *kamerat* to find her eyes wide. I don't think she even realizes she is clutching her familiar in her lap or that wisps of her magic are pulsing upward, the first hint of it I've seen. *Interesting.* She seems lost in thought, frozen in some far-off place in her mind.

I walk over to her and bend down until my eyes meet hers. "If you don't want to return to my father, we need to leave." I watch her blink rapidly to clear the fog before nodding quickly.

SIX

-Carmine Family Grimoire

Astrea

When he asked me why I left, I truly didn't know what to say. But feeling that? The pulse in me? Whatever Ciaran was thinking pulled at a bond between us. One that isn't just from a spell. *Mate.* The word bounces through my brain like a tiny metal ball in a ping-pong arcade game. The mate-bond feels like coming home. It feels like being wrapped up in a warm blanket on a rainy night with your favorite book. It's warm and golden. No spell could manufacture that. *How had I not realized that?*

Mate. I'm his *mate.*

The breath whooshes out of me as the truth settles deep into my bones. Why didn't he tell me? Did he not want me as his mate? That simple question unlocks old feelings of insecurity and inadequacy that my mother did such a *wonderful* job instilling in me. I can feel my eyes tearing up, and I hate it. Hate that the rejection burns through me like a wildfire; that confidence I had gained is slowly being eaten up by those ravenous flames until all that's left in the ashes is the girl who wasn't enough, who will never be enough.

Attempting to stop the tears from flowing, I focus back on the task at hand. My movements are quick and efficient as I pack my bag. Poppy sits calmly next to me, her steady presence grounding me through each breath I try to take in. She's kept herself bigger than usual, remaining in her form closer to wolf than fox. I appreciate the protection. The last thing I do is pull my twin blades from their hiding place and strap each to a thigh. Left behind for me by my sister Hansley, the blades have intricate runes etched into them. Spells for protection and strength. Blood spells. The metal glints in the dim light of the cabin, the spelled blades hungry for blood. I found them with a note:

Astrea,

If you have these blades, it means what I saw was true. You will need these before the end. I'm sorry we aren't there to help you. Every fiber of my body wishes the outcome of all this was different, wishes I could have prevented this. You don't deserve the hardships you've been put through, or any of the hardships to come. Our family is a

The handles used to be leather but have long since been stripped and are now wrapped in delicate golden rope. Another part of the spell work laid in them.

"Are you ready?" Ciaran's deep voice sends shivers through me as I turn around, drinking in the sight of him. His blonde hair has been thrown up into a messy bun, exposing the shaved sides of his head decorated with tattooed runes. He's grown out his facial hair over the year, and his trimmed beard paints him as a warrior. He's beautiful, but under that beauty is someone who has seen far too much death. Far too much darkness.

I used to think that darkness was what allowed me to feel so comfortable with him despite knowing he was the son of the enemy. But now, I know it was that mate-bond. Thinking back, I wonder if I ever had any choice in how I behaved around him, if the lust was real or fabricated from that bond.

I take one last look around the space. I know this is the last time I am ever here again. Once I step through the portal Shadow has created, I won't ever come back. I close my eyes, trying to take in the smell, the warm wood. Memories of Hansley humming as she sketched by the fire invade my brain. When I open my eyes, I look at the small bed where the two of us would sleep, curled up and happy. This small house is the only place that has ever held joyful memories for me.

And now, it will be gone.

Just like my family.

Grief threatens to wash me away as I say goodbye to this place. The waves are so large I wonder if it would just be easier to collapse into them. But like the tide, the wave edges back out to sea, giving me a moment's peace.

I finally look at Ciaran, tears stinging my eyes again, and nod before turning toward Shadow. "I'm ready." I let my hand graze over Poppy's warm fur as we take a step forward into a future that will be uncertain.

<hr>

We step out into an elaborate penthouse, Ciaran moving in silently behind us before the portal closes, shutting out the last piece of my family I had. Both men move with ease through the space. Their movements are comfortable. It hits me, then: a home. This is their home. Shock ripples through me, followed by disbelief and then jealousy ribbed with anger. They've had a home where they got to live free of fear.

"Welcome, *kamerat*, make yourself comfortable," Ciaran offers while walking over to a bar top that looks out over the river, and just beyond, the glittering city of Gothic Grove. When the founding families built the sprawling metropolis, they hadn't intended to actually take care of it. They had created jobs for the inhabitants, but as time went on, those opportunities seemed to disappear, leaving so many jobless and eventually homeless. People turned to drugs to cope and crime to fill their pockets.

The stark contrast between my home in the woods and here is jarring. Here there is no snow, only rain streaking down the windows like the tears I refuse to let fall. The skies over Gothic Grove are a deep, stormy gray and the wind seems to scream, as if it too were demanding justice for the city. For its people. From my vantage point high above, I can pretend it's thriving. Up here, no one can see how rotten it is, how the streets are littered with souls trying to find a way to survive. Souls that have been taken advantage of by the founding families and vampires alike.

Dropping my backpack on the dark hardwood floors, I slip off my worn boots but leave the knives attached to my thighs. Poppy remains at my side as I tentatively look around the space. The place is warmer than I expected, the colors dark grays and bright whites. Shadow and Ciaran have both moved on and are now sitting in a living room full of plush couches and chairs, drinks in hand. The walls are lined with bookshelves on one side, and the other has floor-to-ceiling windows. I look at the furniture longingly.

"You can sit," Ciaran motions.

I shake my head before asking, "How is it we are safe here?"

"My father cannot get past my wards. And if those do fail, he will meet Shadow's next. You are safe here." Ciaran seems so certain, so at ease. Something I've never seen in all the time I've known him. "You would have been here, had you waited for us. Had you not run."

The sharp sting of his words makes me bristle immediately. "How was I to know that? You bound me to you. In my eyes, I no longer had an option. And I guess I really didn't, did I?" I cross my arms, and Ciaran furrows his brow. "Yeah, I felt that Ciaran. Felt that pull that isn't from some gods damn spell you used." I want to ask if he just didn't want me. If he only wanted my power, and now that it's gone, I'm not worth it. But I don't, again refusing those tears that threaten to out me. My voice breaks as I growl, "Mates, Ciaran? Why didn't you tell me?"

"Shit," Shadow mutters from the corner, and I shoot him a glare before refocusing on Ciaran.

He rubs his hands down his face. "I had my reasons for using that spell, *and* for not telling you at the time we were mates. But I'm not my father, and you should know by now you *always* have an option with me. If that isn't apparent already by me not completing the bond, I don't know how to prove it."

People who have never lost freedom don't understand how even a well-intentioned controlling move can feel like having your head held underwater. Under that feeling of insecurity, I can sense my anger rising; a living creature moving beneath my skin, pushing outward. I welcome the feeling. Anger is safe; it's what keeps me alive and lets me avoid opening the chest of nightmares in my mind.

That living beast rolls out of me in a tidal wave as I let myself drown. "So, I should trust you because you didn't *force* me to fuck you like everyone else did? Or because you asked before you sank your fangs into me and drank my blood and magic?"

My body is tense, and Poppy growls low next to me as she feels my energy changing. She's waiting for a signal; if she's needed, she'll burn them alive. I wrap my arms around my middle and dig my nails into my sides. I know he doesn't wholly deserve it, but I can't stop myself from spewing the visceral words at him. As if everything I've kept inside needs an escape.

"I barely knew you, Ciaran," I spit venomously. "All I knew was that you were promising me a way out. A means to an end. I had no idea if I could actually trust you. I spent so long in that place, so much time lost. I have scars all over my body from those times. I barely sleep and my magic is fucking gone because of whatever the fuck spell you used to bind us. So, I'm sorry if as soon as I was out, I didn't just automatically know you would protect me. Maybe, had you been honest, things would have gone differently."

Ciaran and Shadow stand, and I can smell their magic at the ready. It only adds gasoline to my already burning rage. *How dare they.*

"You don't just get my trust. No one does. Just because you saved me doesn't mean I owe you anything." My body is warm, my hands shaking, as my biggest fear spews out at them like venom. "You are just going to use me. Just like your father did!" I explode outward in that moment, gasping as my magic suddenly appears in a familiar darkness that wraps around me. The swirling smoke and shadow create snakes that move like a lover's caress across my arms and chest. I can hear Ciaran saying something, but I can't seem to understand him as I allow my magic to flow freely. I can only focus on the feelings of pure ecstasy flooding my veins. The feeling of coming home overpowers the anger I felt. Relief that my magic is back makes me shudder out a sob.

"Astrea!" Ciaran's voice penetrates the cloak of magic around me and my eyes snap to his. It's one of the few times I've seen him look worried. I cock my head to the side, assessing him. "*Kamerat*, take a breath. We aren't a threat. I know you're angry; you have every right to be. But don't let your magic take control. Let the magic go."

He begins to approach me like someone might approach a feral dog, hands held out in front of him. *He's scared of me.* The thought sends a thrill through me, bringing me more joy than I think is healthy. His eyes have shifted to crimson and his teeth have come down, but his magic is held back. That oh-so-tempting magic that I've always smelled. The magic I'm not entirely sure he even knows about.

His magic is old. Like ours, a dark, soothing voice says.

I look at my shoulder to find one of the shadowy snakes looking at me. Talking to me. It rubs its head along my face like a pet, then gingerly wraps itself around my neck. Another appears, this one holding tighter to my arm.

I take a breath as he takes another step forward, and another as his scent hits me. I can feel my magic dropping its hold on me, until as quickly as it came, it snuffs out. Exhaustion hits me like a freight train, and I feel my body begin to fall. Ciaran is by my side in a heartbeat, his strong scent invading my nose and awakening that familiar ache in my chest as he scoops me up bridal style. I can hear Shadow say something about "that animal" contaminating his chair, and I know Poppy has made herself at home amidst my breakdown.

"You stubborn witch," Ciaran murmurs in my ear. I feel him push open a door, and a moment later, he lays me down on the most comfortable bed I've ever felt. A low moan escapes my throat. "Careful, *kamerat,* make another sound like that and I might not be so honorable."

I think I feel his nose drag up my neck, but my body is finally giving out, the adrenaline leaving me in a whoosh. My eyes drift closed, and the last thing I'm aware of is covers being pulled over my body.

Ciaran

I watch over Astrea for a moment longer before I back out of the room, leaving the door ajar so I can hear her if she wakes. I drag my hand down my face and walk back out to the living room.

"What was that?" Shadow is standing next to the window. His back is to me, but I can tell by his voice that he's worried. I walk over to him and look out at the city across the river. From above, the city looks like any other metropolis. It's not until you hit the ground that you realize what it is: a city infested with vampires, hunting witches and shifters alike. A city that will soon be dead if someone doesn't step in.

My voice stammers as I reply, "That was her magic... which she hasn't had access to in a very long time." I try to keep my breathing even as I think about what she looked like as her magic exploded. She looked every bit the part of The Harbinger. I'm horrified at what she told me earlier, what my father has been doing. But what scares me more? That she has no idea what type of power she holds. "I don't understand what happened when she ran – that spell never should have interfered with her magic. Neither should the mate-bond. As soon as that collar was off, her magic should have come back."

"You didn't notice when you took it off?" he asks.

I shake my head. "No. I was so focused on the mate-bond, I didn't even think about her magic. I was a fucking idiot."

He sighs when I don't say anything more. "This is a dangerous game, brother," Shadow offers. "You need to tell her everything. The more you keep from her, the more things like what just happened will transpire. She's already pissed about you not telling her she's your mate." He cracks a small smile. "No one likes the secret-keeping, miscommunication trope."

I shoot a glare at him. "Let's not throw stones when we live in glass houses."

Shadow only shakes his head. "You know that's different." He claps me on the shoulder before walking away and opening a portal. "I'll give you guys some space. I don't want anything to do with that conversation."

"Pussy," I mutter, and I see him flip me off as he disappears. I look back out over the city before moving back into the bedroom I laid Astrea in. Her scent has infiltrated the room, a hint of lavender mixed with smoke, and I know I'll never get it out. No matter how this ends, I will always smell her in this room.

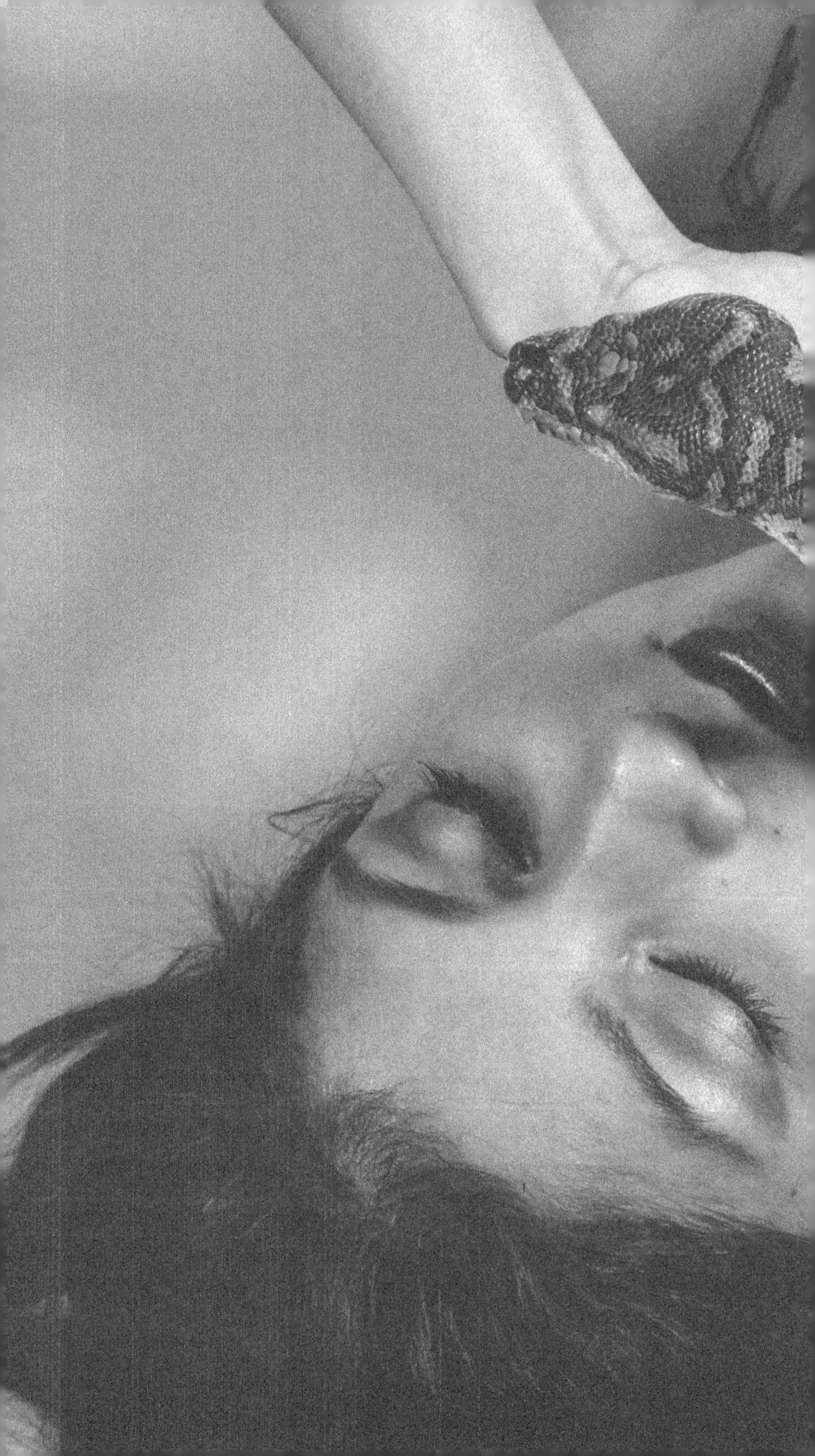

SEVEN

Mates are a dangerous business.
Dangerous if your family doesn't have a bonded
pair.
Power is everything, and they give you power.

– Mori Family Grimoire

Astrea

The soft sheets enveloping my body beg me to stay asleep, but I'm pulled awake by the awareness of another person in the room. I crack my eyes open to find the dark room illuminated only by small, twinkling lights embedded into the ceiling that make it look like the night sky. I glance to my left and see Ciaran sitting in a chair in the corner of the room, rubbing his temples. From this angle, I can see the slight tremor in his hands.

As quietly as I can, I slip from the bed and move over to him. "How long has it been?" I ask softly.

He glances up at me, his blonde hair falling into his

eyes. Those ocean-blue eyes that have always grounded me at times I would rather have floated away. The edges are tinged with a red gleam. *Hunger.*

He drags his hand down his face and rubs his beard. "A few weeks, I think."

My heart and mind war with one another. My mind keeps yelling for me to leave him be, walk away. Don't get more involved than I have to. But my heart, the traitorous little heathen, is whispering for me to help him, take care of him. *After all, he did give me blood; it's my fault he's so hungry,* the heathen says.

I never have been good at listening to my mind.

I lower myself down onto him, straddling his lap and praying he can't see that my hands shaking from the tumultuous emotions coursing through my body. His hands loop around my waist in an automatic move as I tilt my neck to the side. "Drink," I murmur, silently fighting myself in the process.

"Astrea . . ." he groans.

I almost think he is going to say no, but he moves a hand into my hair and pulls my head to the side even more before tracing his tongue along the vein. I let out a low whimper, which transcends into a moan as he sinks his teeth into my neck.

The feeling of him pulling my blood and magic from me shoots straight to my pussy, flooding me with arousal. The scent makes him pull me in closer, grinding me down on his hard cock.

He unlatches from my neck only to tell me how good I taste and then he dives back in, his hands now roaming over my body. He's fed from me plenty of times but this feels different. It feels like we are doused in gasoline and with one spark, we'll go up in flames. I could fucking care less if we burn. The feeling of him feeding from me has made me lose my damn mind. I want everything he can give me. Because this feeling? It's all that matters, and it's keeping me away from the tsunami of darkness that threatens to consume me.

(No light, no light- Florence + the Machine)

"Fuck, Ciaran," I moan, grinding against him unabashedly, more desperate for release than I have ever been in my life. My hands grip his shoulders, nails digging into him. My body has a mind of its own and is desperate to find release with him.

"Yes, little *kamerat*, take what you need." At some point, he pushed my shirt up to expose my breasts. He grips them harshly before pulling on my nipples, all while drinking from me deeply. I moan louder, his name falling from my lips in a breathy prayer. He stops feeding from me at the sound, only to slam his mouth into mine. The taste of blood invades my mouth And I'm so close to cuming. His hand slips into the band of my shorts, where he lets out a low growl as he feels how wet I am. His fingers pull some of the arousal from me to circle my clit, and I lose the battle with holding back. Stars burst behind my closed eyes as I feel him push his fingers into me.

"*Fuck*. Yes," I scream, fucking his fingers through my release. Not caring about how I look or sound, I ride his hand until he's rung me out.

I slump forward onto him as I come back down, breathing deeply. I'm quickly flooded with an arsenal of feelings that overwhelm me. Ciaran has always felt like home, even when I lived in hell, and this? This felt like the homecoming I've been desperate for. And that is terrifying. I slam back into reality. I go to push off him, to get distance so I can think clearly, but he holds me tight and shakes his head. I watch him bring the fingers he just had inside me to his mouth and lick them clean.

Ciaran growls, "I don't know what I love more, the taste of your blood or the taste of your cum on my fingers." I shiver as he leans in close to my ear. "I want to taste your sweet cunt with my head buried between your legs. And after that, I want to fuck you with my teeth in your neck so I can feel you squeezing me while I drink you down. You'll be so full of my cum, it'll be dripping out of you the rest of the night. Would you like that, Astrea?"

His voice is low and deep, eliciting shivers all over my body. I'm losing the battle to keep myself unmated. My damn heart is screaming to stay in his lap. It's drowning me in feelings I don't—no, I *can't* face yet. I push to stand and his strong arms release me. His crimson eyes track me as I slowly back toward a door that I can only hope is the shower so I can have a few moments alone. I just need a few moments to convince my body to calm the fuck down. Because in the end, he still chose not to mate me. And that can never be forgiven.

Ciaran

FUCK. My brain is screaming at me to follow Astrea, the taste of her blood and cum lingering on my tongue. The incomplete bond is riding me even harder now that she knows who I am to her. And in her emerald eyes, I saw the struggle she had in walking away. It brings me a very small measure of comfort that she is just as affected. I scrub my face with my hand as I listen to her turn on the shower. Her scent is still clinging to my body. Getting up, my bare feet take me out of her room and into the kitchen, where I pour another drink and continue to convince myself not to break the door down and fuck her senseless against the shower wall.

I hear Astrea move into the kitchen behind me and pour herself a drink to match my own before she enters my vision, moving over to the plush couches that overlook the giant windows. She's been gone for a while, and now she smells of my soap, her damp hair in a messy bun. Seeing her like this makes my chest clench. This place was only half of a home without her, and if she chooses to leave I know I won't recover.

"Where is Shadow?"

I opt for the truth. "He thought we might want some space."

"Why would he think that?" she asks me.

I scoff. "Because he's a pussy and doesn't want to be around if I piss you off."

She cocks her eyebrow at me. "And is that likely?"

I snort out a laugh. "I hope not, but I can see why it would be. I'm just hoping you can understand and forgive me." I continue to watch her as she tucks her bare feet under her legs. The movement is so domestic. So comfortable.

"I will assume part of this story is why you kept the fact that we were mates from me." The edge in her voice has me clearing my throat.

But it's the hint of hurt underneath her words that worries me.

"You have to understand, Strea, my mother gave me no information about that binding spell. She told me I would know when to use it, and who to use it with. That was it. I honestly assumed it was just a binding spell. Nothing more."

A look of deep hurt flashes across her face before it's

schooled back to the same indifference she's worn since she came out of the shower.

When she doesn't respond, I add, "I shouldn't have been reckless. I knew how you smelled, how you tasted. I knew what you could be to me, and I still used the spell. I had no intention of starting it that night. . . I am sorry."

For a moment, I think she still won't say anything. Then, she quietly replies, "I'll help you with your father, but after that, we can break this. Or at least avoid it. I'm sure we can find something. At the very least, if I can get far enough away, hopefully it'll disappear."

Everything comes crashing to a halt. "What?"

She looks confused. "Well, I don't imagine you're thrilled to be mated to a witch with no power. I mean, I don't know how my magic flared, but I wouldn't count on that happening again."

Even as she is talking, I'm shaking my head. "*Kamerat*, no. I don't give a fuck about your magic. I still want you—it's been hell knowing my mate has been alone. That you've been hurting. I'm happy to be your mate."

Astrea doesn't look convinced, but I keep pushing. "I'm not my father. I don't give a shit about any of this, but we need to stop him. And your magic is the best way to do that."

"My magic isn't anything anymore. I've had access to it twice in my life: once when your family slaughtered mine and once last night. I don't know what you think I can do, but I can't." She fidgets as she talks, her hands alternating between clenching and relaxing. I watch as every now and again she brushes her neck, as if she is expecting that collar to still be there.

I take another steadying breath before continuing, "I

think you have the magic you spoke of earlier. I think you hold that Harbinger magic."

Her eyes snap to mine. "That's impossible," she breathes.

"Is it, though? You taste different. Your magic tastes different."

She shakes her head like she's trying to convince herself more than anything. "No, that's the mate-bond."

"Astrea, it's not." I run my hands through my hair, searching for the words to explain. "I can taste the difference between them. The bond is light. The magic? That's dark, and . . . smoky."

I don't think she realizes she has started crying until I glance up and see tears running down her face like the rain on the window. My heart is breaking at the wild look in her eyes while she jumps to her feet. "If this is true, I'm a huge threat! That magic has a life of its own. Why didn't you tell me?!" She starts pacing, and I can see the panic and fear settling into her. "If your father gets this, no one will survive. Oh, my God, Ciaran. He has to know. He had me for so long, had my blood." She turns those wild eyes on me. "You have to kill me."

A deep rumbling leaves my chest. "Stop talking about dying. You aren't dying. That's not on the table, Astrea. My father will never lay his hands on you again. We will figure this all out." I try to step forward, but she moves back. "Astrea. *Kamerat.* Please. Just trust me on this. We can beat him, and we can fix this city. Together. As mates."

She shakes her head at me, and her voice comes out thickly. "You're a fool, Ciaran. If the magic is here, so is the soul of the one who had it before. She'll be looking for it. If it's not your father, it will be her. You should have killed me in the first place."

I move fast, my anger lashing out as I slam her back against the door of the bedroom she's been inching toward, caging her in with my arms bracketed on either side of her head. "I will say this one time, Strea. Just one. I was an idiot not to tell you up front when I realized it. But you will not be dying. *We* won't be dying. Mated or not, I refuse to let my father get you or the power you hold. So, yes, take time to process this, but you better believe I'll be on your ass if you try to fucking run again. And if you even think of trying to do something stupid to yourself, I will tie you up."

I have to pause to take a steadying breath before I can continue. "When you are done thinking, we are going to go find someone to help with your magic. You aren't a victim, Astrea, you're a goddamn queen, and that magic you have will bring my father to his knees if you stop fighting and embrace it."

I push off the wall and stalk back into the living room, leaving her alone in the hallway.

***

Astrea

My thoughts come like rapid fire as I stand in the middle of the room, Ciaran's scent envelopes me while I try to hold myself together. All I've wanted is my magic back, but if what Ciaran says is true, if it is released from wherever it's held, I might be more dangerous with it. The type of power my mother described when she told the stories was catastrophic. The Harbinger laid waste to the covens, killing off as many of the lines as she could find before they put a stop to her.

The worst part? The part I didn't tell Ciaran? I can empathize with the witch who previously held this power.

She lost everything. And when you've lost it all, why wouldn't you burn the world around you to the ground? Even now I feel the temptation deep in the pit of my stomach to take this power and seek retribution against those who have harmed me.

A deep ache has formed in my chest, and I rub it absently. I think it's coming from Ciaran; our bond is growing stronger and stronger the longer we are together. Eventually I won't be able to stay unmated if we remain together. I yearn to give into the part of me that wants to mate. I hadn't realized how much I was *craving* family. The pain is almost crippling, thinking about spending the rest of my life away from him. Another potentially bigger part of me is terrified of dragging him down with me.

Poppy bumps her soft black nose into my hand, as if to remind me I'm not alone. I smile softly at her before flopping down onto the bed.

I'm not sure how long I lie in the bed, but eventually, my stomach grumbles and I realize the room has become dark again as night breaches the windows. I exhale for a long moment. I know I'll need to face Ciaran at some point. My thinking has shifted from being scared of the power to agreeing with Ciaran that I need to figure it out. Regardless, I have it, and if people are coming for it I should at least have access to it and know how to use it. That mate-bond still pulses in me, desperately searching for its other half, but I'm still not convinced it would be smart to bond. Can I willingly put my mate in danger by binding him to me and this power?

Folding over onto my side, I push myself up from the

bed and pad over to the giant bathroom. The porcelain calls my name, and ignoring that I just showered, I begin filling it with hot water and bubbles. Once it's full, I strip down and ease myself into the serenity of the space. Piling my hair up into a loose top knot, I let my head rest on the edge and close my eyes.

"I'm not sure I've ever seen you so relaxed." Ciaran's voice penetrates my relaxing moment, and I crack an eye open. He's propped against the door with his arms crossed, his black Henley shirt pulled taut over this chest. I'm struck by how normal he looks wearing that shirt and a pair of black basketball shorts. He pushes off the door frame and stalks toward the tub before sitting on the edge. The closer he gets to me, the more my tension leaks from my body.

"Normally, I have more to worry about. But it seems I'm safe here. After all, my mate wouldn't allow anything to happen to me, right?" Humor flows in my voice, but I can't miss the way his eyes flash when I say mate.

"You're right, I wouldn't," he replies softly. I see the tortured look on his face for a moment, a look that reads *I've already let too much happen to you.*

I sink further into the water and ask, "So, do you know why my magic isn't working? I thought it was the spell, but the more I think about it, the more I realize that spell didn't actually do anything, did it? It only helped the mate-bond show stronger."

"Honestly, I don't know. I think you are correct about the spell, but the magic?" Ciaran pauses, collecting his thoughts. "I'm not sure. However, I know someone who might."

EIGHT

Ciaran

After watching Astrea dunk underwater, I stand and grab her a towel. When she emerges from the bathwater, she looks like a goddess as the water streams off her body. I try to avert my gaze, but I can't help taking in her beauty. The damage my father has done to her doesn't escape my notice. Her body is littered with scars.

Guilt hits me hard, and I have to physically force myself not to stagger backwards. "My father will never suffer enough for all he did to you," I growl, wrapping the towel around her.

Steel laces her voice as she snaps, "You're right." She brushes past me into the bedroom, heading to her pack to pull clean clothing from it. I can't pull my eyes away from the outline of her body beneath the towel as she walks away. "I can feel you staring," she murmurs.

I huff out a laugh. "Can you blame me? My mate is gorgeous."

Holding the towel to her chest, she turns toward me, her green eyes catching mine. "I'm still mad. But part of me also understands it. I know I ran. And I trust you when you say you would have told me once we were out. You make a good point about the magic—I need to learn how to use it if I'm going to be able to defend myself, if we are going to bring down your father."

I step toward her, but she holds her hand up to stop me.

"But," Astrea continues pointedly, "until we get my magic figured out, I'm not doing anything about finishing the mating. We need all the information before permanently binding ourselves to each other. You have to understand what you would be forever connected with."

As much as it hurts to hear her say it, I know why she's doing it. And I can accept that. In the end, I have no doubt we'll be completing that bond. She sees herself as something evil. Dangerous. And while I also have no doubt she could ruin her enemies, I don't think she is evil.

I prowl forward, crowding her space. She clutches the towel tighter but I can smell the need coming off her. "I will wait as long as you wish, *kamerat*, but know that when we do finally complete this bond, I'm going to have you begging for release." I plant a soft kiss on her neck, and her breath shutters out of her. "I'll start by sucking on your tight little nipples as I let my hand trail down you. I'll let you feel my fingers playing with you, but only for a moment, just long enough to bring you to the edge. After that, I'll make you suck my cock so you can understand what will be inside you. And after I've brought you to the edge and back so many times that you're begging to be fucked, then and only then will I fuck you so hard, you'll forget your own name." She whimpers a little, and I smile as I step back from her. Her pupils are blown so wide that the emerald is only a small ring. "Now, get dressed—we have a meeting to get to."

Astrea

I both want to murder Ciaran and allow him to fuck me senseless for leaving me as he did in the bedroom. His powerful body walks away as if he hadn't just turned me on so much that I was already close to begging him. He keeps smirking at me across the room as I squirm in my seat. I shoot him a glare, hoping it conveys my extreme annoyance in his decisions.

When Shadow returns, he is cautious of me. I think he is trying to determine if I blame him. I offer him a warm smile before walking over to him and wrapping my arms around his body. "I'm not mad at you."

He laughs. "Good to see you didn't murder Ciaran." I ignore how tense his body has become. He's never enjoyed being touched. I have my theories, but I keep them to myself; after all, it's his trauma and if anyone understands that it's me.

I shrug as I pull off him, his body immediately relaxing. "Honestly, it's to be determined. But for now, I've deemed him more useful alive."

"Jesus, Astrea," Ciaran mutters before he moves around the apartment to gathering his jacket.

Shadow lets out another laugh, but he asks Ciaran, "Where are we going?"

"To Ava," Ciaran says simply.

I sit up a little straighter at Shadow's sharp inhale of breath. "Do you think that's a good idea?" His question has me narrowing my eyes, irrational jealousy already creeping its way in.

Ciaran shrugs. "We don't have any other options at this point. She might have the answers we need. Besides, she's not mad at me." He clasps his hand on Shadow's shoulder and squeezes. Shadow just glowers at him.

"Who is Ava?" I'm hoping I've masked my jealousy with curiosity, but judging by the way Ciaran's eyes flash in delight, I don't think I've done a very good job at it.

"You'll see." It's the only warning I get from him before Shadow opens a portal. Stepping through, we enter a large garage. Various bikes line the walls on the left, while an assortment of cars line the right. Ciaran and Shadow move toward a black SUV.

"Wait, we're driving? Why don't we just use a portal?" I don't reveal that I will feel safer and less vulnerable using a portal. Panic is trying to worm its way into my chest, trying to cut off my breathing at the idea of being back in Gothic Grove. Back in a city that broke me apart.

Shadow turns to look at me. "We promised Ava no unexpected portal-ing. This is how we get to her. Don't worry, we'll be relatively safe."

I don't mention how the word "relatively" doesn't help me feel better about this. As if sensing my impending panic attack, Ciaran takes a risk and grips my hand. The relief is almost instant. The panic and fear ebb away until I feel grounded. He catches my eyes with his and offers a small squeeze of my hand before pulling us into the SUV.

The city passes in a blur. The streets, once so familiar, now feel like ghosts haunting me. While Gothic Grove has always been gritty, I don't miss just how dark the city has become in the years of Alexi's reign. And judging by the tension in Ciaran's body he didn't miss it either.

My mind is still stuck on all the revelations today has brought me. Really, what the week has brought me. It feels like only yesterday I was standing on my porch, drinking my coffee. We are still on the relative outskirts of the city as we park outside an old brick building. The walls are weathered: what was once red and vibrant is now covered in moss, faded and grim. An old "open" sign flickers off and on above a metal door, giving no indication of what exactly is open.

The smell of the city hits me as soon as the car door opens. It's putrid and rotting; a scent that not even the endless rain can wash away. One that I became very accustomed to, spending so much time in the underbelly of that prison.

Ciaran and Shadow are both tense and box me in between their bodies, Ciaran in front and Shadow behind me. My fingers gently stroke the blades strapped to my legs as a measure of comfort and a reminder that I can take care of myself, with or without magic. The "open" sign lets off a low buzz like it's about to short out, the only sound to pierce the otherwise eerily quiet surroundings.

(Lights- Ellie Goulding, bassnectar version)

Before we can even knock, the door swings open and a hulking man ushers us inside without a word. A shifter, if his eyes are any indication. Glowing as they look us over, assessing us, as he steps aside to reveal a hallway. I can feel the thrumming base as soon as we're in. We move through a darkened hallway before coming out into a large open space. The music, previously just a ramble of bass drops and vibrations, becomes clear and I gasp as I look around. The entirety has been converted into a bar, but it's not the bar that has my mouth dropping open—it's the windows lining the top of the room, where various couples are on display writhing in pleasure. Around the room are red velvet couches and tables that bracket a dance floor and main stage area. Cocktail servers are busy bringing drinks and food to the tables. People are drinking and laughing, genuinely happy. A door in the very back has a bouncer posted in front of it, and couples continue to disappear through it. Seductive smiles are plastered on their faces.

"What is this place?" My voice comes out barely above a whisper, but Ciaran catches it anyway.

He turns and leans in close. "Welcome to The Play-ground," he replies in my ear, causing me to shiver.

Gothic Grove has a thriving nightlife—after all, it's ruled by corruption and sin—but the theme throughout the city is very obviously controlled by the vampires now. Alexi made sure that the remaining witches, "lesser witches" as the covens had called them, knew who was in charge. When you walk into a club like this one, you would normally see witches in servitude to vampires. But as I look around the dark environment, I see nothing to indicate anyone is here against their will.

"How does this exist?" My eyes keep bouncing from area to area in awe. I see a vampire leaning in to feed on a male witch, whose magic flares out to meet him as their bodies come together tightly in a lovers' embrace. I see two witches laughing, and a vampire kneeling at their feet. I even think I see a few shifters, their distinct MC vests standing out amongst the other patrons.

It's Shadow who answers, his voice thick with emotion. "Ava."

Ciaran guides me over to the bar and nods at the man behind it, but no drinks appear in front of us. Instead, the bartender tilts his head at us before he disappears into another room behind the bar. After a few moments, he comes back out and waves our group in. Shadow remains at my back, sticking a little closer than before. His anxiety and tension are not helping my own.

The room we enter is dark with small fairy lights twinkling throughout. It's a similar layout as up front with couches around the edges, but in the center of the room stands a large bird cage. A man kneels in the center of the cage, and outside the bars stands a woman holding a riding crop. She has bright pink hair that is braided on one side and shaved on the other. The dark leather bodysuit looks wrong, given how bright her hair is in the dark room. She is a wisp of a human, her body looking like it could be carried away by a swift breeze. When she turns and looks at us, her smile is bright and her eyes delighted as she takes in Ciaran, but they grow cold when they land on Shadow behind me.

Ciaran hasn't disclosed how they know each other. Both he and Shadow have been cagey about it, and jealousy has become a constant companion, especially when I think about anyone being near Ciaran. I imagine it's the incomplete mate bond pushing me. Magic like that has a funny way of trying to get what it wants.

"Oh, how wonderful!" The slip of a girl prances over and hugs Ciaran, and the involuntary growl that escapes me has her raising a brow before her smile turns into a frown. "I see it's business and not pleasure." She makes eye contact with Shadow once but doesn't address him. Her gaze appears to ghost over him, as if actually acknowledging his presence would shatter her.

"Hello, Ava. We have some questions we're hoping you could help us answer." Ciaran moves so his hand grazes my back before he steps back, leaving Ava standing in front of me. "This is Astrea Mori."

She claps her hands like a child might, with pure glee. "Ooh, a Mori!"

(Lilith- Halsey)

"Astrea can't access her magic. She's used it twice in her life, both times under duress. Theoretically, she should have access now; would you know why she doesn't?" Ciaran crosses his arms over his chest and waits for an answer from the pixie woman.

She cocks her head with clear intrigue and begins slowly circling me, tilting her head back and forth as she assesses me. I manage not to squirm, though the feeling of being examined crawls under my skin like a bug. "Can you tell me about those two times?" she asks gently.

Nothing in me feels comfortable telling her anything, but I shove those feelings down. "The first was when my family was killed. I managed to take out a few of the men who tried to get me before they placed a collar on me," I answer hesitantly.

I don't miss the sneer that moves over her face when I mention the collar. "Those things," she hisses. "Fucking Alexi." The shock on my face has her shrugging. "You aren't the only one who Alexi tried to break," she explains.

I see it then, in her eyes. Trauma leaves a mark on the soul. Physically, one can heal rather quickly, but the soul takes much longer. People often forget that, and once the physical evidence is gone, it's easy to forget the trauma even happened. Unless you know what to look for in the eyes.

"Ava." Ciaran is starting to sound impatient.

The girl, Ava, takes a candy out of her pocket and pops it into her mouth, making her appear more childlike than she already seemed. She tilts her head to the side as she looks at me, her braid falling and exposing a savage bite mark at the juncture. My eyes zero in on it, curiosity hitting me hard.

"Who did that?" The question is out before I can think better of it.

The room stills. The air itself is suddenly heavy; the same feeling before a storm breaks. She shifts her braid back over to cover it. "No one," she answers. Her silver eyes are hard and tinged with sadness. "The collars weren't the only things holding people's magic back. They would implant pieces of them, too, just in case the collar was removed," she explains, a clear dismissal of the conversation.

I freeze and look over at Ciaran. "But you were able to get me out. If I have that in me, how was I able to escape? How was it able to break through at the penthouse?"

Ava sniffs at me, causing me to step back slightly from the sudden invasion of personal space. Something tells me this girl has no idea what personal space actually is. "Oh, you are tricky, Ciaran, using a binding spell like that on her," she taunts. "Where on earth did you get that magic?" She doesn't wait for an answer, just continues talking. "Those pieces were really a safety measure against the use of magic, not to keep you in prison."

"If she has one, how do we locate it and get it out?" Ciaran asks.

Ava smiles and shrugs. "Your guess is as good as mine. I never warranted one, not powerful enough."

Shadow scoffs, and it sounds a lot like, "That's a lie."

She glares at him, her eyes going icy before she turns

back to me. "Can you think back to any times that might have been particularly invasive?"

I shudder, and the box in my brain rattles against the chains I've wrapped around it to keep the memories in. "I don't have a lot of memories from the experiments, to be honest. They drugged me a lot at first, and once they refused to drug me, my mind decided it wasn't worth remembering once I got out."

"They stopped giving you drugs?" she asks, her head tilting to the side again.

Ciaran's rage vibrates in my chest, that annoying bond poking at me. I glare at him before continuing to talk with Ava. I think back. "They started to realize I enjoyed the drugs. They didn't want me to enjoy anything." My own anxiety is starting to pepper me again but I keep pushing the emotions away and keep focusing on the moment at hand. "I imagine it would have happened early on, right?" She nods in confirmation.

Closing my eyes, I think back, trying to remember anything I can. I'm assaulted with fear and panic, swallowing it down the best I can as I search my memories. "So, I guess it would have been my very first time being in the lab," I finally say, my eyes opening back up.

"Can you show me where they worked on you?"

I nod and lift up my shirt, pointing to a thick scar right below my breast.

"May I?" She holds her hand out, and I nod. She lets her fingers dance over the scar, pressing slightly in. When she steps back, she looks proud of herself. "Right there. I would say dig in a few centimeters and you'll find a piece of metal. That should work. But I would be careful—not having full access to her magic for that long can be overwhelming once it's back."

Shadow speaks up from behind us. "She was able to access it earlier."

"Oh, look, you can talk instead of just muttering behind her. Good to know." I can hear the hostility in her tone, but more than that, I can feel the hurt that lies just under it. Clearly, something happened between them.

Ciaran sighs, bringing Ava's attention back to him. She waves a hand in front of her face, as if to clear the anger and hurt away before touching my scar again. "Given how powerful she is, based on the need of the collar and the piece of metal, her magic most likely weakened it. So, in times of high emotion, she would be able to access it—or, say, if she were near a certain someone." Her too-perceptive eyes glance between the two of us, but neither of us confirm or deny the question in her gaze.

"Okay, so, let's cut me open." I palm one of the blades from my hip, but Ciaran grabs my wrist.

"We aren't doing this here. Not if what Ava says is true. I don't want us doing it in a space we can't control."

"You can use the basement." Ava wraps her hands behind her back, teetering on her feet. "Her magic won't do any damage. No one will detect it. You know that."

Shadow growls, "Our place is safe."

She rolls her eyes. "I know you think it's safe, but have your wards truly been tested? Because mine have, and they've stood up."

Shadow growls again, this time causing the hair on my neck to raise. "Who?"

Ava glares at him. "Don't pretend to care now," she snarls.

Something in me roils uncomfortably at the thought of taking this out here, at being in a basement. I involuntarily flash back to my cell in the prison, and a shiver of apprehension rattles me. In my heart, I know things will change once this piece of metal is removed, and I don't want it happening in the basement of some sex club with this girl around.

"I want to go home," I blurt. Ciaran's eyes dilate, and I realize my slip of the tongue. "I mean Ciaran's home. I trust them."

The little pink-haired demon just shrugs. "Suit yourself. Now, if you'll excuse me, I have someone waiting on me." But before she turns from me, her eyes go unfocused for a moment before they snap back to clarity.

"Now that is something I haven't seen in a very, very long time." Ava's gaze bounces between us, but instead of moving closer to me, she goes toward Ciaran, her head tilting. "How did I never see this before?" she murmurs.

Suddenly it hits me, what just happened. "Wait, you're a Seer?" I ask quickly. She's the first one I've met since Hansley died.

"Among other things, yes," she shares absently as she continues looking Ciaran over. "Ciaran, who was your mother?"

He frowns at her. "Kara. Kara Helvig. But in the witch community, she was known as Kara Carmine."

A small gasp escapes me. "She was a Carmine? They were an original family." I remember their home—it was the smallest, and I always loved how cozy the cottage looked compared to the monstrosities the other families, including mine, lived in. I was too young to ever get to know Kara, but Hansley had spoken kindly of her. "Wait, it was your mom who married Alexi when the treaty was formed!"

Suddenly, it all clicks into place: Ciaran is desperate to save his mother's people.

Ava rocks on her heels, sucking her lips into her teeth. "Oh, Ciaran. You've gotten in very deep." She then turns and looks at me. "You need to be careful. You both do. You're playing with very old magic."

"What do you mean?"

Despite the tinge of fear I can hear lacing my own voice, she simply shakes her head, the braid swaying with the motion. "You'll find me when you're ready to know."

NINE

What is true power?
A corruption of the soul.

– Carmine Family Grimoire

Ciaran

Ava has always been cryptic. She's never been your typical witch in all the time I've known her. In fact, I've never been one hundred percent convinced she is fully a witch; her scent is abnormal. I've never felt magic like hers before. I drag my hand down my face in both exhaustion and frustration. She refused to give us any more information, and with Shadow glowering behind me, I knew I couldn't push. Instead, we thanked her for the information and chose to leave.

Glancing over at Astrea, I see her gaze is vacant as she looks off into the distance. Bringing her to see Ava was risky. With us being unmated, our emotions are unstable. The whole time we were in the club, I could feel her anger and jealousy pushing against me. I watched her hands twitch to grab the blades at her hips. But bringing Shadow? That was stupid. As we get into the car again, I can feel the tension pouring off him; it'll be a few days before he comes back down from seeing her. As much as I want to push him on this, I know he'll only dig his heels in. He won't go back to her.

"I'm sorry," I murmur to him. He doesn't say anything. "Why don't you go see Dr—"

He cuts me off with a glare.

"Okay, okay, I'm sorry," I concede, raising my hands in defeat.

He just shakes his head and turns the car on, putting all his focus into driving.

Astrea is practically bouncing in the backseat. "Anyone gonna tell me how y'all knew her?"

"We helped her escape," I answer, hoping she drops it.

"Like you helped me?" she snarls.

I turn and look at her. "You mean, have I fucked her?"

She stiffens before she flashes her teeth at me in a feral growl.

"No, little *kamerat*, I did not fuck her. We got her out in a different way." I don't look at Shadow; if he wants her to know anything, he'll need to be the one to tell her.

The drive goes fast, and soon we are pulling into the parking garage of our home. Shadow doesn't say anything but immediately steps through a portal once he's exited the car.

"Where is he going?" At some point, Astrea's hair came out of its bun, and it gathers now in soft waves around her shoulders as she glances to where he disappeared.

I walk to the elevator and press the button, then step aside to let her get on before I step in. "He needs some space. He and Ava have a complicated relationship. I shouldn't have brought him, but while we trust Ava, we don't trust everyone who works for her. It would have been too big a risk to not have him at our backs. And before you ask, I'm not telling you a thing about them. If he wants you to know, he'll tell you."

She frowns but nods. The elevator dings and we step into the penthouse. "So, what's the plan?" she asks, attempting to change the subject. Anyone else might take her tone as cockiness, but I know her. I know that body language, the way she is digging her nails into her palms. Even her burst of energy in the car. She's nervous.

Pulling my shirt up and over my head, I gesture for her to follow me and turn toward my room. I don't wait to see if she is or not before I go straight to the bathroom and flip the shower on. I unbutton my pants and slip them off first, followed by my boxers, before finally looking over my shoulder. Her eyes are raking over my body unabashedly and her mouth is slightly open. Arousal perfumes around us. It feels good to know I have the same effect on her that she has on me.

"We'll do it here. Blood can wash away quicker that way."

"How very practical of you. And we need to be naked for it?" Her voice is hoarse. She crosses her arms, almost shielding herself.

I shrug before stepping in. "I don't want to ruin perfectly good clothing." It's a lie. I simply want to feel her naked body against mine. Turning on the rainfall shower, I let it rinse over me.

It takes only a moment before she disrobes and steps in. My body is immediately aware of hers. I turn around, drinking in the sight of her. She chews on her bottom lip, another nervous habit, and I raise my hand to cup her face and let my thumb brush over her bottom lip, pulling it out from between her teeth.

"What's going through your mind, *kamerat?*" I ask softly, but the only sound is the water raining down from the ceiling.

(this is me trying- Taylor Swift)

Her big green eyes lock onto mine, and I'm more than a little surprised to see tears shining in them. "This is a lot. We remove this and I will have access to my magic. Magic we think comes from the Harbinger. That's not exactly comforting." She steps under the water, allowing it to flow over her, but she doesn't move out of my touch. I can feel my canines descending, but I remain still. "And then there is the mate-bond to consider."

"I won't force you."

She shakes her head. "No, it's not that. I do want this. I'm still mad you kept this all from me, but I want it. I think it clicked as soon as I saw Ava near you. I wanted to rip her throat out." She closes her eyes and leans into my hand before stepping closer and wrapping her arms around my bare torso. "I've always felt safe with you, Ciaran. It's just hard, after everything, to trust this. And I don't think you fully understand what you are tying yourself to with this magic."

I hold her to my body and nod against the top of her head. "I understand. So, let's do this one step at a time. Let's get this out of you first. Then we can figure the rest out. Okay?"

(Walk Through the Fire- Zayde Wolf and Ruelle)

She lets out a long sigh before looking back up at me. The steam is swirling around us, and her eyes are almost luminous. Her hair is plastered to her body from the water, and the makeup she was wearing earlier is slowly starting to run down her cheeks like tear tracks. I let my hand trace down to the scar beneath her breast before dropping my body down so I'm eye level with it. She looks down and simply nods, giving me all the confirmation I need. I grab the small blade I brought in with me from the seat next to us and make a quick slice across the puckered skin. She doesn't move, doesn't make a sound. I watch her face carefully and I can see the moment she dissociates.

"You're here with me, *kamerat*, no one else." I keep murmuring variations of this as I press my fingers into the wound and begin searching. The minute my finger grazes the metal, she gasps, and her eyes refocus as I pull.

Shadows burst forth from her and her head is thrown back in a silent scream. I stand quickly and pull her to me, letting the offensive piece of metal drop with a clang to the ground where her blood is swirling into the drain at our feet. "Strea, you're here. You're safe," I whisper in her ear. She thrashes under my hold, but I keep her close, repeating the same assurances over and over until I feel something slithering up my legs. Looking down, I see two snakelike creatures of smoke and shadow moving up my legs. Astrea goes still as soon as they touch her body, and then she finally relaxes into my hold.

(Revolution- Ruelle)

Quick as lightning, her mouth is on me once the snakes are tattooed on her body. She has my hair fisted in her hands and her tongue slips over my lips. "Mate," she whispers against my mouth, and the otherworldly sound of her voice has my cock going rigid. I groan as I feel her come alive under me, and then I'm slamming her back against the tile wall as the hot water pours over us. I sink my teeth into her neck, pulling her blood and magic into me. The full taste of it hits me right in the chest. The smokey, dark flavor spiraling into me is utterly intoxicating.

She screams out my name, and I slide my fingers down to find her soaking wet core.

"Fuck me, now," Astrea demands, but I drop down to my knees in front of her instead.

"No. I want to fucking worship you first." I dive into her like she's my last meal. My tongue moves over her clit in circles as I continue to push my fingers in and out of her pussy. The sounds she is making have my cock weeping.

"Ciaran. Please," she whimpers.

I huff out a laugh against her tender flesh. "Please what, *kamerat?*" Her taste is divine as she drips down my chin and over my fingers, so close to falling over the edge.

"Please let me cum. I'm so fucking close." I pull my fingers out of her and stand, eliciting another whimper.

I lift her up so her legs circle my waist and I'm lined up with her entrance. "The first time you cum today, I want it to be on my cock," I command, and then I slam home into her.

"Oh, FUCK, god." Her pussy flutters around me, squeezing me like one of her snakes. "Don't stop," she begs.

I grab her throat in my fist and growl, "What did I tell you about paying homage to false gods, *kamerat?*" I drive into her hard. "I'm your god now."

"Oh, Ciaran. Fuck, yes."

I pull back and look into her beautiful face, knowing beyond a shadow of a doubt this is the moment. "Bite me," I order her breathlessly. "Let me in, *kamerat.*" I feel her dull teeth scrape my neck and she bites down hard. The pain swims over my body, but under that pain I feel our bond snap into place, whole at long last. The moment she accepts that glittering bond, I feel our souls mingle, intertwining, mine the light to her dark. That ancient magic is no longer hers alone but ours. It lazily strokes against something already within me that comes alive next to it. A warm glowing light to her darkness.

"Cum with me," I demand, pushing my hand between us and pressing down on the tight bundle of nerves where we're joined. She comes undone in seconds, gushing around my cock as she finally falls over the edge, and I slam home one more time before I'm unloading deep inside of her.

She pulls off my neck and smiles, blood staining her teeth. I drop my forehead to hers. "Mate," she whispers again.

I'm panting, desperate to catch my breath, but I plant another deep kiss on her mouth while slowly pull out of her. Already, I miss the warmth.

"Fuck," I growl as I see our combined release dripping down her legs. I can feel her magic has toned down, settled, and I pull back to look into her eyes. They are on fire. The emerald is so bright it almost hurts to look at.

She tilts her head as if she is listening to something. "They say you should let your magic out to play."

My body freezes, "I don't have magic."

She shrugs and kisses me lightly. "They say you do."

Feeling a glimmer of trepidation, I search her gaze. "Who are 'they,' Astrea?"

She sighs in contentment and closes her eyes again. "Mmm, my snakes. My magic. It talks to me."

She nuzzles into me before I can comment, and I let it go . . . though my concern remains, both about her magic speaking to her and what it says regarding my own.

They tried to take her power, so we gave her more.
They created a monster.
We created a reckoning.

– Carmine Family Grimoire

Shadow
(Ease My Pain- Solr and Cece mix)

Taking a long, deep drag of the Eufori-laced cigarette, I allow the buzz to work through my body. Seeing Ava never goes well for me. It brings back too many memories I've long since tried to ignore. When we got back to Ciaran's, I didn't want to be around them. No, I *couldn't* be around them. They reeked of their mating bond, the scent like a dagger straight to my chest after being around Ava. After hearing what she said about the mark on her neck. So, I left to the only place that I could think of: the rooftop apartment that my stepbrother keeps for me in his building. The empty space is nothing more than a hiding place for when the demons are too loud to be in our home. A space where they can come out and no one will see me break.

Another deep drag of the drug has my head swimming, but it's doing nothing to drown out the pain that keeps pushing into my brain. *I deserve to feel this pain.* The demons laugh at me; relish in the pain I'm in. "Fuck!" I scream. My power lashes out, cracking the plaster in the wall in front of me and adding to the fractures that match my own heart.

"You know, at some point I'll have to replace this whole building if you keep doing that," my stepbrother's deep voice says from the dark. He steps out, his arms crossed and face hard, but his eyes shimmer with concern. It makes me sick. "And I rather like this place. It would be a shame to have to move."

"Fuck off, Drago. I have no interest in talking to you," I snarl.

"No," he says as he walks toward me. "You just want to spiral while high on *my* drugs in an apartment *I* gave you." Drago's bone-white hair is almost blinding in the dim light as he runs his ringed fingers through it, despite the shaggy length already being slicked back. His body is decorated in just as much ink as mine is, though you wouldn't guess it; he keeps the tattoos mostly covered by the pristine suits he wears. The only hint of them are peeking up his neck and out onto his ring covered hands. My father loved that about him. He also loved that Drago was built like a fighter; his muscle powerful on his frame. He surveys me with his blue eyes; eyes that make me feel like he can see straight into my soul. I shiver involuntarily and he smirks at the reaction.

My words slur as I ask, "How did you know I was here?" I already know the answer, but I crave the pain that his answer will bring.

"Ava."

I laugh. "She should stop trying. Leave me the fuck alone."

Drago lets out a low, uncharacteristically hostile growl. It's the only warning I get before he's got me pinned against the wall behind us. More plaster cracks from the force of it. "I won't keep watching you do this to yourself. I refuse." Drago is using all his magic to hold me in place, but he doesn't have to. I would let him kill me right here if that's what he wanted. *Because that's what I deserve.*

I take another long drag and blow the crimson smoke into his face, begging the voices to stop, if only for a moment. Drago shakes his head and lets me go, and my body drops to the ground. My dark hair falls into my face, and I don't bother moving it. I keep my eyes locked on the ground. Dragos' shoes are still in my line of sight as he squats down into a crouch. "This is the last time you can come here to get fucked up. I'm not going to find you OD'd because you couldn't face your shit."

"Fuck you, *brother*, you don't know anything about my shit," I sneer. My father insisted on me calling Drago my brother, despite having no relation to him. His mother had been sold to my father after my own died. *No, after she was killed.* He was thrilled to have a son like Drago in the family, someone who wasn't a fuck-up like I was.

He stands back up, straightening his suit jacket. "I know enough. And I know if you keep this up, you are assuring the destruction of not just yourself."

He doesn't say another word as he blends back into the darkness, leaving me and my demons alone.

And I let them pull me back under, let myself get trapped under their weight while I pray for the drugs to make quick work of me.

Astrea

We stayed in the shower until the water ran cold. Fucking twice more, both times with less urgency; simply enjoying the feeling of our mating. Once out, Ciaran puts a small bandage over the wound the damn shard came out of, before grabbing the piece of metal and placing it in a small sandwich bag. He plants a kiss on my forehead before he exits the bathroom, as if he knew I just needed a moment to breathe.

I clean the fogged up mirror and finally take a look at myself. My body is covered in marks from our mating. Between fingerprint bruises and bite marks, my body tells the story of the last few hours in a way that has me blushing. But, despite the glow behind my eyes and warmth to my cheeks, I still struggle to see the scars from Alexi.

Shifting my gaze from the mirror, I look down and see those shadow snakes are now curled around my arms. Nestled deep in my skin like two dark tattoos, one has its head on my right hand while the other's head is sitting on my chest, just under my collar bone. My magic feels alive, rolling under my skin, ungrounded and ready to burst out. Just below that, I feel my mate bond with Ciaran pulsing. I can feel him as he moves about his apartment.

"You say you're my magic, but what does that mean?" I ask out loud, despite feeling crazy.

All witches have magic. But not all magic is alive such as we are. You will see.

"That's not disconcerting," I mutter as I move out of the bathroom. It's not the first time in my life that I've cursed my mother for never teaching me more. Or even Hansley.

Sure, I didn't have magic at the time, but would it have killed them to prepare me just in case? She was a Seer, for gods' sake, there is no way she didn't see this coming. Which means she *chose* not to warn me. Something akin to a slow burning rancor pushes through the grief I have of losing her. It's an unsettling feeling that makes me feel volatile.

I grab a pair of shorts and an oversized white sweatshirt and pull them on as I head out to the kitchen, not just desperate to ignore this newfound feeling but also to find Ciaran. Rounding the corner, I see him cooking something that smells of garlic and tomatoes. He hasn't looked at me, though it's easy to feel that he knows I'm there. His tattooed back faces me, and I lean against the wall and take in his beauty. A calmness washes over me like a balm to the rancor that's eating away at me. His muscles ripple below the whirls of black ink. His hair is still down and hanging wet to just below his shoulders.

"Keep staring at me, *kamerat*, and I'm going to fuck you right on this counter."

I snort as I push off the wall and walk over to him, circling my arms around his broad waist. "You say that like it's a bad thing." I nip playfully at his shoulder blade before moving around him and popping myself up onto the counter. I attempt to pull him in with my legs.

Ciaran manages to dodge me. "I need to feed my mate, then I will happily fuck you again." His voice is deep and gravelly, and it sends shivers through me.

He finishes up the pasta and plates two helpings. I slide back off the counter and follow him into the living room, where we sit on the couch. We eat in relative silence, comfortable with each other and enjoying the meal. The rain plays a soft melody in the background. Poppy pads out of wherever she has been hiding, plopping herself directly in front of Ciaran.

"She wants some food," I giggle as she lets out a chitter before poking him with her snout. The giant Viking of a man looks at her as if confused by the attention before he grabs a small piece of meat and holds it down to her. She snatches it happily from him and bounces over to the fireplace to eat her prize. She appears to be perfectly at peace with her new home.

Everything is changing so rapidly. I can't help but wonder if we should have waited until I was more settled into my magic.

"You're thinking a lot there," he ponders after setting his emptied plate aside on an end table. He shoots a warning glare at my fox when she starts to stand back up, heading towards the plate.

I shrug. "I just went from no magic to now having two magic snakes tattooed on me and having a mate. A lot has happened in a very short amount of time."

He nods slowly. "I'm sure it's a lot to adjust to." He hesitates, and I can feel his discomfort flash to me. "Do you regret it? The bond?"

I pause before I answer. Do I regret it? Part of me is still upset with Ciaran for keeping it from me. But I also know I was in no headspace to understand. I was constantly in fight-or-flight, and him telling me a mate bond had started to form would have been bad. A deep, dark part of me doesn't trust that I would have kept myself safe if I had known. What his father had done, and tried to do, had tainted my view, and I would have stopped at nothing to make sure I was never attached to anyone. Even if that meant dying.

"I don't regret it," I finally reply, causing Ciaran to visibly relax. "I do still worry about this power and how it will impact you. I don't think you understand how dangerous it is. And now you've permanently bound your-self to me. To this magic. I can feel it, Ciaran, it's wild and untamed. It makes me feel out of control."

He shrugs. "I'm not worried about being bound to you, Astrea. I've known from the moment we met that you were someone important to me. My worry is making sure you learn how to control your magic, along with the fact that your magic seems to think *I* have magic."

He's not the only one with that curiosity, but before I can open my mouth to say anything, an awareness shoots through me. Almost as though turned by force, my head whips toward the elevator doors.

(I'm seeing red- Tommee Profit)

She's here. That voice ruptures in my head a moment before the elevator doors shatter inward. Bringing chunks of the plaster with it. Ciaran jumps up and throws himself over me as debris rains down. He rolls off as soon as we hear the first growl. As I push myself up, I can see three Hell-beasts pushing their massive bodies through the hole that was once the elevator. Instinctively, I reach for one of my blades and silently curse when I find nothing—they're on the floor in the bedroom. Ciaran is still blocking me from the beasts with his body, and the mate-bond vibrates with his rage. The first beast launches himself at us, but Ciaran grabs it by the neck and squeezes until it snaps, before tossing the mutt to the ground.

The other two beasts hold. Long seconds tick by, leaving the four of us poised in a tense standoff. "What the fuck are they waiting for?" I mutter.

"Hello," a shrill voice sings through the dark hole, and I shut my eyes as a familiarity that I can't place pings through me. A female comes into view, stepping through the massive hole behind the Hellbeasts. Her hair is long, black and matted. Her face might still have been beautiful, if not for the crazed look in her black eyes, but her figure is almost emaciated. The woman's arms and legs are spindly and her cheekbones pop out in sharp points. It makes me wonder how she's alive. And then I see it—the shimmer of a glamor over her. This isn't her real form.

"Oh, my goodness, what a mess we've made," she coos as she pats the closest beast's head, and it leans its massive form into her body. Then she looks up and tsk-tsks at Ciaran. "I'm sorry about that. But really, with all the magic you had layering this place, you would think you didn't want anyone to find you!" She steps around some of the debris, and the glamor shimmers around her like a mirage in the desert.

I grit my teeth, narrowing my eyes at her. "Who are you?"

She laughs loudly. "You don't need to know that right this second, little Astrea." Her patronizing tone grates my nerves. The woman moves forward, which causes Ciaran to emit a low growl. She halts, pouting a bit. "Really, Ciaran, that is awfully rude."

"What are you doing here, *whore?*" he all but spits at her.

The change in her is instant, her face morphing to show venomous rage. "Do not disrespect me like that," she hisses.

"Sucking my father's cock doesn't make you deserving of respect."

I feel the magic just a moment before it tries to hit us, and I shove Ciaran over and fling myself down to the other side. Fury flashes across her face before she sends another wave of powerful magic directly at Ciaran. It slams into him before I can react, and his body goes rigid and drops to the floor. The mating bond pulses out a wave of pain before going silent.

"Ciaran!" I scramble to his side, but my hands reel back at the feeling of the dark magic moving over his body.

"Oh, calm down, he'll be fine. I have no interest in killing him," she replies.

Glancing up, I can see her picking her long red nails, the level of boredom playing across her face almost insulting. She moves further into the room, her beasts flanking her as she walks toward me. I expect her to use her magic again but she just sits cross-legged in front of me. As she does, she unwinds a long whip that she had twisted around her center And sets it right to the side of us. My magic flares to life, those shadow snakes uncoiling off my body and poising to strike as I position myself over and in front of Ciaran.

Her eyes brighten with a feverish gleam. "Ah, there it is. I wouldn't have found you if you hadn't removed that piece of metal he put in you," she purrs, "I told Alexi he never should have used it on you. Men think they know everything." She rolls her eyes as though this is an inside joke between us.

Her words bring the world to a screeching halt around me. "What did you say?"

"You heard me," she answers as she pets one of the beasts. "Alexi was a fool to take as long as he did to try to control you. And to allow Ciaran the freedom he did. But it doesn't matter. Now we are here, and you've got that delicious magic back. Though, having the magic awake as it will make it a little harder to retrieve from you. But I suppose if we can't pull it from you, we can just use the binding spell."

I almost laugh at her. "You won't be touching us. And if you try, I will gut you where you sit." The beast to her left huffs and moves closer to Ciaran and I.

I catch the wicked smile in her eyes before she snaps her fingers, and it launches itself at us. I snap my arms up, my magic flowing out in a long arc of black smoke that the beast slams into. A sick, crunching sound vibrates through me as the creature falls limp, its neck snapped, the bones protruding from its neck.

"That's a fun trick." I can feel her own magic touching the shield I've created around us, black and crackling with lighting. "But it won't hold against me, Astrea, not like this. It isn't yours yet." She steps closer, inspecting the shield before dragging a long fingernail down it, which cuts through it like a butter knife. I don't even have time to blink before I'm hit with her magic and flying backward, slamming into the wall behind us.

(Revenant- Izzy Reign)

I'm slow to get up. I can feel blood dripping down my face, and my head is fuzzy from the impact. My magic still swirls around me, but those snakes have tattooed themselves back on my skin. *Think, think, think, Astrea. We need to get out of here.*

You cannot win with your magic right now; the bond isn't strong enough. Get your blades, the snakes urge in my mind.

I watch her smile wickedly, her own magic still at the ready. Thinking quickly, I gather my strength and slam my palm into the floor, sending my magic out in waves of crackling black energy that fracture outwardly. It's the distraction I need, and I take off at a dead sprint for the room my blades are held in, praying the magic will at least slow her down.

I hear the pounding of paws behind me and I dive into the room, tucking into a ball and rolling into the bedside table. I hit it hard enough to knock the wind from my lungs, but I reach up and grab for the first blade even as I wheeze.

As soon as I feel the hilt, I wrap my fingers around it and slash out just as the Hellbeast attempts to grab at me. I lodge the blade up into its jaw and twist, and it drops dead to the ground.

Panting, I grab the other blade and sprint back out to the room to find her standing over Ciaran's body. Seeing her touching him is all it takes for me to snap and I scream. My power blasts out from me as a primordial rage flows through me. I watch as it shoves her back from Ciaran. Her eyes flash in something akin to shock before she shakes it off. Holding both ancient blades at the ready, I move fully back into the room. As I'm about to lunge, I hear the soft padding of paws come up next to me. Poppy stands tall, paws digging into the ground and her tail long and full of flames. She bares her teeth at the intruder, getting ready to launch her now massive body at her, but suddenly a solid wall of flame erupts between us and the woman.

Shadow.

His tattooed body steps out of the portal with a Eufori cigarette in hand. He takes a long drag of it before flicking it to the ground, then looks at me briefly, his dark eyes focusing on the blood streaming down my face before he nods his head toward my mate's body. "Get Ciaran. I'll hold her off." For a moment, I think I see gold flash through his whiskey eyes, but I simply nod and rush forward. My magic helps lift Ciaran up, allowing me to pull him toward the still open portal.

"I was wondering where you got off to! Your kind is, oh, so fun." The strange woman squeals in delight as she takes in Shadow. "Another thing Alexi was a fool about—he never should have let Ciaran remove that collar from you."

He sends out more flames that block her from moving forward. I can hear her shriek behind them as she attempts to break through, her frustration evident as she realizes she won't be able to. "You can't keep them from me! You know I'll find them!"

He looks over at me where I've stopped to watch them. "Go!" he yells, and I quickly hustle through the portal, my magic still holding Ciaran. Shadow follows, keeping his back to us and holding his fire shield strong until he can drop it and close the portal behind us.

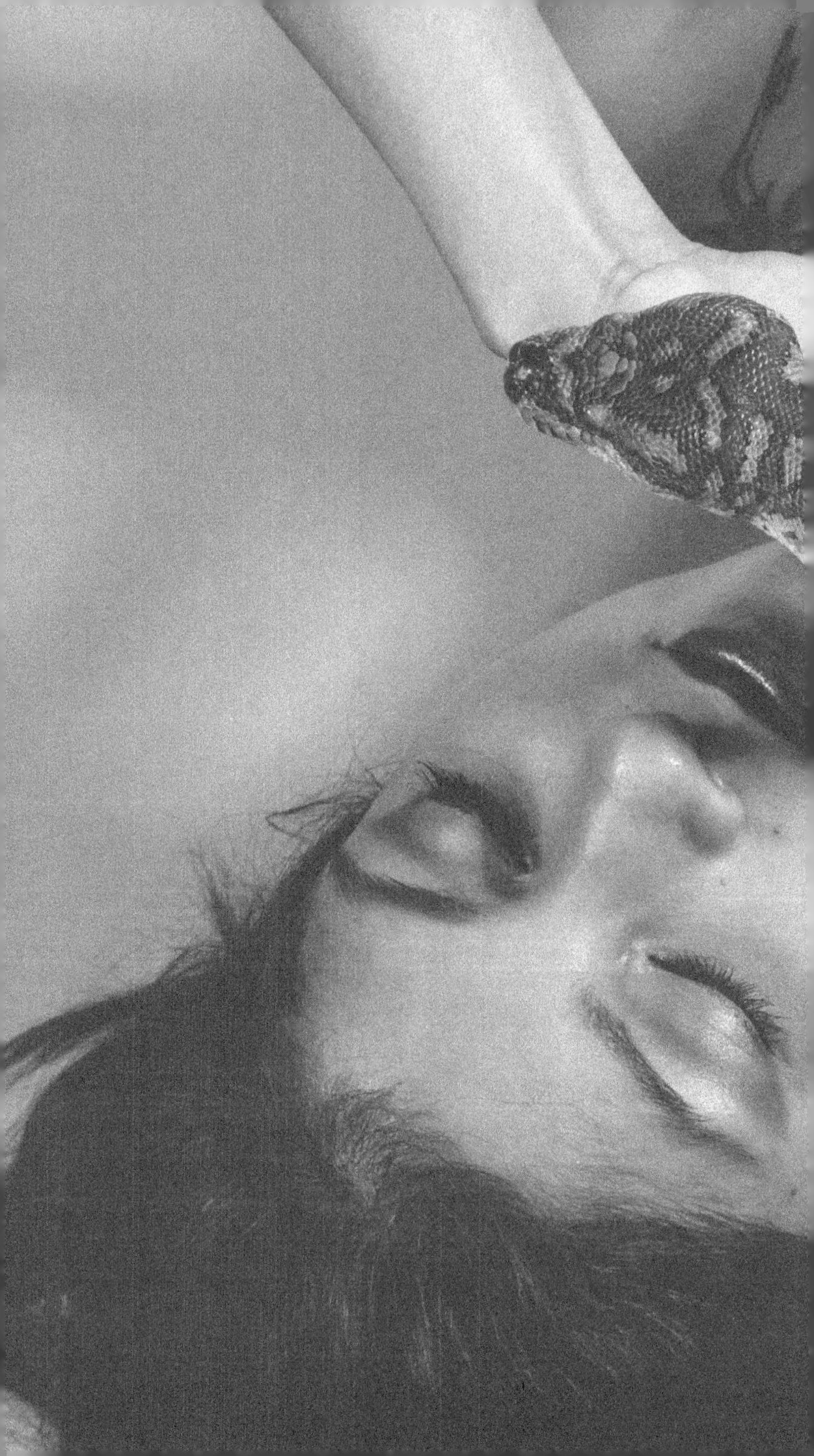

ELEVEN

Astrea

The sudden silence throws me off briefly, the only sounds being my own heavy breathing. I brace myself on my knees, my vision swimming from the sudden use of my magic and the physical exhaustion. *Or, you know, all the fucking blood dripping down my face.* Taking another deep breath, I glance up at Shadow. His back is still to me, and he's standing ready as if he expects her to follow us. She may have been Alexi's whore at one time, but the magic she had around her was powerful. That glamor was powerful.

I'm pulled from the thought when Ciaran groans—my magic has dropped him to the ground as it slithers back into me. Stumbling over my feet, I rush to his side and drop to my knees. The fear I had been holding at bay through pure adrenaline floods through me.

"Ciaran?" I shake him, but he doesn't move. "Ciaran, I

need you to wake up for me. Please," I beg, my voice cracking in the quiet room. My sister's dead body flashes before my eyes as I see him unmoving. That box in my mind rattles again, threatening to spill out all the nightmares it holds. I know if I allow it to, it will drown me.

"We need to get him up and move, Astrea." Shadow's rough voice echoes through the space. "She could follow us through. This place isn't safe."

Anger flares. *Good, I can survive with anger. Keep the anger.* Glaring up at him, I snap, "Well, then get us someplace safe. I don't know what the fuck she did to him."

He glances back at us, looking almost annoyed as he takes a deep breath. "You're mated, right? Use the bond."

"Yes, we mated maybe an hour before she broke in! I have no idea what the fuck I'm doing."

Spinning on his heel, he drops down and lifts Ciaran's massive body up, then jerks his head for me to follow through another portal. I step into a familiar room, to a familiar voice.

"Shadow, what the fuck? You know the rules!"

"Ava," I groan.

Shadow

My head has started to pound, the hangover kicking in, and Ava's voice sounding in my ears threatens to push that headache into a migraine.

"Oh, my God! Poppy! She didn't follow!" Astrea shrieks. She whirls on me. "You have to go back for her!"

The last thing I want to do is go back into that apartment, but looking at the tears streaming down Astrea's face, I know I don't have a choice. Ava is looking between us all in shock, her mouth open. She's only wearing shorts and a small tank top. Her breasts push against the fabric.

Suddenly, the apartment with the crazy witch and the rabid familiar sounds better.

"Fucking stay here," I grumble and portal back into the bedroom I used to call home. I don't have to look into the living room to know the witch is gone. The feel of her magic is no longer present. The sensation before was like oil dripping down my skin, and now it's just empty. I breathe a sigh of relief. She knows what I am, who I was to Alexi. I send a prayer to whatever gods still listen that Astrea didn't catch onto that.

"Poppy?" I call out for the cursed little ball of fluff. The silence in the apartment gives way to a tiny chitter, followed by its fluffy head peeking out from my old closet. "Please don't fucking bite me," I say as I walk over to pick her up.

<hr>

Ciaran
(Deep End- Ruelle)

My body isn't my own. Nothing is working right. My blood burns as it moves through my veins, and though I know nothing is coming out, I still try to scream. Still try to beg for someone to end me. The silent plea echoes through my body, desperately reaching for that thread of darkness tied to my light. I wish I could wrap myself up in it and let it take away the pain I feel.

Shh, pet. Shh. Don't worry, I'll end the pain.

I know deep down if that voice reaches me, I will suffer more. Through the darkness, I see a white light framing the body of the woman's voice.

Her long white hair glows like a halo. As her whole body comes into view, I can see she is naked, her breasts standing at attention. Her eyes glow a vibrant green so similar to Astrea's, but they don't hold any of the warmth or genuine familiarity. Something sinister lies underneath her beauty.

Finally standing over me, she kneels beside me and lifts a finger to my cheek, gingerly stroking me. The path her finger takes feels like liquid fire on my skin, and that internal scream once again echoes through my mind.

She has what is mine, and therefore, I will take what is hers. Her voice is everywhere in my mind. She keeps petting my cheek and running her nails through my hair. *You'll help me get it back. You'll be mine.* She's leaning down as if to kiss me, and I'm begging my head to move, to not allow those lips to touch mine.

In the back of my mind, I can hear someone else shouting, can feel someone tugging on me. The woman before me snaps her head up before she can kiss me and narrows her eyes, the illusion of beauty suddenly faltering to reveal someone else. But before I can truly place her, I'm pulled backward. I can hear her scream in rage as my body and consciousness abruptly snap together, and that's when the real pain begins.

Astrea

When Ava had originally invited us to stay in her basement, before we removed the shard, I had pictured an *actual* basement. Something dark, damp, and cold. But as I descend the stairs, I realize how wrong I was.

While the upstairs is outfitted in reds and blacks, down here is full of deep colors that make it warm and inviting. The stairs dump into a deep purple hallway with black marble floors. I see a living space off to the right full of black velvet furniture, with gold accents throughout the room that make it look regal. To the left is the biggest chef's kitchen I've ever seen. State of the art stainless-steel appliances, concrete countertops, and black cabinets make me want to spend hours cooking in it.

"My bedroom is down through the living room," Ava says, pulling me away from drooling over the kitchen. "Yours is this way." She motions to continue down the hall. "You'll have your own bathroom, so you won't need to worry about sharing. And this place is warded beyond measure, so you can heal here."

"Ciaran's place was warded, too," I mutter.

"Not with magic like mine," she replies. "You're safer here."

I open my mouth to ask how she can be so certain but close it again when she opens a door to reveal a four-post bed covered in black linens, the centerpiece of a lush bedroom. My eyes are unsure of where to settle. The room is dimly lit by a gas fireplace that has two deep-green armchairs in front of it. The plush, cream-colored carpet and walls lined with books and artwork communicate a comfortable home.

"I can have clothes brought to you. You've got a walk-in closet over there"—she points off to a pair of French doors—"and this way is the bathroom." She pulls open the door at the far end of the bedroom and flips on the light. I almost cry at the sight of the bathtub and shower. Both are big enough to fit at least three, if not more, grown adults.

"Now," she says, turning to look at me, "let's go see if we can't get Ciaran back."

Ciaran has been unconscious for too long. To many days of being in the basement of Ava's club. While I was originally wary of her, we've now formed an unlikely friendship. Or, at the very least, I don't want to rip her throat out when she comes near us anymore. Shadow will never let me live down the fact that he had to restrain me with his own magic when Ava went to look Ciaran over that first day. He had returned with Poppy to find me growling at her, snakes at the ready. Well, one shadowy snake—the other had been oddly observant of Ava.

"He's trapped in some type of magical hold. His mind is linked to someone," she said once I had been restrained. She paused, continuing to hold her hands over him, and tilted her head down as if to listen to something being whispered, then suddenly demanded Shadow release me and feed Ciaran my blood.

She worked tirelessly with me for two days to pull him back to where he is now. I've never experienced spell work like she wove. My own magic feels depleted, the two snakes firmly planted on my skin again, neither moving. That voice is silent.

"He'll wake soon." I snap my head up as she walks into the room we've been staying in. She crinkles her nose as she takes me in. "Astrea, it's been weeks. You need to shower and see to your wounds. You smell horrific." Ava looks tired. Her face is a little paler and more drawn than before she helped us.

I push my hair out of my face and shake my head. "I'm not leaving him until he wakes up." Since she told me someone was in his mind, I have kept a tight grip on him, constantly touching him when I'm not feeding him. Constantly whispering in his ear that he needs to come back. That I'm here. I'm waiting. My panic is barely under control at this point. Any time my eyes close, visions of my sisters flash before my eyes. I'm on edge, the magic pulsing under my skin as I try to keep myself from burning down the city to find the witch who did this.

The small woman crosses her arms over her chest. Today, she's got her hair up in pigtails and is wearing overalls over a bandeau top that barely covers her chest. "You aren't going to be much use to him if he wakes up and you're half-dead. And truly, that smell is something straight from Hell."

Deep down, I'm aware that what she is saying is accurate, but in those first few days, all I could think about was the fact that I might lose another person I love. I can't leave him now. Won't. *And if you stop touching him, what's to keep you from giving into the darkness and killing everyone and anyone who threatens to harm him?*

Shadow has also tried to pull me away, though he's never around when Ava is. The two seem to avoid each other expertly.

Exhaustion creeps into my body, the weeks catching up to me. Like quicksand pulling me deeper and deeper, I know I can only fight it for so long before my body is going to be fully pulled under. "How do you know he'll wake soon?" I ask, fighting the yawn.

She plops herself down on the bed he's lying in and grabs a candy from the bib of her overalls. The girl has a serious sweet tooth. She pops it into her mouth and says, "Samhain told me." Her familiar, a fussy raven who has taken a weird liking to Poppy but seems to hate me. "Go shower, at least. Your smell alone might be keeping him under. I'll sit with him." She does a shooing motion, pushing me toward the bathroom connected to the room.

Reluctantly, I concede to her request and step into the

bathroom. Looking in the mirror, I cringe. My hair hangs limply around my shoulders, and the blood from my head wound has matted into it, discoloring the white strands that frame my face. My face looks pale and gaunt, the freckles stark markings on my ivory skin. My reflection looks eerily reminiscent of the woman who spent all those months in Alexi's prison. Again, that fucking box rattles in my head. I hate it.

Avoiding falling into the nightmares that box holds, I strip and walk into the shower. The hot water burns my skin but I don't move away until I'm bright pink and the water runs clear. The weeks I've spent next to Ciaran has allowed me ample time to spiral and overthink. Since the interaction with that woman, something has been tingling at the back of my mind. To my knowledge, I never saw her with Alexi when I was held . . . Yet she felt familiar. But every time I think I have the answer, it slips away like sand in the wind.

It's not just my inability to figure her out that has led me to spiral, but also that she was led to Ciaran by this power. By me. Maybe it's always been me . . .

And that's when it hits me straight in the gut, so hard I double over. *It's my fault my sisters are dead.* It's my fault so many have been hunted down and murdered. All for this power I never wanted or asked for. Tears blur my vision and mix with the water.

A sob escapes me as I collapse to the shower floor. I finally found my mate, my family, only to need to flee. *It's not fucking fair.* But my magic was nothing against whoever she was, and I can't let her get to Ciaran again, or take me. If she were to take Ciaran, I would stop at nothing to get him back, even give her this power. And if she tries to take me, well, I made a deal with myself long ago that I would never be taken again. Taking a deep, shuddering breath, I shove my grief down and turn off the water that's now gone cold.

First step, I need to get out of here. I wrap the towel around my body and step out to talk with her.

"Ava, I—" But I'm cut short as I see Ciaran sitting up in bed, awake and looking at me. *Mate.* My heart bottoms out and a small whimper escapes me as all other thoughts flee my brain.

Ciaran

A deep wave of despair down the bond pulls me from sleep. Disoriented, I look around, expecting to find Astrea's emerald eyes, only to see Ava's silver ones looking back at me.

She smiles at me. "Welcome back, friend."

"What happened?" My head feels groggy as I sit up in bed. My chest is bare, but I notice the sweatpants I wear under the thick blanket.

"You, my friend, had a very close call." I think she's going to say more, but then her eyes go unfocused briefly. "Watch your mate, Ciaran, she's feeling desperate. She will need us all to keep her grounded here." And without any explanation, she moves out of the room, the door snicking closed behind her just as I hear Astrea's voice.

My mate steps out of the bathroom and stops in her tracks, her eyes going wide. She's near enough I can see the exhaustion on her features, the healing cuts and abrasions. She lets out a small whimper, and I'm out of bed in a heartbeat, scooping her up in my arms and burying my nose against her neck.

"Ciaran," she breathes out in relief.

"*Kamerat.*" I lift her so her legs wrap around me and move us back to the bed before pulling the towel from her body. An urgency pushes through my veins to claim her. I waste no time dropping my mouth to her rosy nipple. She arches into me, releasing a breathy moan as I suck the tight bud into my mouth, and the room fills with the scent of her need.

"Please," she utters the broken word. "Please, Ciaran. I need to feel you."

I stand, shoving the sweatpants down to my ankles. My length bobs out, and she parts her legs, exposing herself to me. I sheath myself in one long stroke. She cries out at the sudden intrusion before it gives way to a low moan.

"*Kamerat*. Fuck, you feel too good." I pump in and out of her slowly, and she meets each stroke, her pussy flooding each time I thrust in. I can feel her bond against mine, her magic against me. The snakes that decorate her skin seem to move and shimmer.

"Oh, fuck, oh yes," she screams.

I lean down to her ear as I snake my hand down to her clit. "Say my name as you come on my cock, *kamerat*." And I press down. She comes with a shout, my name a prayer on her lips. I keep thrusting into her, once, twice, and then I'm filling her up, her name spilling out of my lips before I fall down on top of her. I take a second longer to enjoy the feel of our skin melding before I plant a kiss on her forehead and carefully begin to pull out, looking down at our combined release. "*Fuck*, you're beautiful like this."

Possession flares inside me and I'm hit with a deep hatred for the idea of my cum leaving her. I trail my hand up the inside of her thighs, catching my release with two fingers and pushing it back in. Her pussy clenches around my fingers, and I watch as she flushes.

"Is my mate hungry for more?" I ask as I crawl up her

body, my fingers still slowly pumping in and out of her, the sound deliciously obscene. "Can you cum for me again?"

She shakes her head and tries to scoot back as I bring our release up to her clit and press down. "Oh, God, Ciaran, I'm too sensitive. No, I can't."

"Are you telling me to stop, little *kamerat*?" I playfully nip at her neck. She lets out a long moan and shakes her head again. I circle around her clit again and again before dipping back into her. Lazily, I kiss her breasts, sucking each nipple in before I move up to her neck. "You'll give me another one because I own them. This pussy. Your release. You. Belong. To. *Me*."

"Fuck. Fuck. Ciaran. Oh, God." She's thrusting her hips now in time with my fingers.

I pull back for a moment, earning an angry snarl from her before I plunge my fingers back in. "I believe I said you say my name, and my name only, when you're cuming." I bite into her neck, and she squirts into my hand as she screams out my name.

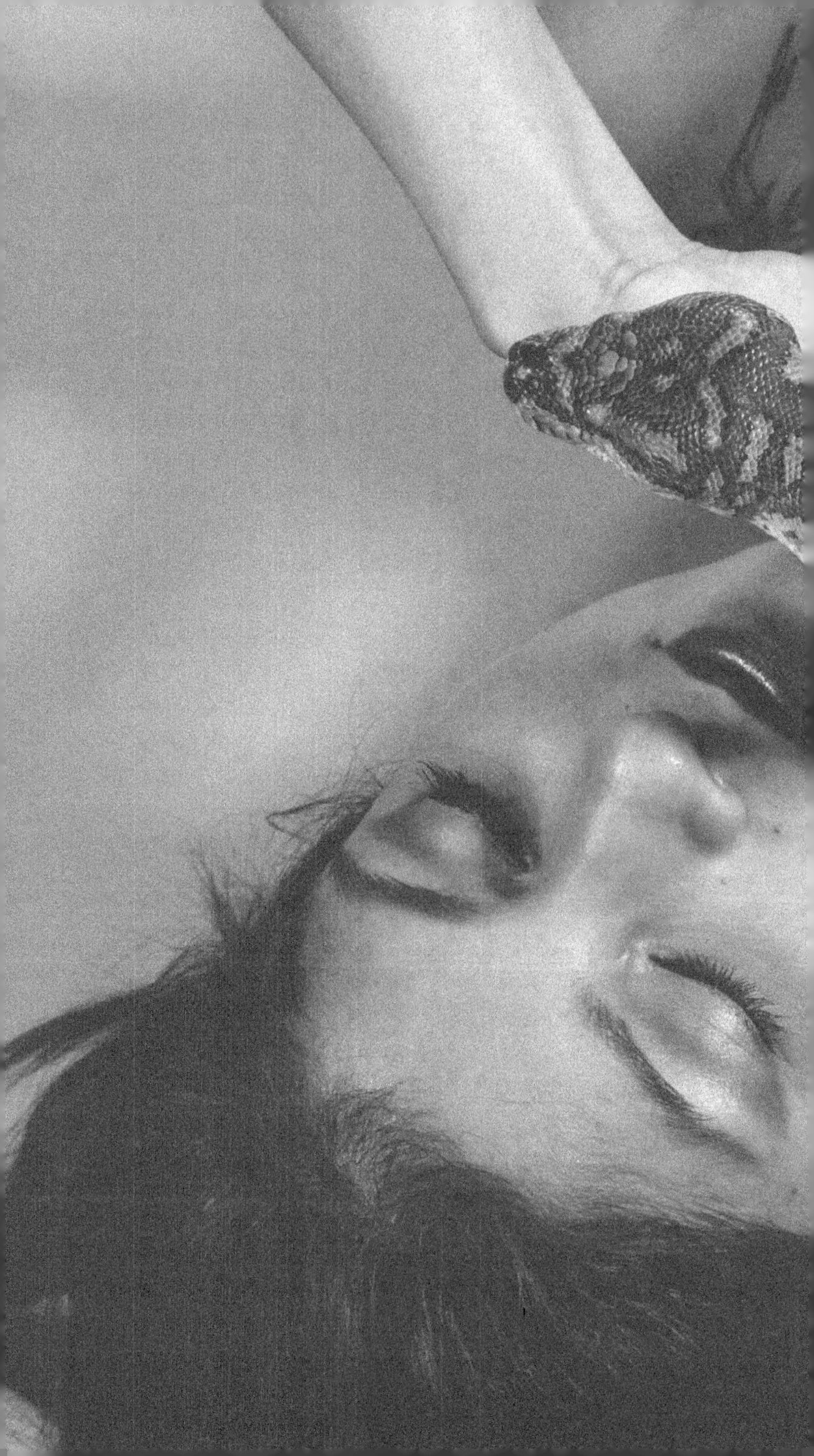

TWELVE

– Carmine Family Grimoire

Astrea

I black out as I cum on Ciaran, his fingers deep inside my pussy while his teeth are deep in my neck. When I wake up, he's lazily licking my neck and tracing circles over my stomach with his fingers. His cock is still hard, pushing into my hip.

"Mmm, you taste so good," he murmurs.

I smile at him. "My cum or my blood?"

"Both." He laughs and pulls himself up so he brackets my upper body with both hands.

I look him in the eyes and let my fingers trace his face.

"You scared me." The admission slips out too quickly for me to pull it back.

He frowns before kissing me on the forehead. "My apologies, *kamerat*. It won't happen again."

My bond hums in my chest, but despite the promise, the worry is still there. Being with him makes it that much harder to follow through with leaving. But I can't deny the logic, the absolute certainty that if I leave, they won't hunt for him, they'll hunt for me. It'll keep him and Shadow safe. Even Ava will be safe. And that's worth it to me. Even if it slowly kills me. Because this time I don't think I will survive running from him. *Maybe the difference is that now I don't want to survive without him.*

"Hey." He nuzzles me. "Where did you go?"

Shaking my head, I put my mask of calm back on and smile. "Just thinking about how you need to relax."

He scoffs and starts to kiss me again. "What I need is to bury myself in my mate's pussy while she drinks from me."

And maybe because I'm selfish, I let him distract me by doing just that.

We spend the next few days in each other's arms. Neither of us are willing to close our eyes, but at some point Ciaran loses the battle. Carefully, I slip out of the bed and pad over to my pack. We haven't spoken about where he went for the weeks he was passed out. I know we need to, but the temptation to indulge in his body has been too great to ignore. Pulling on his hoodie and a pair of leggings, I scoop my hair into a messy bun and sneak out the door. The club isn't open yet, so I make my way through the main area in search of Ava. I made the mistake of looking for her during business hours my first few days here, and the bartender quickly ushered me back into the basement before any of the guests could see me. At the time, I was offended, but now that I've seen what I looked like, I can understand.

"You're planning to leave, aren't you?" Her voice comes from the office doorway behind the bar. Ava's leaning against the door frame with her arms crossed. She's got black-rimmed glasses on and her pink hair up in a bun matching mine, her shaved side freshly cleaned up. Today, she's wearing a black corset cinched tightly atop a black skirt that's cut short in the front but trails long in the back. Her feet boast matching black stilettos.

I want to shrug, to seem indifferent about it, but my chest heaves and a small whimper escapes me. "I have to. Not right now, but soon," I admit, and the finality in my voice shocks even me. My magic scratches at me, restless. "They'll follow me, it's this magic they are after. Not Ciaran or you or Shadow."

She moves behind the bar and pours us both a coffee, followed by a shot of whiskey. "Look, I know you don't know me. And have only recently started to like me." I open my mouth to apologize, but she holds up her hand. "I get it. I would have been the same in your shoes. But let me offer you some advice: wait to leave. Don't make the decision now. Right now, it's based on fear."

Taking a sip of the coffee, I allow the warm liquid to soothe my soul as it slips down my throat. I don't look at her, instead focusing on the cup in my hands and the shot still untouched. "I woke up to them burning. My whole family is gone because of this power. She told me she *found us* because of this power. How can I stay when I know that?" What I leave unsaid is the unease the magic leaves within me. How restless it makes me. It's taking a toll on me in the short time I've had access to it.

"No, they are gone because the original families were a bunch of power-hungry fools. They are gone because they allowed the vampires to take part in magic, they should have no knowledge of. Because of that, Alexi Helvig is being controlled by something that never should have woken. If you leave, you'll still be hunted, and Ciaran won't just let you go. You aren't facing this alone anymore, Astrea."

I frown, stuck on something else she said. "You said something is controlling Alexi? What is it"

Ava takes a long, steadying breath. "The power you hold...when it woke, it also woke *her*, and she took control of the body that held her. I think she has been using some kind of magic, and whatever influence the witch's body she inhabits had, to get him to look for her Harbinger magic. The magic *you* have."

I shake my head in disbelief. "But my power never manifested before the night my family died." Flashes of that black smoke ripping people apart as I ran fly through my head. I remember the feeling of my ankle snapping as I tripped and that collar closing over me, shutting the magic down. A shiver creeps up my spine. "If I've always held this powerful magic, why would I have spent my whole life without it?"

"If you can trust me, we could maybe find out. Could you do that?"

Can I? Can I trust this witch to help me? Looking at her, I realize I've trusted her from the moment I allowed her to help my mate. I nod.

"It won't be comfortable," she continues. "Finding the truth rarely is."

"I survived eing tortured by Alexi. I can handle whatever you throw at me," I reply, my voice nonchalant despite the pressure on my chest and the urge to run moving through my limbs.

She looks at me, really looks at me. Uncharacteristically sad, she says, "Physical pain is one thing. Emotional suffering at the hands of loved ones? That is an entirely different beast."

<hr>

Ava's magic continues to puzzle me. She went on to explain how she's able to go into a witch's mind to uncover memories. To have that power is rare, even amongst the most powerful coven. And on top of being a Seer? It makes me curious what else she may be hiding. With power like that, she is not an average witch—if she is a witch at all.

Ava prepares tea for me, something she says will help me relax so she can get into my brain more easily.

I can only hope the memories she is after aren't in that chest that's rattling in the corner. She doesn't move to wake Ciaran, though she tells me she checked on him. Surprisingly, she insisted Shadow be present, so he sits on the chair opposite me, a frown plastered on his face.

"I don't like this," he grumbles. "Ciaran would want to be here for this."

"No," I reply harshly. "This is my choice, and he needs rest."

When he moves to argue again, Ava steps in. "She said no, *rakkaani*." He freezes at the name. "Sorry," she murmurs. Her cheeks redden and she avoids eye contact.

The air around them crackles with tension, and I wisely keep my mouth shut, though my eyes dart between them.

He drags his hand through his already rumpled hair. It

has started to grow out, giving him an unkempt appearance all the time. "Let's get this over with."

Ava gives a small nod. "You'll keep me grounded here while I go into her mind. You know when to pull me out."

He gives a shake of his head but seems to know exactly what she is talking about. "This better not be like last time."

Shooting a glare his way, she snaps, "Sure, you get lost in someone's mind one time, and suddenly, it's always bound to happen." She turns back to me. "Okay, Astrea, you'll stay seated and restrained. You'll feel my hands on your temples and my magic. Please don't let your snakes eat me while this is happening."

I nod, but my palms are sweating and it's taking all my strength to keep my legs from bouncing with nerves. Being restrained is not something I cope well with anymore.

"We don't have to do this," Ava says quietly. Empathy and concern are displayed openly on her smooth face. Until this moment, I never realized her eyes are a unique silver, similar to the color of a twinkling star.

"Yes. We do." I let my resolve flow through my words.

She only nods before wrapping rope around me and placing her hands on either side of my head. My skin is crawling from the feel of the rope, but I refuse to allow myself to back out. I need the answers more than I need to be comfortable at this moment.

"Remember, it's all in your head; nothing can physically hurt you." I note the distinction, not that nothing can hurt me, but that nothing can hurt me physically. It's the only warning she gives before I can feel her working her way into my memories and the room goes black.

Ciaran

I'm startled awake by fear and pain shooting down my

bond. I'm disoriented and confused. But it's the screaming that has me jumping from the bed and sprinting upstairs into the empty club. I jump over the bar and push into Ava's office, only to barrel into Shadow. His hands splayed across my bare chest.

"You can't break the connection yet!" he shouts at me. Looking over his shoulder, I can see both Ava and Astrea on the opposite side of the room, their eyes closed. Astrea is bound to a chair, tears streaming down her face. Ava is behind her, fingers pressed into Strea's temples. Sweat covers her face, plastering wisps of her pink hair to her forehead.

"Let me go, Shadow," I growl as my teeth descend. I shove against his body again, but he holds firm.

"No. If you pull Ava before she's finished, you'll do more damage. Let it play out."

I see Ava grit her teeth, and another long cry escapes Astrea. My heart breaks with it. I shove against Shadow again, knowing it's a futile gesture but having nothing else to do with my frustration.

"She wanted the answers, man," Shadow says.

I force my body to relax enough for him to deem it safe to let me go, and then I move over to the couch, knowing there's nothing I can do but sit with my head in my hands and watch my mate endure more torture.

Astrea

I wake to screaming around me. The voices become clearer by the second.

"How dare you sleep with him! Do you know what you've done?!" It's my father's angry voice I make out first.

"I made us stronger," my mother hisses. I move from the floor, quickly getting to my feet and approaching my father's

study. I round the corner to see him pacing and my mother simply lounging.

"You are a gods damn fool, Kathrine! Having both is a fucking liability."

I watch my mother wave her hand, dismissing him. "You just don't see the bigger picture." Her tone is patronizing.

I don't even track my father's hand as it smacks her hard across the face, he moves so swiftly. "You've doomed this family. Maybe the whole community. All for what?" It's the first time I've seen my father look genuinely afraid. All my life, I had never seen him look fearful. "Astrea!"

I startle, thinking they've somehow seen me observing them, but then I see ten-year-old me trot into the study.

"Yes, Daddy?" Never in my life have I called my father Daddy. And the fact that I promptly hug him, and receive one back, makes my eyes go wide. The look of devotion on my young face is enough to almost bring me to my knees.

My father bends down to my level. "Astrea, can you tell me what happened today?"

My mother gets up and grabs my younger self, dragging me back away from my father. "I told you what happened. That little shit Carmine thought they could cheat me out of what I was owed, and so our little Astrea here taught them a lesson. Isn't that right, doll?" I feel a phantom tingle in my scalp watching the way she grips my younger self's hair.

"Mommy you're hurting me." My younger self whimpers but my mother only rolls her eyes.

It's in this moment that I see them, those same twin snakes that I have on me now, curling up my little body. My mother yanks her arm away, and my father's face turns white. The younger version of me looks between my parents as the magic unfolds.

"Do you see now, Kathrine?" my father whispers. His

voice is shaking. "Do you see now what you've turned our daughter into? She won't be able to control this, and the families will find out. We cannot have both."

My mother says nothing. Her horror is evident, but just beneath it, I can also see the cunning side of Kathrine Mori; the side that always found a way to get what she wanted, and more often than not, that was power.

"So, we already have the spell. Link her to someone else, they'll use the magic so she won't be able to." And there it is, the solution my mother's brain cooked up.

"She'll die, Katherine! You do that spell and she'll fucking die," my father screams, his face red. My mother only shrugs. My father shakes his head vehemently, "No. We rebind her. Erase the memory and pray that she hasn't woken with the magic being active."

I'm ripped from the memory and dumped into another one just as quickly and unceremoniously.

Chanting resumes around the flame lit room. I'm laid out in the middle of the circle, the cold stones biting into my back, screaming and writhing. Surrounding me are the founding families all dressed in ceremonial garb. The dark fabric is meant to obscure their bodies and faces but I know better. I could name each person in this room. I pause and look around the circle, until my eyes snag on Hansley off to the side of the room. Tears fill my eyes at the sight of her. Her hair is half down, fallen from the bun she had it twisted into. Her own robes are thrown off to the side, discarded as if they are nothing more than wash rags.

Another ear-piercing scream rips from the young me. "You're killing her!" Hansley screams, moving to break the circle. Someone I can't see holds her back. The flames that provide the light in the room flicker and flare upward as the chanting gets louder. The shadows they cast on the old stone walls transform each person into demonic wraiths, their forms dancing behind them.

"We have to bind her—we almost have it," someone yells, and I feel the spell the moment it lands in my body, like my magic is being slammed into a box. My younger self thrashes, head thrown back in a silent scream as my back bows off the ground, almost levitating. My fingernails scrape against the dirty ground as they search for purchase. I can feel it in my chest now just as before, the pain of it being taken, and I drop to my knees. Tears pour down my face as I grieve for what was taken from me in that moment.

I watch as my body suddenly drops back to the ground. I wince at the impact on the hard ground. Hansley flies into the middle of the circle and grabs me, gathering my limp body against her chest. She glares at the families around the circle.

"Get her up, Hansley. We can't have her waking up here. She can't regain this memory, or that magic won't stay contained," my father says.

I watch my sister lift my body into her arms and begin to move through the crowd. Suddenly, she stops at the edge of the musky room. Her voice has the Seer's tone to it; a far-off, almost dreamy quality as it rings out through the room. Shadows are cast across her, obscuring half her face. "You will all face the consequences of this. No one will be safe when they awaken."

THIRTEEN

Should the power awaken, it must be fully claimed by that witch, or its original owner will take it upon her waking.
To claim it, she must take ownership of it, give in to the darkness.

— Mori Family Grimoire

Ciaran

Astrea jolts into awareness at the same time Ava stumbles backward, unconscious. Shadow catches the small woman before she can hit the ground, scooping her up without a word and leaving the room as I rush to my mate. I unbind Astrea from the chair and catch her weight with my body as she curls forward. Her frame still shakes with deep, heart-wrenching sobs.

Kneeling in front of her, I cup her face between my hands. "Talk to me, *kamerat*."

She heaves another sob. "They bound me, erased my

memory." Her body shudders. "My mother had an affair; she slept with someone else. My father was never really my father." The words tumble out of her rapid-fire.

I pull her into my arms, letting her soak my shirt before she finally pulls back, her emerald eyes glowing with an array of emotions. One of those snakes is now curled up around her neck. The longer she has her magic, the more those snakes seem to be in tune with her emotions. "We need answers, Ciaran. And the only place we could possibly get them is within one of the family grimoires." She pauses for a moment, her breath pulling in deep before she lets it back out. "I think my family had the spell your father wanted, the one to link him to this magic."

My body goes absolutely still and a wave of dread moves through me in cold waves at the idea of my father having access to a spell like.

"We'll have to go to the coven grounds," she whispers.

Despite Astrea being correct, I know that in order to make it across the city and into that cursed place, we'll need help, and the best one to help us is going to piss off my best friend even more. No doubt he's already on edge having been here for weeks. His anger—no, his rage—burns deep within. This will not make anything better.

Grabbing her hand, I pull her up. "Come on. We need to go talk to Ava and Shadow."

This body is new to me, but being stuck in this world without my mate isn't. My awareness came quicker this time around, which makes me believe my magic is—or, *was* —awake. In generations past, it wasn't until the end of my life that I would become aware of who I am, and that my soul would be able to take control.

The woods around me are quiet; the creatures sensing a predator in their midst are wise and remain hidden. Even the birds are avoiding this part of the woods. My bare feet brush delicately over the bed of dried pine needles and dirt, the connection grounding me. The further my soul gets from my original life, the less in touch with nature I've become. Witches these days don't seem to live in nature; instead, they dwell in that cesspool of a city.

The snap of a twig pulls me from my thoughts, and I whip my head to the right, where two glowing eyes peer out of the darkness at me. I let out a small sob as the massive Hellbeast pads into the clearing. Its black fur gobbles up the dim light around us, making the sharp white teeth in its maw stand out even brighter. It moves toward me, its head a little above my own. It bumps my forehead with its snout, scenting me, before I fling my arms around its massive neck, squeezing it in a hug. Behind it, I see five more of them pad out of the darkness, but none are as large as this one. And none hold the same connection to me that this one does.

HER

NOW

(Snake-Halflives)

I stare at the wall in front of me as Alexi fucks me from behind. He's pathetic and not the Helvig I want, but he's the one who has served my purpose to get me here, albeit slower than I intended. The witches have done an excellent job of hiding who holds my powers, but all it took was a little nudge for Alexi to build the prison and start hunting. He's been a useful servant helping me through the years, though he's been unaware it's been me every time. One of the only good parts of my reincarnation each cycle is a different body with different magic.

"Oh, yeah, take it like the good slut you are."

I will be thrilled when I can finally snap his neck. I roll my eyes, glad I never allow him to fuck me in a way that lets him actually see my face—I can truly only fake it so much. I moan out the appropriate sounds before allowing my mind to return to the issue at hand.

Astrea Mori. She has my magic, and I want it back.

If the man fucking me had been smarter, I could have taken it before it awoke. She might even have survived it.

But he was blinded by his own hubris, as men normally are, and she escaped with the help of his own son. The mate-bond they created is stronger than I expected, too, and the frustration I feel that my spell didn't hold him is a palpable companion at this point.

Alexi suddenly grunts, and I feel his release splashing out. He's barely finished before I shove his doughy body off me and walk quickly to the bathroom to shower. I refuse to allow him to feed on my magic. Because of that, his immortality is slowly creeping away and his age is starting to show. I throw a small bit of magic back into the room so he won't follow me. The witch I'm currently occupying didn't have extraordinary power, but she did have the power of illusions. This, in addition to the arsenal of powers I've collected over the years, has been far more helpful than I originally thought. I doubt the original families had any idea I would be able to collect powers through the lifetimes. If they had, no doubt they would have done something different to keep me trapped.

This witch's body is one of my favorites, now. I built up her muscles and curves from the body she tried to keep so small for her family. Too many witches these days treasure small frames, but I know there is value in a sturdy one. I squeeze my breasts, enjoying the weight of them, enjoying being able to drop the glamor I normally have on. While this witch has stark white hair, the glamor I wear has ink-black hair on an emaciated frame. Again, if Alexi were at all intelligent and not just thinking with his dick, he might have noticed I *feel* different than I look. After all, a glamor can't change how something feels, only how it looks.

Keeping the shower ice cold, I make quick work of scrubbing his sweat and cum off before hopping out, pulling my glamor back up, and padding out into the room.

"One would think you didn't get enough, walking out here like that," Alexi grunts from the bed.

Because I didn't, you disgusting pig. No one will ever give me enough. My heart still cries for my mate, and no amount of sex will fix that. Nothing will *ever* fix that deep ache in my soul. It's why I will never stop waging war on this city. Why I will someday follow through with my threat to burn it to the ground. Hopefully, the flames will be taking my own soul with it.

"Mmm, maybe later. We need to find your son and the girl," I purr, pulling on my black jeans and then the leather bustier that zips up the front. His hungry eyes latch onto my neck, and I force myself not to scowl. "Find someone else to satisfy *that* hunger," I snarl. "I have work to do."

"You're forgetting who's in charge here." Alexi stands, still quicker than someone his size should be, and grabs me by the throat before shoving me into the wall. "I think I want a taste of you."

He forces my head to the side to gain access to my neck, but I've had enough. My power lashes out at him, shoving him off me. The black Hellbeast sidles up to me, appearing from the dark with a low growl toward Alexi. People are under the impression that Alexi controls the beasts, but they are *mine.* They have been with me since the beginning and answer only to me. They are immortal, and they have served me well. They are my only family at this point.

"I've had enough of you today, Alexi. Test me again, and I'll rip your heart out," I growl and storm out. I don't stop walking, nor do I allow my magic to drop him, until I'm out the door, where my Hellbeasts flank me.

"Let's go hunting, boys," I purr.

FOURTEEN

Ciaran

"This is an awful idea," Shadow vocalizes. "We can find another way." We've gone back and forth the past few days on what we should do, and we've continued to land back here. The space that Shadow continues to avidly protest against.

I watch my mate dig her feet in and cross her arms over her chest. The frustration is clear in her body. "It's the only way," Astrea retorts. She has no idea why Shadow is being so difficult, and not for the first time, I wonder if I should have clued her in.

Shadow looks at me, but I just shrug. "Seriously?" he asks me. "You know this is a bad idea; we can't keep using *him.*"

I blow out a very long sigh. "Getting his help is the only way to get across the city and onto the covens' lands. If we don't do this right, my father and whoever is controlling him could get to us first. Besides, Astrea is going to do this with or without us. Isn't that right?"

She smiles wickedly and nods.

Ava sits silently off to the side. She hasn't recovered well since her dive into Astrea's head. She's currently sitting on her couch, while the rest of us are spread out across her living room. She has a fire going but is still wrapped up in a deep-red velvet blanket, her face leached of color. Shadow looks at her every so often, deep worry etched across his face.

"If I may?" she finally interjects.

"By all means," I reply.

She clears her throat, and Shadow shoots her a concerned look. "I think she needs to go. We need answers. If there is even a snowball's chance in hell that the book is still in the ruins of her home, we need to grab it. We can't have that type of power fall into the wrong hands. And we won't make it there without Drago's help, we all know that."

Shadow flinches at the name. "The whole point of all this was to stop Alexi. Why are we so focused on this? We can stop him without the use of the grimoire." His eyes are still glued to Ava. My friend wears his heart on his sleeve, and he doesn't even realize it.

I shake my head and huff, "My father is a moron. Up until a few years ago, the most he wanted was to rule the drug trade. He had no ambition outside of that. When he suddenly decided to start taking witches, it made no sense. It wasn't going to help him get rich; if anything, it would make it worse. He broke a decades-long peace treaty with them out of nowhere. Someone else is pulling the strings."

"I think he is helping the original witch who had it," Astrea jumps in. "Why else would he take us? The only way he would even know The Harbinger magic exists is if a witch told him."

Shadow groans. "I'm not going to win this argument, am I?"

Astrea's face breaks into a wide smile. "Nope!"

"So, it's settled: we all go," Ava says and moves to stand, but Shadow pushes toward her, his agitation clear.

"Absolutely not. You aren't going anywhere."

"You can't keep me from him, you self-righteous asshole," Ava growls at him, her cheeks flushing red.

The room goes silent. Astrea may not know their history, but the way she sucks in a breath shows she guesses enough. I motion for her to follow me out of the room, leaving Shadow and Ava to stare each other down.

"Not our fight," I whisper in her ear as we ease down the hall toward the room we are staying in.

Shadow

Holding my stare, the little hellion in front of me crosses her arms across her chest. If looks could kill, Ava's would be spitting venom at me, and I would be dead. Wisely, Ciaran pulls his mate out of the room.

"When are you going to get over this, Shadow?" Her voice hurts to hear. Everything hurts when I'm around her.

"You don't get to ask me that," I growl. "I'm keeping you safe."

She moves to stand, still wobbly from being in Astrea's mind. She gets weaker and weaker every time she uses that damn power. *And whose fault is that?* "Bullshit! If anyone gets to ask you, it's me," she snaps at me.

Her small frame moves toward me, and panic courses through me as she reaches her hand up to touch me. I practically trip over myself to get away. The pain that moves over her face is utterly devastating. "You say you want to keep me safe? You're killing me every day that you continue to follow this path." Ava shakes her head in sadness, backing away from me and turning toward the hallway. "We won't wait forever. We *can't* wait forever."

The panic is clawing at my chest, the demons screaming in my head, but instead of saying what I should, I lash out. "Good. Go fuck him, for all I care. I want nothing to do with either of you."

Rage, followed quickly by anguish, moves through Ava's silver eyes. "You're letting them win, Shadow. Every day you keep yourself in this prison you've created, you are letting them win." She shakes her head, her pink hair swishing with the motion. "I hope the day never comes where you wake up, ready to let yourself out, and realize you're alone."

She walks out of the room, leaving me alone with the voices telling me how unworthy I am. How unclean I am. I can't allow that to touch her. So, I light up another Eufori joint and breathe deep, praying for it to take me away from this hell on earth.

"I want her out, Ciaran, now," I demand. I'm barely hanging on; barely keeping myself under control. The drugs are doing nothing to keep me calm. The silver-eyed demon is the only thing occupying my mind now. The fact that she's still here is killing me. Having tasted her, I can't keep her near me without eventually losing control fully.

"If we pull her without a plan, everything will be fucked. You know that. She's a favorite, which means she's a lot fucking harder to get out than the average witch," he replies. I growl at him, and Ciaran flashes his teeth at me, his eyes blazing red for a moment before he regains control.

"Fuck!" I yell, pulling my black hair through my hands roughly. "Fuck, fuck, FUCK." I unleash my fist into the wall, and the pain grounds me for a moment. Ciaran's eyes are wide as he looks me over, suddenly realizing how serious this is. How serious I am.

He takes a deep breath, steadying his own emotions. "If you want her out, you know who we need to go to. He's the only one who can help us hide her for a while. Are you okay with that?"

No. "Yes. If it gets her out, that's fine," I say, even though the words taste bitter on my tongue.

"Alright, I'll set it up," he replies. He pauses a moment before leaving the room. "You know, Shadow, you could leave with her. You could be free. I wouldn't fault you for wanting that."

My chest constricts. "No." The word is out of my mouth too quickly. Ciaran may think I deserve to be free, but I know better. I know I need to pay up for the damage I've caused, and that bill is never ending.

"So, you need my help?" Drago's voice is a lover's caress across my body, and I hate how much I still react to him. He demanded a meeting with me over Ciaran, which is irritating me to no end. Ciaran has always handled our interactions.

I grind my teeth. "We just need you to hide her for a little while before we get her out of the city." I take a long drag of the Eufori, and the red smoke whirls around me as it exits my nostrils. Drago's powerful form leans against the wall as he watches me, his arms banded across his chest. Those powerful arms I know would feel so good bracketed around my body. I shake my head, trying to clear the thoughts and hating myself for still wanting him after he betrayed me.

Drago's face shifts to sadness. "Shadow . . ." he murmurs as he steps forward.

"No," I say firmly, stepping back toward the wall of windows behind me. The low rumble of thunder breaks the tense air in the apartment; the sound of rain splashing against the large windows masking my uneven breaths.

Drago strains to hold himself back, to refrain from crowding into my space, but he doesn't stop talking.

"No, you are going to listen, Shadow. I'm done with this." He presses forward one step, his blue eyes flashing golden momentarily. "I'm *sorry*. I know that's not enough. I do. But I am. You have no idea how hard those years were."

I snap forward, my body shoving into his. "Oh, *I* have no idea?" I hiss.

He holds his hands up in surrender. "Wrong choice of words. I won't know what you went through, but I can tell you being out here wasn't any easier. I had hard decisions to make, and one of those was not getting you out. I *couldn't* get you out." Drago's voice cracks and he pauses for a moment, squeezing his eyes shut briefly before continuing. "He was watching me, and until the moment he died, there wasn't anything I could do. I didn't have the things I have now. I had to build that up." He fists his hands at his sides as his body vibrates. "I hate that I couldn't rescue you, couldn't save you. I had to listen to everything happening and know I couldn't do anything."

The heartbreak and regret is evident, but I can't—no, I won't allow myself to cave. Anger is the only thing that keeps me standing, and if I forgive him, I have to let that go. So, I don't give him the out. Instead, I school my face, taking in my drug and blowing it out in his.

"We are bringing her soon. Be ready." The portal opens behind me, and I step through backward, ignoring my heart breaking and pretending I don't see the shimmer of tears in Drago's eyes.

FIFTEEN

It's awoken.
And now we will all pay the price of those before
us, long dead.

– Carmine Family Grimoire

Astrea

We make it three steps into our room before I turn and jump into Ciaran's arms, slamming my mouth onto his. I sweep my tongue out and into his mouth, moaning at his taste. His strong hands grip my ass so hard, I know I'll have marks tomorrow.

"I need you," I breathe out between kisses.

He emits a savage growl that shoots straight to my pussy. He walks us backward until we hit the bed, and he drops me down. Looming over me, Ciaran looks untamed, wild, beastly. He strips off his shirt, showing me his deliciously muscular chest, and shoves his hair back from his eyes.

"Strip," he commands. The authority in his voice sends deep, body-wracking shivers through me. I often forget the man in front of me is a vampire. That he is a predator.

I quickly discard my clothing and lie back down on the bed.

"Spread your legs and let me see you," he demands. Slowly my legs fall apart, exposing my already soaked core. His eyes zero in on me, and I watch his tongue peek out as if he's about to have a five-star meal. "Touch yourself. Show me how badly you want me." He starts to unbutton his pants. My mouth waters at the idea of tasting him. "Astrea," he cuts in, snapping my attention back to his face, "now."

Pushing my hand down my soft belly, I dip one finger inside myself, grabbing my arousal before pulling it up onto my clit. I cry out as I rub the sensitive nub and my hips start bucking. I move back down and push two fingers in, a poor substitute for Ciaran's, and try to meet the aching need to be filled.

As I watch, Ciaran takes his hardened length out of his pants, gripping it roughly at the base as that thick vein pulses. Precum glistens on the tip, and he swipes his thumb over it while stroking himself. His eyes watch my fingers with unhinged delight, his pupils fully blown out. Faster and faster, I pump my fingers before circling my clit. My eyes fall closed, lost in the moment, so I'm not prepared when Ciaran pushes his tongue into me. I shatter over him, my release coating his mouth. My scream pierces the room.

Before I'm finished, he replaces his tongue with the head of his cock and pushes into the hilt before pulling back out again. My breathing stutters as I try to adjust to being so full, followed by being so empty. "Fuck, Astrea," Ciaran growls. "You are so tight. You were fucking made for me."

I tip my head up to look at him. He's watching my pussy

devour his cock. The sight of the hunger on his face brings more arousal to my body.

His eyes meet mine, brilliant red now, and he smiles devilishly. "I'm going to fill you up so when we walk into that club tonight, my cum will still be dripping out of you." And then he strikes, his teeth burrowing into my neck and his cock going hard and deep. True to his word that I'll be full of him, he brings us to climax together three more times.

Ciaran

Astrea and I spend another hour feasting on one another before she finally asks me if I remember anything from the past few weeks. Other than mind-numbing fear, I tell her I remember nothing. She lets out a long sigh but nods before slipping from the bed to get dressed. It wasn't the full truth—I remember a female voice, one that is still haunting my mind. But worrying her, or them, over a voice isn't something I'm prepared to do just yet.

I get up and walk into the closet behind her, my cock still hard and bobbing out in front of me. She turns around, and a wicked gleam lights her eyes before she drops down in front me. "Fuck me," I groan as Astrea darts her pink tongue out to lick up my length.

"I want to taste you all night," she purrs, pulling my cock into her warm mouth until I hit the back of her throat and she gags. I grab hold of her hair and start to move her head up and down my length.

"Does my mate want to choke on my cock?" I growl, staring down at her. She moans around me at my words, and I smile as I thrust harder, hitting the back of her throat. "You look so pretty like this, with my cock shoved into your mouth. Tears trailing down your face."

I pick up my pace and watch as she moves her own

hand down between her legs. I pull my cock out of her mouth and slap her in the lips with it, causing her to glare at me. "I didn't say you could touch yourself, did I?" I snap.

"But—"

I don't let her finish before I shove myself back in between her pouty lips. I keep up a relentless pace, watching spit stream from her mouth to match her tears. "You can come tonight, if you are a good girl and listen to me." She growls between thrusts. "Oh, fuck, Astrea, I'm so close," I moan. "Your mouth feels almost as good as your pussy." The hum that vibrates from her pushes me over the edge and I unload into the back of her throat.

Like the good girl she is, she swallows it all down with a smile on her face.

The room is tense as we prepare to leave for the club. Ava is shooting daggers at Shadow. Shadow is seething in the corner, refusing to look at anyone. And Astrea is testing my limits with her outfit—I want to both drag her back into the room to mark her up again and demand she wear a burlap sack out. She's filled out more over the weeks we've been at Ava's. Her curves are delicious.

"Alright. Let's go," Shadow grumbles.

"Oh, yes, please have fun while little ol' me is staying back at the homestead waiting for the menfolk to come home." Disdain drips from Ava's voice as she storms out of the room. I pinch the bridge of my nose in frustration but don't say anything as Shadow opens a portal and we step through to directly outside Club Eufori.

Astrea

Standing in the club, I can still taste Ciaran's release at the back of my throat. My pussy continues to throb with need. I glare over at my mate, who smirks. Ciaran motions for Shadow and I to move over toward the massive bar. It's packed with witches, vampires, and even humans. I can smell the Eufori in the air, and my nose crinkles. The scent rattles the box in my mind, poking at it, trying to unlock more memories that I don't want. I shake my head in an attempt to clear it; I need to stay focused. My mate brushes my back in a grounding gesture before planting a kiss on my neck.

We agreed he would go to Drago, not only to avoid a confrontation between him and Shadow but to keep me out of his line of sight. Not because he's afraid I can't hold my own but because, in his words, "I'd rather not rip out his heart when he looks at you." It's hard to say no to that. So, I sit with Shadow at a table near the bar, casually sipping on a vodka soda water and waiting for my mate to return. I'm praying we get out before I break and beg for a hit of that drug. It's been a very long time since I was rocked with a craving for Eufori.

I look over at Shadow, who seems equally tense, his knee bouncing up and down under the table. His long fingers dance across the table as if he is tapping out his nerves. I slowly sweep my own hand over and grip his hard in a comforting gesture.

"You can leave, Shadow. I'll be okay here on my own." Even as the words leave my mouth, I worry that, should he leave me alone, I'll seek out what my body is vibrating for. I send a silent curse towards Alexi and hope someday I can repay him for everything he did to me.

The flames of anger are suddenly licking the insides of my body, stroking my dark magic. I'm assaulted with visions of Alexi's body in pieces as I stand over him, his warm blood dripping through my fingers. My fingers flex and twitch in anticipation, the hold on my magic loosening.

"I'm not leaving you. Ciaran would gut me." Shadow's voice pulls me from the intrusive thought. My magic settles back down like dust over my body.

I shrug and go back to people-watching, praying for my mate to hurry the fuck up. But as the time ticks on, my body becomes more and more restless. Downing the drink in front of me I stand swiftly and announce, "I'm going to dance."

Shadow looks taken back by my sudden statement. "That's an awful idea," he growls.

I roll my eyes. "Everything is an awful idea to you." I turn toward the dance floor and glance back at him again. "You can come with me or you can explain to Ciaran why I'm alone out there."

He's up and out of the booth immediately, following me into the dense crowd while snarling under his breath.

Ciaran

(Playground- Bae Miller)

"Drago, it's been a long time." I walk up to the giant of a man currently holding court at the back of the club. Crimson smoke fills the room. *Eufori.* I pinch the bridge of my nose again, trying to stay calm. The drug may have little effect on me after all these years, but my witch will be affected should it filter down toward the bar where she and Shadow wait for me. No need to mention how much Shadow should be avoiding this. I need to speed this along. Like hell am I going to introduce her to Drago. And Shadow has no interest in seeing his stepbrother again.

"Ah, Helvig. It has been awhile," his voice booms over

the music. "Care for a drink?" He gestures to the two witches who move to vacate the area.

I shake my head. "No, but thank you."

He nods his head and gestures toward the open seat next to his throne-style chair. Drago has owned this club for longer than I can remember. Ever a figure in the underworld, even my father respects him—or maybe fears him—as he has so many loyal followers. "What can I do for you, friend?"

(Purple Lamborghini- Skrillex, Rick Ross)

"I can't just swing by and say hello?" I ask as I take the whiskey offered to me. Drinking a sip, I look out over the club. I can't see Astrea, but I can feel our bond pulsing, giving me some relief. *Shadow may have been right; coming here was dumb.*

Drago laughs again. "You are many things, Ciaran, but you are not one who just 'swings by.'"

"How's business?" I ask.

He raises an eyebrow at my blatant attempt to avoid the subject. "Everyone wants an escape. But that isn't why you are here, is it?"

I shrug noncommittally, which brings another laugh from him. Drago has the body of a fighter. Honed and powerful muscles ripple under his white dress shirt. Colorful tattoos on his chest peek out of his shirt where he has a few buttons undone. He could best anyone in this club with pure physical strength, and if that's not enough, his touch of death makes him feared by even the most powerful. Not to mention the other talents he keeps hidden.

He sips his drink before offering, "Why don't you grab the woman and Shadow, and we will retire to my office?" I freeze temporarily at his words, and he tsks. "You didn't actually think I wouldn't notice when powerful creatures walk into my territory, did you? That woman you brought is leaking magic." He smiles. "Not to mention she's currently dancing on top of the platform."

Trying my best to control my reaction, I glance out to where he points. Sure enough, Shadow is glaring up at my mate who is enjoying herself a little too much. I curse under my breath; I should have known better. Even if Drago hadn't sensed Astrea, he would have known immediately that Shadow was here. Louder, I reply, "I just didn't want to intrude on your hospitality." I catch Shadow's eye and jerk my head up toward the stairs that lead to Drago's private office.

Drago stands and moves past me, gesturing for me to follow. His hair has grown since I saw him last, now styled in shaggy layers that hang around his face. The white offsets his blue eyes, giving him an eerie look.

We walk past two guards, which is laughable given Drago is the most dangerous creature in here besides our group. His office is exactly as I remember it, a modern, clean and crisp design. It looks more like a boardroom than the private office of a drug dealer at the back of a club. I can feel Astrea move into the room behind me, and I squeeze her hand when she slips it into mine a moment later. Shadow takes up position a little further back, watching for any threats that might come up the stairs.

"Now," Drago says as he looks over Astrea, "who is this beautiful creature?"

"Astrea," she answers. I'm cursing her choice of outfit again now that she's in front of Drago. The corset-style bustier under the leather jacket shows off her filled-out cleavage and stomach. Thankfully, only one snake is showing. But its smokey body is resting on her toned thigh, drawing attention to the hem of that short skirt, and it doesn't help that her black combat boots lift her almost to my height. She has her hair pulled up in a high, slicked-back ponytail, and her smoked-out eyes give her an ethereal look, like a dark angel. My only peace of mind is that her twin blades are strapped to her thighs, though they're invisible to the naked eye. "It's a pleasure to meet you. Ciaran has spoken highly of you."

Drago barks out a laugh. "Now, I've heard everything. So, tell me, Astrea, what are you in need of?"

I can feel myself tensing, hating her name on his tongue. The fresh mating bond is chafing me and ruining my normally excellent patience. She lets her thumb trace my palm as a way to calm me.

"We need to get to the coven grounds. I hear you are the one who can make that happen." Astrea pauses, only for a moment, before adding, "And when the time comes, we may elicit your help killing Alexi."

Astrea

The deep thrum of the bass pulses through the club below us, but the office is so quiet you could hear a pin drop. Without Drago's help, we won't make it back through the city to my old home. So while it was a risk asking so directly, it was one I hope pays off. The only other alternative is to pray Alexi and whoever he's working with won't notice us sneaking back into the city. It's not a prayer I think will be answered.

"You have found quite the woman here, Ciaran. Do you support this?" Drago asks, taking a long pull from the glass in his hand.

I growl, and my magic flares slightly through the limited control I have on it.

Instantly Drago cocks his head toward me, his face

paling. Ciaran has already put his body in front of mine before I realize anything is happening. "What have you done?" Drago growls. "You've woken something that should not have been allowed back—Harbinger," he hisses. When he speaks the name, I swear something golden flashes through those ice-blue eyes.

I freeze before stepping back out in front of my mate. I look at Drago cautiously before asking, "What do you know of that name?" My heart pounds in my chest at the idea that someone else knows this magic.

He smiles wickedly. "I know that the snake on your leg is no mere tattoo. I know you've got another one. And I know that if that power is alive and well in you, its original owner is alive and looking for it. Tell me, has Kallen come calling yet?"

As if those snakes suddenly have permission to move, they slither over my body to visible spaces, the magic vibrating under my skin. I move to step forward, but Ciaran latches onto me, dragging me into his front and placing his hand across my stomach. A show of possession if I've ever seen one. "You seem to know a lot about this, Drago," he snaps.

Drago snorts with amusement. "I have been around for a very long time. I would be a fool not to know all the power players, alive or dead. But you didn't answer my question—has the witch shown up yet?"

It's Shadow who answers this time, stepping forward with disdain etched across his face. "Are you going to help us or not?" He spits out the question like it's a foul taste in his mouth.

"What did I miss?" I whisper, looking between them and back up at Ciaran. The subtle shake of his head has me tamping down any further reaction. If I didn't know better,

I could have sworn hurt flashed across the other man's face before he schooled it.

"I told you long ago, I would do whatever you asked of me to make amends. If this is what you ask, I will do so." Drago's voice is low, hard, eerily close to sounding afraid.

"Nothing you do will make amends," Shadow spits. "Help us or don't, but it won't fix us."

Drago takes Shadow in, his eyes swimming with an emotion I can't place. "Someday, you will have to let this go. For *her,* you will have to." He looks back at us. "That magic you have needs to be claimed as your own. Right now, it still belongs to the witch it was taken from. Once you do that, you'll be unstoppable. But you didn't answer the question, has Kallen hunted you down yet?"

It suddenly clicks. "That's who was in the apartment," I say under my breath. "That's Alexi's whore. Oh my god." The revelation that the owner of this power has been so close burns through me, my heart beating hard in my chest.

Ciaran's other hand comes to my hip and squeezes gently. "How does she claim it?" he asks, and his voice is steady and calm. It's the opposite of everything I'm feeling right now. I try to lean into that, to breathe in his steady presence.

"I don't have that answer; I'm not a witch," Drago responds as he stands. "I can get you into the city and out the other side so you can search the old family estates, and I'll make you a deal for help beyond that."

Shadow is vibrating with anger next to us. "You are in no place to make deals," he snarls through teeth clenched so tightly I worry he'll break his jaw.

"How else do you expect me to gain an audience with you?" Drago shouts. "You think you are the only one hurt in this? Your refusal to let the anger go isn't just hurting you.

It's hurting all of us." Drago slams a shot of clear liquid back before continuing, "Here's my offer, Shadow. You stay here with Ava and I for three months. If, at the end of that, you still want nothing to do with us, that's fine. We walk away for good."

If Shadow's rage were a living creature, it would have swept out and slaughtered us all. "I can't make a deal *for* her. She has a life. And I won't stay here for three months."

My phone vibrates, distracting me from the argument. Looking down, I read a text from Ava. "Uh, Shadow?"

He jerks his head in my direction. "What?" he snaps.

I glare at him. "First, don't you dare get pissy with me. But second, Ava says she'll do it." Ava. The girl they keep referencing. I hold up my phone as evidence of the text I just received. I think I do a good job keeping my shock in check.

Shadow drags his hands down his face, muttering something that sounds a lot like, "Motherfucker."

Drago looks pleased with himself. "It's settled, then! You've got my unlimited help, and when this is over, Ava and Shadow will stay with me for three months!"

Shadow says nothing, just storms out of the room with his cell phone going to his ear, no doubt calling Ava.

Ciaran releases me from his grasp. I can see him shaking his head as he steps up next to me. "Bold move, Drago."

Drago shrugs. "I won't let my stepbrother kill himself, or Ava, with that rage he holds. It's time we face it." He moves back behind his desk and sits down.

"Wait, stepbrother?!" I ask in shock.

"Only in the loosest sense. My mother was very briefly with his father. She died not long after they got together." He pauses and pushes his hands through his hair. "He took a liking to me and kept me around. Shadow was not so lucky. Depending on how you look at it. Now, for you two. I'll get a car to take you where you need to go. I suggest you rest tonight and be prepared in the morning. I'll send the car at dawn."

It's a clear dismissal of the conversation, if ever I've heard one, so I simply say, "Thank you."

He nods distractedly. "I'll contact you soon."

Ciaran pulls my hand, and we head back out into the club.

SIXTEEN

It started with a mate bond.
So, it shall end with a mate bond.

– Carmine Family Grimoire

Astrea

(Bad Dream-Ruelle)

Gothic Grove was founded by five witch families: Mori, Fairmore, Hoar, Cosark, and Carmine. They built the city to sustain their magic, inviting all manner of supernatural creatures to live amongst them. Shifters and vampires lived within the general witch population, but the founding families refused to live among the others. Instead, they built their homes atop a cliff overlooking the city. It was a gated community that looked like paradise but was more of a prison. With one road in and one road out, it was a veritable fortress; protected not only by the location itself but the strong magic that had been infused into the gate and walls surrounding it. They kept out anyone who was not welcome, while keeping the families isolated.

True to his word, Drago managed to ferry us across the city. Our headlights bounce off the cast-iron gates that guard the abandoned kingdom. They're hideous, looping up and around in jagged pieces that connect to the long black granite walls curving around the perimeter. Miles and miles of the dark stone encase the grounds. All around us, nature has reclaimed the roads, but she hasn't touched that gate or the walls. Even she recognizes the evil that was infused into those barriers. I hate them. As a child, I saw them as prison walls keeping me locked in a tower.

"Do you see that?" I ask as I squint past the windshield wipers.

Ciaran looks to where I'm pointing. "Lights . . ." High up on the hill, the flicker of firelight can be seen dimly through the heavy rain. He turns back to me. "Someone is living here?"

I grip his hand hard. "I think other witches have moved in here," I say in a hushed voice, as if speaking too loudly will alert them to our presence.

Ciaran turns off the car, leaving the patter of rain hitting the car top the only sound. "That will make things more difficult," he muses. "It means we can't drive in, we'll have to walk. We don't know who they are or what they are doing here." He lets out a long groan but squeezes my hand, then both of us exit the car into the inky black night.

As soon as I touch the gate to push it open, I can feel the residual magic in that iron beast. It tries to nip at my palm, tries to taste my magic. Gritting my teeth, I shove back, one snake coming off my right arm and squeezing that nefarious magic until it's gone and the gate falls open, the last of its poisonous power dissipated. Whoever is living here now hasn't imbued it with anything new.

"This place feels . . . heavy," Ciaran whispers as we cross the threshold.

"Generations of entitled witches lived here. This wasn't a home or safe place for most of us. That gate may have kept people out, but it also kept us in. I swapped this prison for another when your father took me. And I would venture to say many others felt that way. This place is evil."

I send steel down my spine and stroke those blades on my thighs. The snakes move against my skin. Slithering and unsettled. Hungry to be unleashed. My hold on them is tentative at best. And I'm worried that the longer I'm on this land the harder it will be to keep this magic under control.

"Come on." I motion toward the steep hill. "We've got a couple miles to go before we hit the first house."

"How far is yours?"

I laugh. "Mine is the farthest. After all, we reigned over the families—we couldn't be housed with the rest, now, could we?"

Ciaran groans. "That's a really fucking long way to walk."

I look over at him. The rain has soaked us both already. His hair is intricately braided back, those runes almost glowing. His T-shirt is plastered to his body, and the urge to run my hands over him overwhelming. My hunger for him never ceases. He smiles wickedly when I glance back at his face, as if he knows exactly where my mind wandered.

"With no stops, we could do it in a day. But it'll take time to search for the grimoires." Kneeling, I let my bare palm touch the overgrown road and close my eyes, allowing my power to drift outwardly. "There are a lot of witches here. I can feel their magic. We need to be really mindful to avoid them."

His keen eyes survey the darkness around us. "How far do you think they are?"

I again let my power drift, searching. "East of here. Farther away from the old family homes. If we stay in those homes, we should be fine. But let's be quick about it."

He lets out another groan. "We'd better get moving."

I laugh a little. "Is my big, scary vampire mate afraid of a walk?"

"A walk? No. A trek through magic-infested lands that used to house some truly evil people whom my father slaughtered? Yes. Yes, I am."

Ciaran

(Seven Devils- Florence + the Machine)

From the moment we walked through that gate, it has felt like the air itself is trying to press us into the very ground we're walking on. The hairs on the back of my neck stand at attention, the feeling of being watched so overpowering it's as if I'm being choked by it. I'm not sure if Astrea feels the same, but the farther onto the property we get, the quieter she's become, and her hands haven't left those daggers. The snakes that decorate her body have their heads resting on the backs of her hands. Occasionally, one will smoke off her body, hovering briefly around her shoulders before positioning itself back on her arm.

The dark skies overhead press down on us, and the rain pelts us like tiny bullets as the wind picks up. Lightning cracks overhead, illuminating the ghost town this place has become with each flash. The road has long since been overgrown, with cars abandoned along the shoulder as if we were walking through a post-apocalyptic world.

Even my father's prison felt more comfortable than this place.

Astrea pauses and looks around, her eyes searching the inky blackness. "They've cast a wide net of magic. It feels strange. Not like anything I've felt before."

"What do you want to do?" Part of me is praying she wants to turn around so we can breathe again.

"The Cosark house isn't far. It was the first house, dedicated to the least powerful of the families. We can stay there for the night; hopefully, whoever is around now will leave by morning." I choose not to point out that if they've moved in here, they won't be going anywhere.

We keep pushing forward, against wind that seems to grow stronger the further we walk. Almost as if Mother Nature herself is screaming at us to turn back. That the answers aren't worth this. I grasp Astrea's hand, the mate-bond pulsing and demanding the connection.

It takes another twenty minutes for us to crest the hill. Lightning splits the sky open above us, the rain bleeding down from it. The Cosark property is illuminated below, and the house looks like a tomb. Half of it has been reclaimed by vines and moss while the other half has crumbled down around itself.

"They didn't burn it like they did ours. They detonated a bomb on one side. When the family ran out, they slaughtered everyone minus the girls. Those, they took." Astrea's words are steel.

Hesitantly, I ask, "Did you ever see them? While you were there?"

"I saw the youngest, Justine, once. Her body was being dragged to the incinerator. Whatever they had been doing to her killed her." She looks grim, emotion shining in her eyes. "Let's go."

She starts slowly down the hill with the gravel driveway crunching under her boots. At some point, her hair started to come out of its braid and strands are now plastered to her wet face. Her green eyes are vacant, disconnected. She's pulled inside herself, and I worry that this journey will demand a price that she won't be able to come back from once paid.

Astrea

I can feel Ciaran's unease down our bond; it's distracting and makes me jumpy. I know I'm drawing further into myself. This place is already grinding on me, that internal box flung wide open now. The memories keep assaulting me every place I look. I can see my life here and can see the death that followed. The fresh magic in the air has made me on edge. No one should be here—no one should *dare* to be here. The families struck such fear into the hearts of other witches when they lived. Clearly in death they don't hold the same sway.

My magic pulses briefly under my skin, allowing one snake to come twisting up my arm. Its head perches on my shoulder as we come to a halt outside the ruins of the Cosark house.

"No new magic is present here," I say. Ciaran only grunts, gripping my hand tighter before releasing it and stepping over the threshold of the house. He's carrying a long sword down his back that makes him look like his Viking ancestors. He continues to walk in ahead of me, surveying the empty foyer. Vines dangle down and the smell of earthy decay permeates the stale air. "We should go further in, away from the damaged part of the house," I continue. "With this wind, I don't like the idea of getting crushed in our sleep."

He huffs out a laugh. "No way will I be sleeping while we are here. This place is like a murder house out of a horror movie. We go to sleep and BAM, something comes out to kill us."

"I think we are more likely to die outside." I mean to sound light, humorous, but my voice must come out flat because Ciaran frowns slightly. I move further into the house, trying to ignore his concern, and find us a relatively dry spot to sit down in. The roof is still intact over it and the walls block out most of the wind. Closing my eyes, I take deep breaths, and the deep sense of dread and panic that have been riding me since we began this journey finally overtake me. The memories from that box assault me viciously, demanding I give them attention. . .

It's the smell of smoke with something else layered under it that wakes me up. Reem and I got drunk last night—the empty vodka bottle is still next to my bed, but my sister is nowhere to be found when I blink my blurry eyes open.

"Reem?" I call out tentatively. Her side of the bed feels cold . . . she must have fled my room hours ago. I stand up, my legs wobbly, and move toward my door. When I open it, smoke pours into my room, causing me to jump back coughing. Panic starts to wedge itself into my chest. I call out again, this time for both my sisters. "Reem?! Hansley?!"

I move out of my room, the smoke thick enough that I don't notice my path is blocked and trip over something lying outside my door. Pushing to my feet, I feel something wet on my bare legs—blood. I follow the trail down my leg to the puddle on the floor that lies beneath Reem.

"No!" The word shatters me, and tears stream down my now ash-covered face as her lifeless eyes stare up at me. Her

white hair looks almost like mine, polluted with the red blood that still flows from her slit neck.

I'm yanked from the memory by Ciaran yelling my name. I gasp for breath as though I were in the house again and desperate for fresh air. The scent of smoke is still heavy in my nostrils. My face is wet with tears and my vision swims, Ciaran's form blurry at first but slowly sharpening as I blink.

"Are you okay?" His concern is dripping down the bond, leaking into me and sending an involuntary sob out of my throat. "You weren't responding to me. You scared the shit out of me." He pulls me into his body, and I savor the feeling of it; the safety it brings me.

I take a shallow breath. "I have kept a lot of things locked away, and that box has cracked open." A shudder moves through my body. Everything in me is telling me I am no longer safe. My magic is thick in my veins searching for any danger around us.

He pulls me back and kisses my forehead. "We can leave, Astrea. We can leave right now."

The thought is so tempting. No one tells you how much it'll hurt when you are finally forced to face trauma you've locked away for so long. The overwhelming tsunami of emotions that will be forced down your throat as your body attempts to process everything that happened. Everything you've locked away. I shake my head. "No, we can't. We need the answers. I'll be fine." *Maybe if I say that enough, it'll be true.* He doesn't look like he believes me anymore than I do, but I refuse to turn back. "We've got at least a few more days hiking through before we reach my home. It'll get worse before it gets better, but we don't have a choice. If that grimoire is still there, we need it."

"We should search all the houses. If we can find even one, that might help, even if it's not yours," Ciaran says. "If you are dead set on staying and looking, we might as well take every opportunity we have."

Ciaran

I watch Astrea drink small sips of water before unbinding her wet hair from its braid. The tremor in her hands and vacancy in her eyes would be evidence enough of her distress without the icy terror also seeping through our bond. Moving over, I wrap my arms back around my mate and nuzzle into her neck, reveling in her scent washing over me. She lets out a long, breathy sigh, arching her neck toward me a little more.

"What are you doing, little *kamerat?*" I growl.

"Mmm, nothing . . ." But I can feel her hand creeping down toward the front of my pants.

"That doesn't feel like nothing," I say as she gropes my hardening cock through my pants.

She doesn't reply but drops down to her knees in front of me. Face full of concentration, she works my wet pants down until I bob free, tip glistening in the dim light thrown out by our lantern.

"You don't have to do this," I say.

"I want to," she replies, looking me in the eyes. Hunger finally giving life to the dullness that has slowly leached into them.

Her hand fists me tightly before she pumps me once, twice, and then takes me into her mouth. *"Fuck."* She swirls her tongue around my head before sucking me back down, this time taking me deep into her throat. My hand finds her hair and I slowly begin to fuck her mouth. She moans around me as I start to move faster, the feeling vibrating my cock.

"I bet if I touched your greedy little cunt, it would be soaked, wouldn't it?" She looks up at me, her pupils blown wide. "I'm going to fuck your mouth now, Astrea, and if you drink all of me down, I might let you cum tonight."

She whimpers in response, her hands clutching my ass, and I unleash myself.

Fucking her mouth hard, I watch as tears stream down her face and saliva leaks out of her mouth. The image has me loudly cuming down the back of her throat.

When she pulls off my cock, she bats her large green eyes at me, her lips spread in a full smile. "Will you make me cum now? Please?"

Astrea

Ripping my shirt off, bra going next, Ciaran tosses the remnants aside and latches onto my breast. I arch into his mouth as fire invades my belly and a deep need pulses through me. He releases my nipple as he looks up at me, his eyes going red. He bites into his wrist until blood flows freely, then spins me so his one arm is holding the blood to my mouth while the other starts to inch towards my pant line.

"Drink," he commands.

I don't hesitate to pull his wrist to my mouth and drink in the smokey taste of his blood. At one time, I might have recoiled from the idea, but now I savor the taste of him, the feel of him. His fingers unbutton my jeans and plunge into my soaked underwear.

"Fuck, you're so wet. And all from you sucking me off?" I cry out a low moan as he pushes his thick fingers into me.

My head is swimming from the combination of his blood and his fingers. It's a better high than any drug.

When he suddenly takes his wrist from my mouth to yank my pants off, I have no shame as I beg for him, the words barely sounding like English. When he puts me on all fours and drives his pulsing cock into my pussy, I cry out in overwhelming pleasure. Then I feel warmth suddenly drip down over that small, untouched hole before I feel pressure as he starts to push his thumb inside me.

"Ciaran," I whimper. The blending of pleasure and pain makes my world swim.

"Shh. Relax, Astrea. Let me in." I focus on the burn, and then my muscles slowly start to relax and allow him in. "That's it. That's my good girl." Once his thumb is fully in me, I can't breathe. The feeling is intoxicating, being this full.

"Oh, fuck. Ciaran, oh, that feels so good. Don't stop."

He stops moving and pulls my hair back, so he is in my ear. "That's right. Beg me as you scream my name." He thrusts slightly, making me whimper.

He only chuckles before releasing my hair and going back to a relentless pace. It doesn't take long before I fall over that edge, screaming his name in my release. I expect him to follow me, but he doesn't—instead, he pulls out rapidly. The loss of him inside sends a sob cascading from my lips.

He pulls his thumb from me before I feel him pushing two fingers back in. "Ciaran . . . fuck." He is slow at first as he pumps them in and out of my tight channel, before creating a scissoring motion. After a few moments, he pulls his fingers from me, and I feel the head of his cock press against me. "Oh, fuck, I can't, Ciaran. You won't fit. I can't do this."

He leans down so his mouth is at my ear. "I will take you however I want, *kamerat*. Because every part of you belongs to me."

He slowly pushes in and the burn is unbelievably intense. I squirm, uncomfortable with the intrusion. He pauses, allowing me to get used to it before he pulls out and slowly pushes the same amount back in. After three or four times, my muscles relax and the burn feels pleasurable. I let out a low groan of ecstasy, and he moves to push fully in. His hand goes back around and slowly begins rubbing my clit. The sensation allows him to fully seat himself inside me.

"Oh, fuck," I whimper. His movements are slow at first as he gives me time to adjust. Pleasure shoots up my spine. My entire body is burning in an arousal so intense I no longer feel connected to this world.

"I'm done going slow, *kamerat*, I can't control myself anymore. I hope you are ready." It's the only warning I get before he starts to fuck me hard.

I push my hips back to meet his thrusts. "That feels so good. Yes, yes, yes, yes." I'm panting and moaning, and I know I can't hold on. "You're going to make me cum again. Fuck!"

"That's it, cum for me while I fill your ass up." His dirty words push me over, and the feeling of his hot release shooting into me has me reeling in pure ecstasy.

SEVENTEEN

Ciaran

I slowly pull out of Astrea, careful not to add to any discomfort that she is going to have. The sight of the mess I've left behind makes me want to never leave her naked body. But I need her to rest, and already her eyes are starting to blink more slowly. Grabbing my already dirty shirt, I clean her up before throwing a blanket over her naked body.

"Get some rest, my mate," I murmur as I kiss her forehead. She snuggles down into the blanket and promptly passes out. I want nothing more than to curl up with her, but I begrudgingly pull my clothes on and go in search of the grimoire.

I gave her a good deal of my blood while we fucked,

hoping it would help her sleep. Help counteract whatever is going on to send those nightmares to her. Vampire blood can do amazing things when given the opportunity, particularly for our mates. When I discovered what Astrea was to me, I looked into our lore on mates. According to the old texts, when a vampire finds their mate, our blood can do more than heal physical wounds; it was written that we can force our blood to provide what we need for our mates. In this instance, I wanted Astrea to have some peace. I had hoped I could find out more information, but the other books had long been burned by my father. Another way for him to control our kind.

I look down at Astrea's sleeping form once I return from searching and smile. While I didn't find the grimoire that belonged to this family, at least my mate got a few hours of uninterrupted sleep.

The sound of tires on gravel invades my mind as I blink the sleep from my eyes. Astrea sits up, the blanket slipping off her bare body. Her face is still coated with the exhaustion we both feel. We look at each other for a moment before we register exactly what we are hearing.

Moving as quickly and quietly as we can, we slip our clothes on before creeping towards the front of the crumbling structure.

"Who are they?" I whisper as we spy a handful of people in the front.

"The witches I felt," she answers. Her voice is flat, but the way her hands curl into fists betray how calm she sounds.

We both watch as they walk around the property, never coming close enough to the house to make us run, but also not giving us enough space to sneak out. Astrea starts to fidget next to me as we watch them search around.

"What are they looking for?" I ask, more to myself than to Astrea.

"Us," she says in a hushed voice.

———

The witches stayed outside for most the night before finally loading up back into their cars to leave us in peace. The whole night, Astrea and I switched off keeping watch, but thankfully they never came into the old home.

As we leave the Cosark house the next morning, I can't help but notice how dark it still is. It's as though daylight can't fully penetrate the air. I glance over at Astrea as she finishes putting her hair up in a ponytail. The effect this place has on her is visible. Her normally vibrant eyes are dim, even lifeless at times. The color has been leached from her cheeks, and the red of her hair looks dull. The fact that we have already been here a day longer than we should have been makes me worried about the full effect this place will have on her by the end.

"Did you eat?" I already know the answer; I watched her push the granola bar back into her pack after I handed it to her.

"I'm not hungry." She moves past me, heading up the driveway. "The next house will be the Fairmores'. It's not too far, so we shouldn't need to walk as long."

I frown, following her. "What about the magic you felt yesterday?"

She furrows her brow. "It's faint. I don't think anyone is currently practicing."

"Do you think they know we are still here?"

She shrugs, "I think if they had we would have had a very different night."

I nod. "Let's hope it stays that way."

We walk in mostly comfortable silence, only talking when I check on her or she points something out. The deeper in we get, the more it feels like we've left the normal world and entered another. Ravens caw overhead as they circle like vultures waiting on their next pound of flesh. It's eerie. My hand twitches, aching to pull my blade. I notice Astrea has kept her hands on her own.

Desperate to take my mind off the eerie feeling, I look at her and ask, "Tell me about your blades."

She glances over at me. "My sister left them for me."

"The Seer?"

She nods. "Hansley left them at the cabin for me, I found them the night I ran from you. They have strange magic on them. Almost like they are alive."

I whistle low. "Interesting. I've heard of blades like that but never seen them. What about your other sister? You never talk about her."

She shrugs. "Reem and I had a hard relationship. When I was younger, she and I were close, but after my tenth birthday, she kind of pulled away. Reem always seemed to have hot and cold feelings towards me. The night she died was the first time we had really spent a lot of time together. I think Hansley knew how hard it was for me to be around Reem, so she spent a lot of time with me. That night, Hansley was busy. Reem showed up with some vodka and wanted to make amends. She had been acting weird, but I didn't think anything of it. We got wasted on cheap vodka and passed out in my room. That was the last time I saw her alive."

Before I can comment, she cuts the conversation off, pointing off into the distance. "That's the Fairmore property. Let's hurry. I feel that magic again."

Astrea

Talking about Reem was a bad idea. I feel a current under my skin that has me shaking out my hands in an anxious motion. I'm thankful the Fairmore estate is just ahead. Only their barn still stands, so we make our way to that. I don't have hope their grimoire survived, but I have to rest. I have a concerning bone-deep exhaustion I can feel sinking deeper and deeper into me. My snakes haven't moved off my skin all day, and my magic feels slow here. The disconnect grows with every passing moment. I know Ciaran is worried; I know he can tell something is off. But I haven't told him—even the idea of talking is too much.

When we enter the barn, I practically collapse into a pile of hay. My eyes feel so heavy . . . Sensing Ciaran near me, I let the sleep pull me under without a word.

I scramble backward, swearing her lifeless eyes track my movements. Pushing up, I take off on bare feet to Hansley's room and throw open the door, only to vomit upon seeing her naked body on the bed. I cover my mouth to stifle the sob invading my throat. Her head hangs off the side, upside down with purple handprints vibrant against her pearl-white skin. I'm frozen as the smoke swirls around me, obscuring her body every now and again. Confusion and disbelief at this reality worming into my mind like a parasite.

Somewhere downstairs, I hear a crash that startles me into action. Flames have crept up closer and the smoke is invading my throat. Racing past my sister's corpse, I move to her balcony and shove the doors open. Instantly, the humid air presses down on me. Despite my shorts and sleep tank, I'm dripping sweat as I fling my leg over and start to climb down the trellis attached to the side of our home.

Moving as quickly as I can, I forget about the missing piece that Hansley broke last summer sneaking out. Before I can catch myself, I'm falling down the last story. I hit the ground hard on my ankle, and the resulting crack is loud in my ears, almost vibrating my whole body. I collapse with a thud that knocks the wind from my chest and roll, gripping my ankle.

"Over here!" Disoriented, I look up to see a male in some type of military fatigues rushing toward me.

Move! a voice slithers down my body, and I'm quick to listen. Scrambling up, I try my best to run while dragging my ankle behind me.

A hand grabs me from behind, and a scream pours itself from my mouth at the same moment magic explodes around me in thick, glittering black smoke.

Once again, I find myself being pulled from the memories that have shaken out since being on this property. I gasp for breath, and sense my ankle is burning. It takes a moment for me to realize I'm safe. My ankle isn't broken, and those stormy blue eyes are my mate's. We don't have sex this time. Instead, I let sleep take me again, praying I'm not pulled into more nightmares.

Ciaran

"Are you going to tell me what's going on?" I stop walking, forcing Astrea to turn around to face me. The dark circles under her eyes are getting worse, and her movements are slow and heavy. Almost as though she is pushing through water instead of merely walking. It's part of the reason I forced her to sleep longer, refusing to let us leave until closer to the following evening. She's been silent since the Fairmore barn, and as we near the Carmine house, she has grown so distant. I'm not sure I'll be able to cross the chasm that this place has created.

"I'm fine." Her voice is flat, her eyes haunted.

I grab her arm before she can turn back around. "Like hell, you are. You look worse than you did at my father's prison." She flinches, and I cup her face. "Astrea, talk to me."

She lets out a long sigh. "Being here has triggered a lot for me. But it feels like it's more than that. It feels magical. Something, *someone*, is interfering with my magic. With me."

"So, we leave. This isn't fucking worth it. We'll figure out how to claim your magic some other way. Get our answers some other way."

Astrea's head, now buried in my chest, shakes adamantly. "No. We are almost there. The nightmares are just exhausting, that's all. They aren't real." I'm not sure if she is trying to convince herself or me. "The Carmines are just through that tree line. We can just pass through and keep walking. We don't have to stay the night." I know why she added the last piece. The Carmine house is my mother's house.

"No, you need the rest. We'll stay the night. Come on." I pull her behind me. The rain has never stopped, the darkness never let up. It feels as though I'll never get dry again, at this rate.

"Ciaran." She stops me just as the house comes into view. "Do you want to keep walking? We don't have to go in there." She asks again.

I look at the house; my mother's family home. Something pulls at me, a flicker of warmth that is outside the bond. It's pushing me toward the house. "No. We have to."

My ancestral home is the only one still standing, fully intact. I'm not sure if it was my mother's relationship with my father that kept it standing or if they knew the power wasn't within our family. Either way, as we push open the front door, it feels like opening a time capsule. My memories of my mother aren't much, but the scent that hits me has the few I have battering my mind. The overwhelming feeling of grief has me stumbling backward, pushing into Astrea's form.

"Ciaran?"

I search the foyer in front of us, my gaze bouncing as if I expect a ghost to walk through. When nothing happens, I tug Astrea off the porch and we shut the door behind us. The relief is instant. That oppressive feeling lifts, and I pull a full breath into my lungs for the first time in three days. Glancing at Astrea, I can see color has returned to her cheeks, and her eyes are clear and bright again.

"Holy shit," she mutters, stepping around me. "This place has more magic than I've ever felt." Her eyes are wide as she takes in the house.

"This is my mother's magic." I would know it anywhere. As a child, my room always felt like this, smelled like this a mixture of sage and lavender. A scent that forced my soul into a place of peace no matter what my emotions were. It grounded me when nightmares would fill my dreams. Safety has always been an illusion in my world, but as in that room, in this space it feels concrete and attainable.

"It's powerful protection magic," Astrea says. The front

entry looks nothing like what my father's house looked like. This looks cozy. The floor is dark hardwood, the walls a deep green, and upon glancing to our left, the furniture in the living room looks well loved. I watch my mate move into the living room before she turns and looks at me. "Your mother must have known. Why else would this place be like this? It's completely untouched."

I follow her in and try to avoid feeling overwhelmed. Yes, my mother was good to me. But the only measure for "good" I had was that she was better than my father. She died when I was young. I think the grief I've felt wasn't so much for her but for the idea of a mother, so the thought that she was attempting to take care of me from beyond is unsettling.

Astrea has made herself at home on the old couch, looking more comfortable than I've seen her since we started into the cursed land. She's pulled her boots off and set her knives aside and is now slowly pulling her hair out of its messy topknot and finger-combing it as she continues to look around from her vantage point. Maybe it's my discomfort down the bond, but she gets up and wraps her arms around me. "Do you want a minute alone?" she asks as her scent envelopes me.

I kiss her forehead and reply, "Sure. Why don't you go find the shower? I'll join you in a moment." She nods and skips off back down the hall.

Looking around the room, I take in the mismatched furniture. The stacks of books piled everywhere. The herbs and spice jars strewn about. I didn't know this person. The mother I knew, or remember, was very orderly. Our home never had anything out of place. Everything matched and looked clean. And now I wonder how much of that was my father's doing.

Walking over to the fireplace, I drag my hand over the mantle. Not a speck of dust lines it, which strikes me as odd. When my fingers hit a raised piece of brick followed by the feel of paper, I pause. Prying the top of the brick loose, I see an envelope with my name scrawled across the top in elaborate cursive. I pull it free and drop down onto the couch, holding it in my hand like it could explode at any minute.

Careful not to rip the contents, I gently open the envelope to find several papers. Unfolding them, I take a deep breath and start to read:

> Dearest Ciaran,
>
> If you are reading this letter, you have found your way to my home. It also means I am not with you. For that, I am truly sorry. The burden on you is not one you should bear but nonetheless will have to. Things are in motion that I cannot stop, not now that Astrea Mori has shown her power. Shown The Harbinger power. It will mean, despite what the rest of the families believe, that the witch formerly known as Kallen will have awoken. She'll be searching for it. And this, my dear one, is our fault.
>
> Long ago, your ancestors helped Kallen gain those powers that Astrea now holds. Our family has never been high up in the coven standings, and we didn't agree with what they did to her. We didn't understand what we unleashed by giving her that power. When the covens stopped her, they separated the soul and the power into

two different families. Each passed down, generation to generation. It is my belief that Kallen's soul
has been more aware than the families believe.
That she's been taking power during each life she
is reborn into. The soul is like a parasite and the
body is only a host now. Whatever witch she is in
is long dead.

The power Astrea was given was due to her
mother's affair. That greedy woman put all of us
at risk. The covens will never admit to that,
though; they will fight tooth and nail asserting
that once the power was rebound in Astrea,
Kallen's soul would remain asleep. They prefer us
all to believe the lies they spew.

And trust me when I say they have spewed
many lies.

For the past two generations, we've been
watching and waiting for her to make her move. I
knew Alexi was present during the time the original families cursed her, so I planted myself with
him; hoping that when she did return, I would be
able to right the wrongs of our past. If you are
reading this, it means she discovered me and had
him kill me. Make no mistake: she's controlled him
for a very long time.

Astrea will need to accept that dark power as
her own in order to keep Kallen from magically

stealing it back. Otherwise, Astrea would have to offer it freely to her. You are her counterpart; you ground her. If you don't figure out how to link your magic, she will be lost to its darkness.

I love you, Ciaran, and I'm sorry to pass this burden on to you. Hansley Mori told me she saw two paths. If you are on the one that caused you to use the potion I left you, know I will make Alexi suffer when he reaches the afterlife. While I'm so thankful you found your mate, my heart hurts knowing how much you've both suffered and how much is still to come.

This letter will allow the magic I locked from you long ago to resurface. And with-it memories you may not have possessed prior. I hope you can forgive me for the things I've done. But if you can't, I understand and know that I have continued to pay the price for the choices I've made here in the afterlife.

Trust your mate Ciaran. Trust each other. But most of all trust the love you have for her.

Love Always,
Mom

P.S. Please take care of our grimoire. It's your legacy.

The moment the letter slips free of my hand I'm assaulted by a slithering sensation up and down my spine until it finally lands on those tattoos across my head. My vision swims and the room become hazy as doors deep within my mind start to switch their locks and slowly creep open. When the first one swings wide my knees hit the ground and the world goes black.

EIGHTEEN

Should the covens begin to fall, we must preserve
the found families.
Above all else, we must survive to regain the power
and soul.
A more powerful spell must be used.
The same mistake cannot be made again.

– Mori Family Grimoire

Astrea

I'm frowning as the water officially runs cold. Ciaran never joined me. I step out and dry off, then wrap the towel around my body before going back out to the living room. As I pad down the hall, I hear a crash, followed by a roar of rage.

"Ciaran?" I call out. When I round the corner, he's sitting on the ground, head in hands with an an envelope next to him. There are scattered books and shards of glass on the floor. As my gaze bounces around the room, I search for an enemy, but I find it empty. Only my mate. As I approach, he looks up at me, his eyes shimmering with emotions I can't identify. "What's wrong?"

He holds the envelope up, its age clear through the yellowing of the paper. I see his name etched across it. "I found this." His voice is barely above a whisper. "It's from my mother." Careful not to let my towel slip, I take a seat next to him. The fabric of the couch scratches the backs of my bare legs as I attempt to get comfortable.

"It seems she knew we'd be here. It seems she knew a lot." He takes a steadying breath, hand shaky as he runs it through the golden hair he's unbound from its intricate braid. And then he starts talking. Each revelation feels like a gunshot to my chest. From my mother's affair, to Hansley having seen this. I want to scream at my sister for not warning me. Hansley knew I could be taken, knew what I would endure, yet she never warned me.

I stand up. My rage is a living beast that is eager to strike out. I want to hurt someone. And since I can't reach the people who caused this, I decide the world will do just fine. My magic crackles across my body, ready to lash out, but a sharp tug on the back of my neck has me whirling around. Ciaran grabs my throat, holding me firm, and the pressure immediately grounds me. His eyes are red, and his canines have descended. "You are going to listen very carefully to me."

An inhuman growl comes from my throat, causing Ciaran's mouth to lift into a small smile. "Growl at me. Fight me. But you will not allow that magic to control you." He tightens his grip on my throat, his other hand yanking the towel off me. "Now kneel."

There are times when I don't want him to be so demanding, but at this moment, I know it's what I need.

What *we* need. So, despite shooting daggers at him, I drop to my knees in front of him.

"Good girl," he praises. "Now, take my cock out. I want you choking on me before I paint you with my cum." Clenching my thighs together, I quickly unbutton his pants and pull his thick length from his pants. I salivate at the sight of him and immediately take him into my mouth. He hisses and yanks on my hair. "No rushing." I dig my nails into his thighs in response, which earns a groan from him. It's my small act of rebellion, reminding him my submission isn't total.

Ciaran sets a relentless pace as he fucks my mouth. Spit and tears are streaming down my face as he hits the back of my throat repeatedly. "Such a good girl. You look so fucking pretty when I'm shoved down your throat," he growls. Wanton moans vibrate my mouth around him, and I keep pressing my thighs together, desperate to ease the ache that's built. "Ah, fuck, Astrea, your mouth feels so good." It's the only warning I get before he pulls out and rope after rope of his release sprays my chest.

When he's finished, he smiles and runs his fingers over my chest through the mess he's created. "Clean this up," he demands. He shoves his fingers into my mouth, and I lap him up, savoring the taste. He does it three more times before my chest is cleaned of his release. "Lie back and spread your legs." I don't hesitate. His eyes glow molten hot as he takes in my dripping center. "First, I'm going to feed from you here"—he taps my femoral artery— "then I'm going to feed from you here." He pushes his thick fingers into me, and I scream out at the delicious intrusion, followed by pure ecstasy flooding my veins as Ciaran digs his fangs into my thigh, drinking me deeply.

Her

At some point, a witch I inhabited was a Realm Walker. It was lucky, given how incredibly rare they are; Shadow is the only one to have walked the earth in centuries. The portal I created opens into the old family grounds, and I step out, my Hellbeasts flanking me. I can smell my magic, the tang of it potent in the air. My mouth salivates at the thought of having it back. I move in the direction I feel it emanating from, and my feet carry me over the uneven ground directly to the Carmine home. I scowl at the place. The ones who had been so loyal, only to betray me in the end. I twitch and shake; my glamour is becoming increasingly bothersome. It's not meant to be worn for as long as I have, and I'm starting to think it's no longer worth hiding behind it.

Moving forward with my beasts in tow, I make my way over to the small home. It's the only one that's not a mansion. The cottage shoots a longing through me for the home I once had. The home my mate and I had long ago. It was simple, but it was ours. We had built it together and were excited to raise a family in it, before it was all taken away. I curl my fists, my sharp nails drawing blood as that familiar rage coats my tongue and fuels my steps. *Once I have my magic back, I'll kill them all.*

As I near the small home, I can hear moans coming from inside. While the magic prevents me from entering—*nice touch, Kara, but it won't save your son*—it doesn't prohibit me from looking in a window. Fluidly, another glamour slips into place, one that allows me to go unseen. Silent as a mouse, I peer into the large window at the front of the home, the one they failed to cover in their haste. On the floor, I see two naked bodies, Ciaran feeding from Astrea before he moves up her body and slips his cock into her. She has her eyes closed, head thrown back with a look of utter rapture on her face. My nipples pebble as I watch the power Ciaran has in his body as he thrusts into her. *I want that.*

I shift on my feet, pressing my thighs together and wishing it were me under him. *Me* he was feeding on, fucking, filling with his release. *No, not him. My mate. I want my mate.* I must make a small sound, because he snaps his eyes up, the predator in him sensing something watching. He keeps fucking her, but his eyes remain on my invisible form. Her blood is dripping from his chin, his blond hair a mess in front of his face. Then Astrea grabs his face and drags him back down to her lips, pulling his attention back to her. The moment she finds her release, I can taste her magic in the air. He's not far behind, and I watch him fill her up, then collapse off to the side so as not to crush her when he's finished.

I want that. Again, that thought plays through my mind. *I deserve to find someone again.* Centuries of loneliness have taken their toll. By keeping my soul bound to these infernal witches, they've kept me from my mate. They've kept me from being at peace with him. The ground beneath me starts to smoke as my anger becomes something physical. The beast nearest me nudges my hand, as if to remind me to take a deep breath. I have worked too hard to allow myself to lose it all here. And so, with slow, steady steps, I back away from the lovers to await the next phase of my plan.

I walk out of the portal onto the grounds of the old Mori house. There I can see the witches the coven has lent me. Their leader, a mousy female, walks up with a sneer on her face. None of them are enjoying working with me, and I know that they will end up being a bigger problem at the end of all this. But for now, I need them. I'm not as dumb as she thinks I am; I can sense something *other* in her, something not fully of her making. She reeks like Hell magic. Just as she is my puppet, someone else seems to be using her as well.

"We've done what you asked." Her voice is annoying.

Pinching the bridge of my nose, I take a deep breath, willing myself not to break her neck. "Thank you. Now, is the magic that we need in place?"

She crosses her arms in a bratty fashion that has me wanting to smash her face into the ground. "Yes. But what assurances do we have that you'll protect us from them? Once they figure it all out, they'll come for us."

My Hellbeast growls low, and she edges backward. "You are forgetting who the fuck I am," I snarl. "I don't have to give you assurances. I don't have to do anything. So, get your shit together, or I'm sure my little beasty here would like a snack." As if to prove my point, the beast snaps at her.

She quickly scrambles away from me, the fear plastered across her face sending shivers of delight up and down my body. Someday, I'll have to kill them. But for now, I just need them to be more afraid of me than whatever else, or whoever else, they've made a deal with.

Ciaran

I lie next to Astrea, catching my breath. I have no interest in moving, but I tilt my head up to look back toward the window. An unease moving over my body and down my spine.

Breathlessly, she asks, "What is it?" Looking at her, I can't help but feel my cock grow hard again. The bites on her neck, the way her hair is a mess, and the scent of our combined release has me wanting to fuck her all over again.

Instead, I lean over and kiss her before pushing to a stand and walking over to the open window. "It felt like someone was watching."

This has her standing up quickly and moving over to me. "Doesn't look like anyone is out there," she replies.

But I'm not convinced. "Go get dressed; I'll take a look around." Pulling my jeans on, I don't bother with a shirt as I grab my large blade and exit back into the night air. That heavy feeling on the grounds seems to have multiplied since we've been in my mother's home. The relentless rain ceased at some point, but now a dense fog has descended around us. An unnatural silence is pressing in around me; pushing through it feels as though I'm slogging through thick mud.

Moving as quickly and quietly as I can, I circle around the home until I land at the window. I almost think I've made it up when some uneven ground causes me to stumble slightly. Looking down, I see two smoldering footprints.

"Fuck."

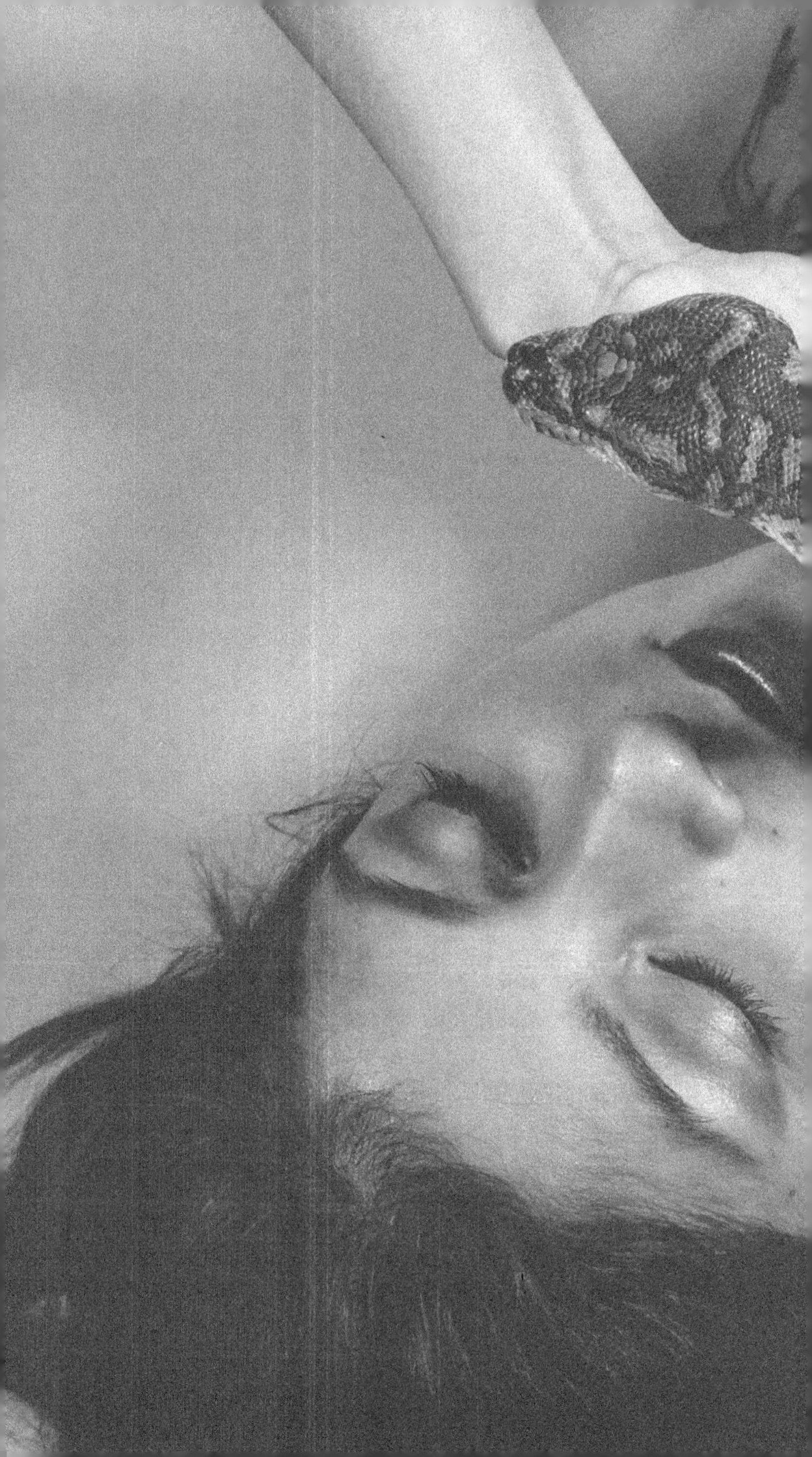

NINETEEN

They will come for The Harbinger and her mate.
They will seek to rip the power away from them.
With that threat, it is imperative we trust the
mate bond.
Trust that magic.

– Carmine Family Grimoire

Astrea

With the discovery of the footprints outside the window, we decide not to stay the night. Ciaran gives me some of his blood to help keep me on my feet, particularly given how much he took during our last round. I can see the guilt in his eyes about it, but I assure him I'll be okay. We quickly repack our bags, grabbing extra clothing from his family's closet, and move out.

The moment I step outside, I'm hit with another crippling flashback.

(Tourniquet- Evanescence)

I wake up to Ciaran standing over me, panic etched on his face. "Astrea?" He's shaking me. I push him away and retch into the dead grass next to us. Nothing coming up but bile. The taste burns the back of my throat, causing my eyes to water.

After a moment, I ease myself up to a sitting position and clutch at my head. It throbs relentlessly. "It's okay, I just got hit with a flashback. I'm fine," I stammer. *If I keep saying it, at some point, it will come true. I'll be okay. I'll be okay.*

"No. You aren't. I felt that. Could taste the terror and desperation you felt. What did you see?"

He pulls me up to stand as I keep trying to take deep breaths, to focus on the ground I'm standing on, his voice; anything to keep me here and not in those memories. "It was my time with your father." I don't realize I'm clutching one of my blades until Ciaran pries my hand off the physical blade and licks the blood off my palm.

"I will kill him, but not before I pay him back for every ounce of pain, he inflicted on you." His voice is so calm it frightens even me. I look up into his stormy eyes, comforted by the hurricane of anger alive in them.

(Haunting- Halsey)

We bypass the Hoar house completely and head straight to mine. The anxiety has turned into a living beast in my stomach the closer we get. I keep swallowing back the urge to vomit all over the decaying grass below our feet. Cold, clammy sweat has broken out over my body, and I keep feeling the ghost of that collar around my neck. Something in me is screaming to go back, clawing at my insides, repeatedly insisting that *the grimoire isn't worth it*. But I shove it all down. Shove it all back into the splintered coffin of the box.

The remains of my family home appear on the road in front of us, first as rubble before we reach the blackened skeleton itself. It's a ghost from my past waiting to be exorcized. The old Colonial-style house is nothing more than cinders. The foundation is all that still exists.

The wind shifts, kicking up that smell of ash and smoke. Maybe it's a phantom scent, but it overpowers me for a moment. I can picture myself trying to escape, snapping my ankle, my power finally appearing before that collar. It all flashes before me in an instant.

"I hate this place," Ciaran grumbles next to me. "I will be overjoyed when we can leave." I don't say anything, only nod and motion us forward.

The cloying smell gets worse as we move toward the husk of my former life, and all I can think of is scrubbing my skin raw to get the scent off me. My hands are twitchy against my blades, and those snakes have moved their smokey forms to my shoulders. Ciaran pulls his sword from his back in response to my unease.

"Let's start searching," I say, looking back at him, distracted.

That was my mistake.

The moment we step across the threshold of what used to be my home, I feel the trap spring. Magic, fast and swift, knocks into us, sending us tumbling forward further into the crumbling space.

Spinning around, I draw my daggers, looking for whoever set the trap to show themselves. Off in the distance, I can feel someone using magic. "Fucking hell, there is a coven here. They are holding us in," I snarl. Dread of being trapped *again* moves over me and I swallow it back, desperate to stay focused on the moment.

Ciaran is scanning the space around us. "This can't be a coincidence. How the fuck did they know we were here?"

A sinister voice drips into the air in answer. "I told them, obviously."

I close my eyes, praying when I open them, it's not the same woman who attacked us before. Who caused my mate to leave me for the weeks in Ava's basement.

It seems the gods no longer care to listen to me.

Her

I smile at my prey. Astrea has pulled her knives off her body, as if those will stop me. Just beneath the anger in her green eyes is the look of desperation. It's the same look an animal has when they know they are trapped by a predator. It's a look I crave.

My voice is laced with cynicism as I tut, "I'm honestly a little disappointed that the trap worked as well as it did. I truly thought we'd get into more of a fight." I let out a dramatic sigh and take a step forward. They both inch back, causing my smile to widen.

"I'm going to kill you, Kallen," Astrea hisses. She hasn't noticed that her magic isn't working as it should. Hasn't paid attention enough to realize that those snakes are now locked firmly back onto her body.

I slow-clap. "Oh, clever girl, figuring out who I am." The smile doesn't leave my face as I walk over the line of magic that is trapping hers; blood magic is powerful when you are the one fueling it. She can't cast, but I have my full power, given its my blood used with the spell. "But you might find it difficult to kill me, given your magic is under lock and key at the moment and those knives, brutal as they are, won't do much to me," I explain sinisterly.

Her face goes ashen as she reaches for her power and comes up short. It's Ciaran who lets out a low, rage-filled growl. "Maybe the blades won't kill you, but you aren't immortal; something will kill you." He launches himself at me, sword raised, but my beasts intercept him.

"True, this body isn't immortal, but my soul is, and I'll just keep coming back until I get what I want," I say conversationally.

Astrea's eyes shift between me and her mate, who is focused on my Hellbeasts as they circle him—they won't kill him, but he doesn't know that. Astrea grips her blades hard, her knuckles turning white, and my eyes narrow at her. I tsk, "I wouldn't try it." But she launches herself at me anyway, and I decide I've had enough. My glamor drops, and I can't help the cheshire cat grin that spreads over my face at her reaction.

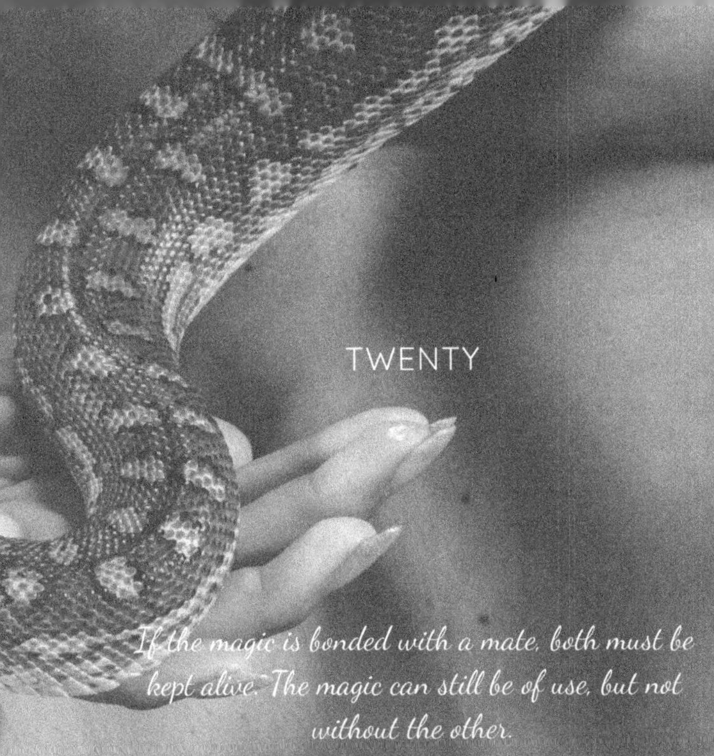

TWENTY

If the magic is bonded with a mate, both must be kept alive. The magic can still be of use, but not without the other.

– Mori Family Grimoire

Astrea

My blades fall to the uneven ground as one hand flies to my mouth and the other clutches my chest, the pain of my heart breaking a physical sensation. "Reem?" I choke out. Her dead body overlays the one in front of me as my reality crashes in around us.

My sister's face smiles back at me, her long white hair blowing in the breeze. Fog swirls around us, and she looks like an ethereal goddess at this moment. "Mmm, not anymore," she answers as she caresses her body. *My sister's body.* "She hasn't been Reem for a very, very long time."

"No." I shake my head in disbelief. My voice is barely above a whisper. "No, no, no. That can't be true."

The witch in front of me dusts off her body like the glamor she's been wearing left her dirty. Her long red skirt drags across the ground and the matching red corset looks out of place in this environment. Her shoulders are bare and only a necklace adorns her chest, the end of the pendant tucked into her—my sister's—ample cleavage. "I must say, this is my favorite body I've been in. Other than my own, of course."

"How long?" I whisper.

She smiles widely. "Since you were ten years old."

The horror that bleeds into me freezes my body as she approaches me. The eyes looking at me, Reem's eyes, crinkle at the corners. Her hand reaches up, and she delicately strokes a finger down my face. The touch burns like acid, and I grind my teeth down, refusing to let out a scream. Her fingers swipe at the tears leaking down my cheek and I watch her lick the salty liquid off them. I'm immobilized in anger and fear and grief.

She leans in, her breath tickling my face. "You are going to give me back that magic, Astrea."

"I will kill you with this magic," I hiss. The truth of the situation finally spurs me into action. I go to shove her away when we both hear a loud screech and the fall of a body. Looking over, I see my mate is covered head to toe in Hellbeast gore—I had forgotten he was fighting them. My focus is only on the woman in front of me wearing my sister like her favorite dress.

Ciaran points his sword directly at the witch in front of me. "Get the fuck away from her."

Ciaran

Fury coats my tongue as I gut the last beast, its body falling to the ground with a loud thud. My vision is red as I gaze up and see the woman from my nightmares touching my mate.

"You! Get the fuck away from her!" I point my sword at her. "Don't you dare touch her."

The woman claps her hands in delight before stepping back. "Oh, I do love a good alpha male posturing. Your father always tried to, but let's be honest, he doesn't have the same bite you do." She moves with lightning-quick speed, speed that no witch should have, and is behind me. Whirling, I bring my sword arching up, but she dodges it. My sword slashes at nothing through the air.

"Ciaran!" I glance back to Astrea for a brief moment to see the witch has appeared behind her. She's holding my mate as if they are lovers, one arm bracketed over her stomach and the other caressing her neck and up into her hair. Something flickers in my chest again; the pulse that isn't the bond but something akin to it. Glowing and warm.

Kallen lets out a low chuckle and purrs, "I forgot how good this magic smells." She viciously yanks Astrea's head back and licks up the side of her neck, letting out a long groan of pleasure as she does. "Fuck, I've missed this. I will enjoy ripping it out of you."

Something pushes forward from me. Bright white light curves and whirls around me and toward Kallen. Her eyes flash in anger and she tosses Astrea to the ground, my mate hitting the dirt hard with a resounding thud. "*You*," she seethes. "You should not have that power." All I see is gold before it blinks out and my vision goes black. The sound of my mate screaming hits my ears before I hear nothing.

There is a roiling inside me, like a sick feeling of bugs beneath my skin. I think I scream, but I can't be sure. That black oil in me is pushing toward wherever that golden light came from, and everything it touches is cut off from who I am. My back bows as I beg whatever gods there are not to let that blackness touch the light, but no one listens, and the moment it wraps around that place in me, I cease to exist.

Astrea

(Cry me a river- Tommee Profit and Nicole Serreno)

The bright light of Ciaran's magic blinks out.

I'm screaming and scrambling to my feet as I watch Kallen's magic wrap around Ciaran and push into him. His eyes go wide before the blue is fully gone, replaced by black, and that bond in us pulls taught before it shatters. My chest heaves as I collapse back to the ground from the severe pain radiating through me. I try to crawl forward toward my mate's unseeing body, but two feet appear in my vision.

"That pain you feel in your soul, in your whole fucking body? Imagine that times a million. That is what your family did to me." Kallen's sharp nails dig into my scalp as she lifts my head up by my hair. "But I'm offering you a choice. You can return my power and I'll give you your mate back. Or...you can keep that power and I will let you watch me take your mate over and over again before I kill you and rip that magic from your cold, dead corpse. It's merciful, really, and far more than you deserve."

"I didn't do anything to you. I didn't ask for this!" I cry out through gritted teeth. My whole body is screaming in blinding agony.

"You're right. You are paying for the sins of your family. Take your complaints up with them." She savagely releases my hair, slamming my face into the ground. My nose cracks, and I feel warm blood gush out. "When you are ready to give up your magic, come find me and my new pet."

Then her feet are walking away from me. My hands

grab at the dirt as I try to pull myself toward Ciaran, who's standing motionless. "Ciaran," I whimper, still desperately reaching for him. "I'll kill you! I swear, I will burn this fucking city to the ground!" I scream in rage.

"Funny, that's what I plan to do." With a final smirk over her shoulder, she pushes Ciaran through a portal, leaving my broken body in the ruins of my old home. Tears course down my face, my body heaving in uncontrollable sobs. I'm grappling for that now empty bond, but there's nothing. Only silence within me.

An unbearable silence.

I shatter.

My power explodes out of me in grief and sorrow and finally rage. The world around me blows apart; the foundation of my old home disintegrating into nothing as my power shoots out. It eats away at everything it touches. Birds fall from the sky. Bugs are pushed up from the ground, their bodies twitching. Nothing survives. *I am the Harbinger. This power is mine.*

Radiating fury, I push my broken body to stand. The snakes writhe across me before pushing out. They drop to the ground at my feet, no longer smokey beasts but fully formed and ready to kill for me. I look around at the death and destruction I've created. I don't feel anything aside from that rage. I *refuse* to feel anything other than that. Because if I let that grief in, that loss? I will drown in it.

As I'm about to move forward toward the city that holds my mate, the one I will bring to its knees, I sense something behind me. Turning, I find Shadow and Ava stepping through a portal with Poppy close on their heels. Their eyes flare wide, no doubt taking in the death I have created around me. It's Ava who steps forward first. My snakes hiss in warning, forcing her to stop.

"Astrea? Where is Ciaran?" Her voice is soft yet hesitant. I can see Shadow's eyes looking around, searching. Desperation laces his features.

"She took him." My voice doesn't feel right with the pure, red-hot rage that is keeping me standing.

She nods, her long pink hair moving in the breeze. "So, we'll get him back." Her hands are splayed out in front of her in a sign that I can only assume means surrender.

"Incoming," Shadow murmurs.

My head snaps to the left in time to see the treacherous covens who helped her trap us. Who helped her take Ciaran. Whatever magic she was shielding them with has dropped. Sacrificial lambs. They should have known better than to align with her.

Ava realizes my intent within seconds. "Astrea, don't!" She reaches out, but it's too late.

I let out a scream and the two snakes shoot forward, grabbing the witches one by one and dragging them to me. Black smoke dances and lightning crackles over my fingers as I look down at them.

"Please, don't!" one begs. "We only did as we were told!"

I sneer at them, their begging falling on unsympathetic ears. "You chose the wrong side." My power shoots out and all four drop dead in an instant; the screams of agony barely leaving their lips before my magic settles in a black mist over their bodies.

The last witch is desperately trying to fight against my snakes. "Where did she take my mate?" I demand in an almost robotic tone.

"Please!" The witch screams and begs. "I don't know where they would have gone! Please, I didn't want to do this."

I look at her, my face devoid of emotion, before letting my eyes meet the two snakes holding her. "She's all yours," I utter flatly and they devour her whole, leaving nothing but a husk behind.

A gasp escapes Ava and I know Shadow has pulled her against him, attempting to inch his body in front of hers. "I wouldn't harm your mate," I say, again in that voice that is so unlike mine. He stiffens at the mention of 'mate,' and I give a low, detached laugh. "It's fairly obvious, Shadow."

"So let it go, Astrea. Show me you aren't a threat to us. Ciaran wouldn't want this," he pleads.

"She took him," I growl. Both snakes, having finished their meal, again create a barrier between us with their black bodies. "She is in his mind. Our bond is gone." The last word cracks, and I can feel the rage falling away. I grapple for it to come back, but only deep sorrow remains as the embers of my anger slowly extinguish.

Ava breaks away from Shadow and steps to me again. One, two steps and she's in front of the first snake, bending down and holding her hand out to its iridescent head. It flicks its tongue out, tasting her.

"Ava . . ." Shadow growls from behind her.

She allows the snake to keep tasting her until it moves away, letting her walk directly to me. The other snake still curls protectively next to me, its night-black head pushed against my thigh. *Crack.* My rage echoes in my mind as the last ember fades away and the grief floods in. Ava catches my body as I start to fall and helps lower me to the ground. Sobs rip through me.

I don't know how long she holds me, but eventually, the grief moves to numbness. My tears are no longer falling. At some point, the snakes have allowed Shadow and Poppy near me as well, and he picks me up and carries me through a portal. My snakes, still corporeal, slither behind us.

TWENTY-ONE

– Carmine Family Grimoire

Astrea

"It's not my fault they hate you. They know you don't like them." Ava's voice pushes into my brain first as I regain awareness of my surroundings.

Shadow's voice is next. "They are snakes! Very large fucking snakes. Of course, I don't like them!"

"You're one to talk," she huffs out before her voice goes high like she's talking to a puppy. "But they are so sweet."

I feel a brush of fur on my face and I breathe in Poppy's scent. The small comfort brings tears to my eyes as I push my nose into her and take another deep breath. She chitters, and the sounds around the room stop.

"Astrea?" Ava's face comes into view. Her large eyes are full of concern. "Are you okay?"

Her question feels dumb. I want to scream that I'm quite clearly not okay, given the hollow chasm in my chest where Ciaran used to reside. But I don't yell; I just try to push myself up to a seated position, wincing as I feel my ribs shift in a way they shouldn't.

"We wanted to get a healer but . . ." She motions to the two snakes. "They weren't keen on allowing anyone near you."

My eyes track to them. They are massive in size. One is true black, almost leaching the color from everything around it. Its energy feels volatile and angry as it uses its body like a barrier between Shadow and the rest of us. The other is an iridescent black, shimmering like starlight. That one seems to be more friendly to those around me, as it curls politely next to Ava.

"They stayed like this?" My voice cracks, and Ava hands me water.

"Mhmm."

The water is cool on my parched throat as I gulp it down greedily. With the glass drained, I hold out my hand and the iridescent one moves closer, laying its head on my palm. Its eyes look into mine intently before they shift back around the room. Poppy moves closer to it, the little fox sniffing it once before curling herself up against its scaly body.

"Seriously? They even like the fox?" Shadow mumbles. It earns him a hiss from the other, who is still using its body to block him from us. I can't help but wonder how they have physical bodies now.

You accepted the magic. We are fully yours. I jump slightly and look down at the one on my hand. *We will still live on you but now we can be this or our smoke version.*

"Yes, but how do I get you guys back on me?"

We refused to go when you weren't conscious. But now that you are, we will rest.

The feeling is almost soothing as its massive body starts to move. As it does, it shrinks down so that it can fit on my arm, its head nestling back on my chest. The other snake moves over and does the same, though it takes up residence on my bare leg under the sheets.

"Were you just talking to them?" Shadow asks, still keeping his distance.

I scratch Poppy's head. "Yeah. They've always talked to me."

"Ooh, what are we naming them?" Ava claps before popping her candy in her mouth.

"Gods have mercy," Shadow mutters and grabs a tumbler of amber liquid off the table. After he shoots it back, I watch as he takes a red cigarette from his pocket and goes to light it.

"If you smoke, I swear to God, I will demand one of these snakes comes back off Astrea and eats you whole like it did that witch," Ava seethes.

Shadow stops with it halfway to his mouth before he puts it back and sits down. I didn't notice when I first looked at him, but now I can see it. His face is ashen, his black hair stark against it. There's also a slight tremor in his hand as he pushes it through his hair.

Withdrawal. He's going through withdrawal. I've seen it happen—hell, I have been through Eufori withdrawal myself before—but I didn't realize Shadow was using it that frequently. I go to open my mouth, but Ava gives a small shake of her head, and I close it again.

"I'm thinking Buttercup and Onyx for the names. What do you think?" Ava asks, laying herself down on the bed next to me

I scrub my hands down my face. "I'm not naming one of my snakes Buttercup."

She reaches her hand up and traces the iridescent snake on my chest before I can slap her hand away. "This one is absolutely Buttercup," she giggles.

"Focus, Ava," Shadow growls. "We need a plan."

"We have a plan," I say in a detached voice, scratching Poppy's head again. "I'm going to burn this city to the ground until there is nowhere left for her to hide."

Shadow

(Lying from you- Linkin Park)

My hand is shaking, and I push out of the bedroom into Drago's hallway. It took everything in me to remain in that bedroom while they talked about a potential plan. My head spun while Ava attempted to reason with Astrea that burning a whole city was not, in fact, the best-laid plan. I finally couldn't stand it any longer. I can barely contain myself as I rush into the bathroom and vomit up the alcohol I consumed.

"Fucking hell," I mutter as I wipe my mouth with the back of my hand. I push off the toilet and move over to the sink. The face that looks back at me in the mirror isn't one I want to recognize, but it's one I know well. It's been twenty-four hours since my last hit, and my body *hurts*. I know if I don't smoke soon, I'll be in for a hell of a ride, one that unfortunately won't kill me.

My eyes catch the razor in the shower. *If I can't use Eufori, maybe that is the next best thing.*

Do it, that dark voice in my head taunts me.

Sometimes, the anger and hate I have for myself gets so noxious that I wish I could turn back time and prevent Ciaran from saving me.

I'm about to walk toward the razor when Ava moves in behind me, taking me away from my thoughts and crowding the space as she shuts the door. I try to move away from her but the bathroom is too small. I watch in both horror and desperation as she slowly pulls her top up and over herself, revealing her breasts. My mouth waters.

"What are you doing, Ava?" I whisper.

She only smiles before pushing off her pants, exposing her naked pussy to me. The small room floods with her natural scent. "I'm going to shower. What are you doing?" she asks, her voice dripping with false innocence.

The little minx turns the water on and steps through the open doorway into the tiled shower. The shower itself is what makes the bathroom so small. The massive structure allows water to rain down from the ceiling. Leave it to my stepbrother to have such an extravagant shower.

The water cascades down her body in smooth tracks. My eyes follow helplessly as it moves over her nipples, now peaked, and disappears down into the apex of her thighs. Hands tracing over her own body, she gives me a small smile. "Are you going to join me?" she asks in a husky voice. My cock is painfully hard against my jeans.

I watch as she drags her hands across her breasts, cupping each one before tweaking her nipples. My resolve is slowly cracking. She bites her bottom lip, right hand moving down past her belly button. "Or are you just going to watch?"

A low, animalistic growl emits from deep in my chest as the scent of her arousal hits me. "Ava." Her name is a warning on my lips.

She cocks her eyebrow as I watch her push her tiny fingers into her slit. "I suppose Drago could help me," she whimpers.

My stepbrother's name on her lips snaps my restraint and I push forward. I lash out with one hand, grabbing her neck and pushing her against the wall. "Keep his name out of your mouth while your fingers are in that tight cunt." I squeeze just enough to know her breathing is impacted. I push the fingers of my other hand into her tight heat, next to her own. She gasps at the rough intrusion. "This. Is. Mine," I huff like the big, bad wolf. Her arousal gushes out around us.

"So fucking take it," Ava snaps.

(Control-Halsey)

I know the moment my eyes glow golden, the moment I lose my hold on that beast I've kept chained away for so long, because hers widen in delight.

"There you are," Ava whispers. Her demeanor switches in that moment—gone is the coy, playful girl, and instead stands before me the dominant queen. "Kneel," she commands.

I obey immediately, fingers slipping from her. This. This is what I'm good at. If our relationship were only this, I would be fine.

She smiles. "You remember how to behave for me...good boy."

I groan at the title, that beast rumbling in my chest. She pulls at my hair before bending down to be eye level with me and asking, "You are going to listen to everything I say, aren't you?" I nod, and she smirks. "Good boy." She licks up the side of my face before standing and spreading her legs. "Now, make me feel good."

It's all the permission I need, and I latch my mouth onto

her pussy. I dip my tongue into her before moving up and sucking on her clit. Her moaning has my cock rock hard and begging to be touched, but she hasn't given me permission.

"Oh, fuck, Shadow. Yes." She starts grinding on my face, and I push two fingers into her tight channel. "Oh, my God, yes. Yes." She's so close. I open my eyes and look up at her. Her head is flung back and she's gripping her breast with the hand that isn't in my hair. "You want my cum on your tongue?"

"Please, Ava. Please give it to me," I beg before diving back in. I eat her like she is my last meal, and just as she is about to cum, I spear her with my tongue so I can keep the taste of her. I let her ride the long wave out before sitting back on my heels to look up at her.

Her hazy eyes look down at me, filled with lust. "What do you want, Shadow?" The implications of the question are not just sexual, and that sends me reeling. The moment is now lost as terror pushes through me, and she knows it. "I asked you a question," she demands, desperate to gain control again. To keep me.

But it's too late; she's broken the spell. She can tell the moment that the beast is rechained. I can feel my eyes returning to normal. The beast thrashes, furious that I'm denying it. Denying us.

I stand up and back away from her with the taste of her arousal still coating my tongue. Her eyes hold so much sadness, it crushes the little bit of soul I have left. I hate the pity. Hate the sadness. I don't deserve any of it. I deserve to be tormented. So, I say what I know will push her away. "I want to smoke. You should find Drago if you want to fuck."

Wet clothing and all, I exit the bathroom, only to hear her yell out, "Fuck you, Shadow," before the unmistakable shudder of a sob.

Astrea

Spending the morning flipping through Ciaran's family grimoire has my eyes burning. The old parchment paper has faded over the years, and it's clear no one thought to update it so it could be read without damaging one's eyes. I rub my hand down my face in frustration. Thus far, all I've learned is about Ciaran's power, which is a balance to mine according to his mother. But aside from that, it gives no indication of why or how it works. Glancing at the clock I decide coffee needs to be consumed if I'm going to continue down this path of self-inflicted torment.

As I exit the room, I watch Shadow throw himself out of the bathroom soaking wet and hear Ava scream after him. I wisely do not go in that direction and instead head to what I hope is the kitchen. Rounding the corner, I find a spacious kitchen attached to a comfortable sitting area. My stomach aches with hunger, but all I can think of is Ciaran and getting him back. So, instead, I reach for the coffee. Ignoring the heavy feeling on my chest that I know will worsen with the caffeine intake.

They brought me to a safehouse of Drago's for me to heal, according to Ava. My injuries weren't bad, minus the broken ribs and nose; both of which healed near-instantly once the snakes came back to my body and one of Drago's staff looked me over. She was an older woman and said little, which was just as well. I have no interest in small talk while my mate is out there with someone masquerading in my sister's body.

"You're up."

I startle as Drago's voice emerges from the shadows, followed closely by the man himself. "Good lord, you scared me!" I yell. "Give a girl some warning before just appearing like a gods damn ghost."

He smiles and shrugs. "I had my reasons for staying quiet. I apologize."

I raise my eyebrow. "Could those reasons be the stepbrother who is currently spiraling and the tiny hellion screaming at him from the bathroom?"

He shrugs once again. It's the only confirmation I need. My curiosity is far from sated, but none of them are willing to talk, so I don't push. I have my theories, and when this is all over, I'll demand Ava tell me. *Maybe while we drink wine and have a girls night.* The thought startles me. I have a friend. I've never had friends before this. Somehow it both warms my heart and sends a jolt of fear through me.

I watch Drago's powerful body as he moves into the kitchen and pours himself some coffee, and I take a sip of my own. Poppy hops up onto the counter and sniffs toward Drago. She narrows her eyes slightly before chittering and running back into the room. "She doesn't seem to like you or your stepbrother. Why is that?" I ask.

He leans against the counter and brings the mug up to his lips, looking at me over the ceramic as he blows the steam. "She knows a predator when she sees one."

I narrow my eyes. "Yet she just cuddled with a giant snake that arguably could eat you."

He lets out a deep, throaty laugh. "If your snakes can take on the likes of me, I will hand my empire over to you, little Harbinger. But trust me when I say they cannot."

I expect them to move under my skin at the challenge, but they do not. "Sure, now you choose to stay on my skin," I mutter.

He's right. We could not eat him in his true form.

My eyes widen, and he simply smiles over the rim of the

mug he drinks from. He's wearing sweats that hang low and a tight black shirt that spans over his muscular body. His tattoos are on display for once. And while he exudes a don't fuck with me attitude, nothing gives away what his true form might be. That it could be different from what stands before me.

Drago must notice the scrutiny because he pushes off the countertop, his eyes flashing to gold. My magic roars to life as I scramble back, almost tripping over my own feet to escape the predator in front of me. I swear I see a ghost form of wings behind him before the image blinks away. He exposes his teeth in a wicked gleam before his eyes settle back to the blue they normally are. "What in the actual fuck are you?" I sputter as my heart hammers.

"That is a story for another day, perhaps." He goes back to casually drinking his coffee. "Now, how do we plan on getting Ciaran back?"

Drago
(Tragic Endings- Eminem, feat Skylar Grey)

I've been around a lot of predators before, people of power to varying degree, but the magic rolling from the Harbinger is unparallel. Even with Ava in the room she radiates pure, uncontrolled magic. It will dwarf the rest of us when she figures out how to harness it. We've spent the last hour planning, or at least trying to plan, how to rescue Ciaran. The fucking vampire getting himself caught is an inconvenience and if it were anyone else I would let him rot.

Not anyone.

I want to tell that voice to shut up but it's right. There are two others I would do whatever was needed to rescue.

You mean you would do more than you already have.

I ball my fists up, wanting to tell that pesky voice to stop talking so I can focus on the two females in front of me. "So, I hunt them down, make them talk." Astrea's voice cuts into my mind finally.

Crossing my arms over my chest I let my gaze roam between her and Ava. Ava looks worried as she watches her friend pace. "Tell me, little Harbinger, have you ever hunted anyone before? Ever killed anyone?" I ask her.

She stops pacing, her green gaze locking onto me. "I have done what is needed," she responds cryptically.

"There is a difference between doing what is needed and what you currently want to do," I reply. And it's the truth. Hunting down her own kind and torturing them for information isn't for the faint of heart. She goes to argue with me, opening her mouth for a moment before the scent I've obsessed over for years now wafts into the space, drawing my beast upward and forcing the golden glow of my eyes to latch onto the source.

My mind is pulled backwards to another time in our life as I see Shadow step into the room. . .

The sound of Eminem echoes out from under my stepbrother's door. I've only seen him a handful of times since his father bought my mother, and every time, he's disappeared before I could say anything. His darkness is a beautiful temptation in this scenario my mother's gotten us into. He's an enigma; never saying much and keeping to his room unless he's with his father in the basement. His father told us that his son is "useless." He's convinced Shadow has no powers and wants nothing to do with him. I hear him sometimes, hurting Shadow to get his power to come out, his last-ditch effort to have a "son worthy of my legacy."

My theory? Shadow is hiding it from his father. The

question is why. Though, given who his father is, I could guess. When we first met, I could smell the power rolling off him in waves of evergreen and citrus. It moved over me like a weighted blanket, and I wanted nothing more than to press my nose into his neck. But he only looked at me with a glazed-over expression before turning away from us. I haven't had many other interactions with him since. I'm desperate to see him again. To catch that scent again.

I ball my fist as I stand outside his door, the urge to demand his attention pushing through me like an addiction. At first, I was furious about my mother pulling me into this deal—after all, I'm not the one who was sold, she is. But she played on my guilt, so here I am. And I can't be upset because it's put me in the path of this new obsession I have. So far, I've only stalked him from the dark, but I can't ignore the need to interact with him anymore.

I pull the Eufori out of my pocket and light it up before pushing through the door. Shadow is lying on his bed with his shirt off, his muscular golden chest on full display. His night-black hair is still wet from his shower, and the scent of him makes my mouth water. I take a deep breath, attempting to control myself. Shadow cracks an eye open before fully opening both and pushing up on his bed. Anxiety moves over his body.

"What?" he asks, tension bleeding out of his body. The scent of it hits me fully in the chest. The sound of his voice sends shivers through my body. Mine. The word bleeds across my mind in shades of gold and black.

I close the door behind me and stalk into his room fully until I'm standing at the end of his bed. I take another deep pull of the drug before holding it out to him. He narrows his eyes but takes it anyway. The sight of his lips wrapping around the joint stirs something deep within me and I have to shift on my feet to keep my dick from hardening.

Blowing the smoke out of my mouth, I ask, " Why are you avoiding me?"

He glares at me before handing the drug back and standing. He is the same height as me but leaner in muscle. While I'm bulkier, his body is almost graceful in its power. I was trained for fighting. He was trained for surviving.

"Why do you care?" He lets out the smoke, the red haze curling around his face. His defiance has the dark part of me demanding to show him exactly why I care. He would look so pretty on his knees for me.

Keeping my voice calm and level, I reply, "We live together, shouldn't we get to know each other?" I take another drag of Eufori to hide the need that is now riding me harder than any craving I've ever had. Mine, mine, mine. Over and over, the word repeats in my mind. Get him on his knees. Let him worship you. Another drag of the Eufori has the voices stopping for a moment, allowing me to gain some control again.

He lets out a laugh as he crosses his arms and leans against the desk to the right of his bed. His room is plain compared to mine, with a basic twin bed that barely holds his body, a small wood desk, and a chest of drawers. It's also clearly the smallest. "I doubt we'll be together here that long. If you're smart, you'll get away from here; get your mother away from here." He shoves his hands through his hair as he says it, a nervous habit. I see him do it often as I watch him.

I push forward and invade his space. His body tenses. "Why are you hiding how powerful you are? I can smell it. Just below your skin." I take a deep breath, my nose inches from his face. "You smell divine."

He shoves me back. "Shut your fucking mouth. You don't know shit."

I smirk before I push forward and grab his throat, my own eyes flashing to gold right before I see the glimmer in his. "Mm, yeah, that's what I thought." The room fills with tension so thick it feels almost suffocating.

His pupils blow out, the whiskey color all but gone from them. His breathing increases quickly, and when he bites his lip I let out a low groan before smashing my mouth into his. He freezes for only a moment before he yields, opening his mouth as my tongue sweeps in. I squeeze his throat and he grinds up against me, his hard cock pushing against my own. I pull my mouth from his and kiss down his neck, nipping as I go. His answering moan has me smiling. Against my nature, I drop to my knees in front of him, pulling his sweatpants down and allowing his long length to bob free. I pause for a moment to look up into his eyes, giving him the option to stop this. But instead, he grabs my hair and pushes his cock past my lips.

His taste explodes in my mouth, causing me to moan in contentment. I let him control the pace, pushing in and out as he sees fit until the need to taste his cum overpowers me.

I pull off briefly and slip my fingers into my mouth before taking his cock in again, then I let my fingers creep back to his tight hole and slowly begin to push one in. The thought of my cock pushing past that tight ring has my eyes rolling back in my head.

"Oh, fuck," he cries out as I breach his body, his cock twitching in my mouth. I smile and pick up the pace with my finger, allowing his dick to hit me in the back of my throat. "I'm going to cum. Oh, fuck, shit, yes, yes, yes." Shadow releases into my mouth, and my own cock twitches, desperate to be buried in him. His taste is intoxicating.

I slowly pull off his cock, allowing my finger to also slip free. Sitting back on my heels, I look up at his face to see ecstasy splashed across it. But it doesn't last long as something twinges in my chest. I frown, rubbing it absently, only to realize he is doing the same thing. The understanding hitting us both at the same time.

His eyes are wide, shock going across his dark features. But the shock leaves rapidly and is replaced by fear. As I reach for him, he narrowly avoids me and runs out of his room, leaving me kneeling in the center alone. And it's at that moment that I realize two things: One, the scars that cover his back confirm what a piece of shit his father is. And two, when I kill his father, I will make him suffer.

Astrea

Drago seems to pause for a moment as Shadow meanders in, smelling strongly of Eufori. The scent that I've never noticed always seems to cling to him. He glances around the room, his gaze hard when it lands on Ava and downright frigid as it lands on Drago. Those same golden eyes flash through Drago, shinning bright before they extinguish back to blue.

"Just in time to know the plan!" Ava says in an oddly chipper voice. I glance at her briefly, the tension between the three so thick it's threatening to choke me. Shadow crosses his arms, his back pressing into the door frame as he leans against it. Ava launches into the explanation, leaving out nothing, before glancing at me to get confirmation she got it all correct.

"That sums it up," I mutter.

"You can't possibly think this is a good idea, Drago!" Shadow's voice carries in the small living space.

"It wasn't his idea, it's mine," I reply. "It's my decision how we get information."

He drags his hands through his messy hair. "Ciaran would never want this for you."

I glare at him. He's right, Ciaran wouldn't want this for me, but I refuse to back down. "Well, Ciaran isn't here to have a say, and you can't tell me he wouldn't do the same fucking thing."

Ava is sitting on the countertop kicking her feet back and forth. At some point, Drago drifted into her orbit, and he casually allows his body to press into her thigh. Shadow zeroes in on it as she shifts slightly to lean into Drago. "It's Astrea's choice what she wants. She's a big girl," she says.

Shadow's eyes are wild with emotion, despite being under the influence. For a moment, I worry he'll launch himself at Drago, but instead, he takes a deep breath, training his eyes back on me. The emotion gutters out of them. "Fine. But I'll be helping."

"Are you sober enough to help?" I don't mean it to be cruel, but if he's the only one coming with me, I refuse to put Ciaran at any more risk.

He shoots me a withering glare. "You've never asked before, so it shouldn't make a difference now."

TWENTY-TWO

Should The Harbinger reclaim the power as their own, you will not be able to seperate them. You will need to keep the host alive to access the power. You will need to prevent the magic from binding to the light.

Should they bind, no one will be able to stop them

– Mori Family Grimoire

Shadow

Astrea asking if I was sober enough to go with her destroyed me. *It's because she knows how worthless you are.* I growl at the voice. They've been so loud around Ava and Drago. Never giving me a moment of peace. And my beast keeps rattling his cage, growing more ravenous every moment I'm with those two. A constant reminder of what I am. I know I'm barely clinging to my sanity. I know the drugs are the only thing keeping me alive. Or at least that's what I keep telling myself.

Astrea's plan to go hunting down witches and gather information is a bad fucking idea. I know what that darkness does to someone; it leaves a blemish on you, a stain that will never come off. I take a long, deep breath as I try to ignore the need to head back to the roof and light up another joint. For Ciaran, I'll do this. For Ciaran, I'll help Astrea hunt them down one by one. For Ciaran, I will endure this torture of Drago and Ava because so long ago he saved me and the blood debt I owe is too large for my liking.

(Last Resort- Falling in Reverse)

I'm lying in my cage, the air above me cool. The wind is blowing throughout the aviary Alexi likes to keep me in and goosebumps break out across my flesh. My naked body is prone on the cold stone floor where I've spent the last hour carving up my skin for every person I killed last night. The rusty piece of metal lies next to me, shiny with my blood. Part of me hopes I'll bleed out before he comes back for me. I've been here for a year now. For the first six months, I thought my stepbrother would come for me; had hoped that the bond I felt flickering in my chest would be enough for him to come. But it wasn't enough to bring him. I wasn't enough. He's left me at the mercy of Alexi after my father sold me. I should have known better than to hope.

My eyes shut and I'm assaulted with the images of him on his knees before it fades away and I see my mother's body lying lifeless. Unseeing eyes peeled open towards the ceiling, her warmth long since gone away from her body. I can hear the sounds of my father as he directed people to remove her body from my room. I can see his disgusted look as he takes me in.

"Motherfucker." I hear Ciaran's voice before I see him, the sound pulling me back from the memories. The clang of keys on the old jail door is loud, but the squeak of the door opening even louder. I see him come into view and look down at me. I think I attempt to offer a smile, but my face isn't working as well as it should.

Though he's the son of Alexi, I learned early on he thinks his father is a piece of shit. We formed a friendship of sorts despite me being here as the product of a business deal between our fathers. And now I can't seem to get rid of him, even when I want to bleed out in my cage.

He bends down to look me in my face. "I'm not letting you do this anymore." He pulls me to my feet, and my head swims. It takes a moment before I realize he's shoved his arm into my mouth, his blood, liquid gold, flowing directly down my throat to my beast. The crushing disappointment that I won't be dying today is overwhelming.

After he is satisfied that my wounds are healing, he slings my arm over his shoulders, and we start the long walk out of the cage I'm held in. The old aviary is housed behind the prison itself. Tucked back in a grove of woods, you wouldn't know it exists unless you were one of the unlucky people Alexi dragged back here to be thrown in with me.

I don't realize we've made it to Ciaran's car until he shoves me in, not caring that I'm naked or covered in blood and grime. "Where are we going?" I ask in a rough voice.

Before he says anything, he grabs at the metal collar looped around my neck, shoving a key into it and releasing the metal. He throws the device to the ground, sneering at it before looking at me again. "To our home."

"How Ciaran?" Because it's not lost on me Alexi is the only one with those keys and guards them like a dragon would hoard jewels.

He doesn't look at me, instead looking at the ground, no, looking at that collar. "I made a deal with my father."

Astrea

(Darkside- Neoni)

Had I thought inflicting torture would be hard, I would have been sorely mistaken. Catching the vampires each night is easy; breaking them is even easier. And none of them have seen Ciaran or Kallen. Each day, I feel myself slipping further and further away. Whether it's due to my missing mate bond, that hollow, deep ache, or the fact that torture is a second language to me now, I'm not sure. We've been at it for weeks now, the endless amount of torture getting us no closer to finding them.

"We need a witch," I say as I wipe warm blood from my face. "It's clear the vampires know jack. But she was working with a coven. They might have information." The alley we are standing in smells like piss, and now the rich coppery scent of blood hangs in the air as well. I have long since stopped caring if we are caught; I welcome anyone who might stumble upon us, as they could have information. But in Gothic Grove, everyone knows you don't look down dark alleys. You won't find anything you want to see.

Shadow looks at me. The colder I've become, the more anxious he seems to get, constantly flipping his lighter off and on. "You want to torture one of your own?" I know he wants to smoke, but all the times he's been with me, he's been very evidently sober.

I hiss back, "They are not my own if they helped her."

I watch him push a tattooed hand through his hair before dragging it down his face. "Astrea, there are things you can't come back from. Torturing a witch? I don't think you'll come back from that."

My chest caves in a little. *He thinks I can still come back from any of this.* The truth is, I knew as soon as I picked my blade up against that first vampire, I wasn't coming back from this. I was giving myself over to something unholy. Unchaining that darkness within me that begs to destroy everything. To be a reckoning against anyone who stands between me and Ciaran. It hasn't escaped me that history is repeating itself. That I have become the very thing Kallen was. And I couldn't care less.

I don't say anything to Shadow. I just walk past him to go in search of my next victim.

For his part, he doesn't try to stop me, but I can smell the Eufori the minute he lights it up.

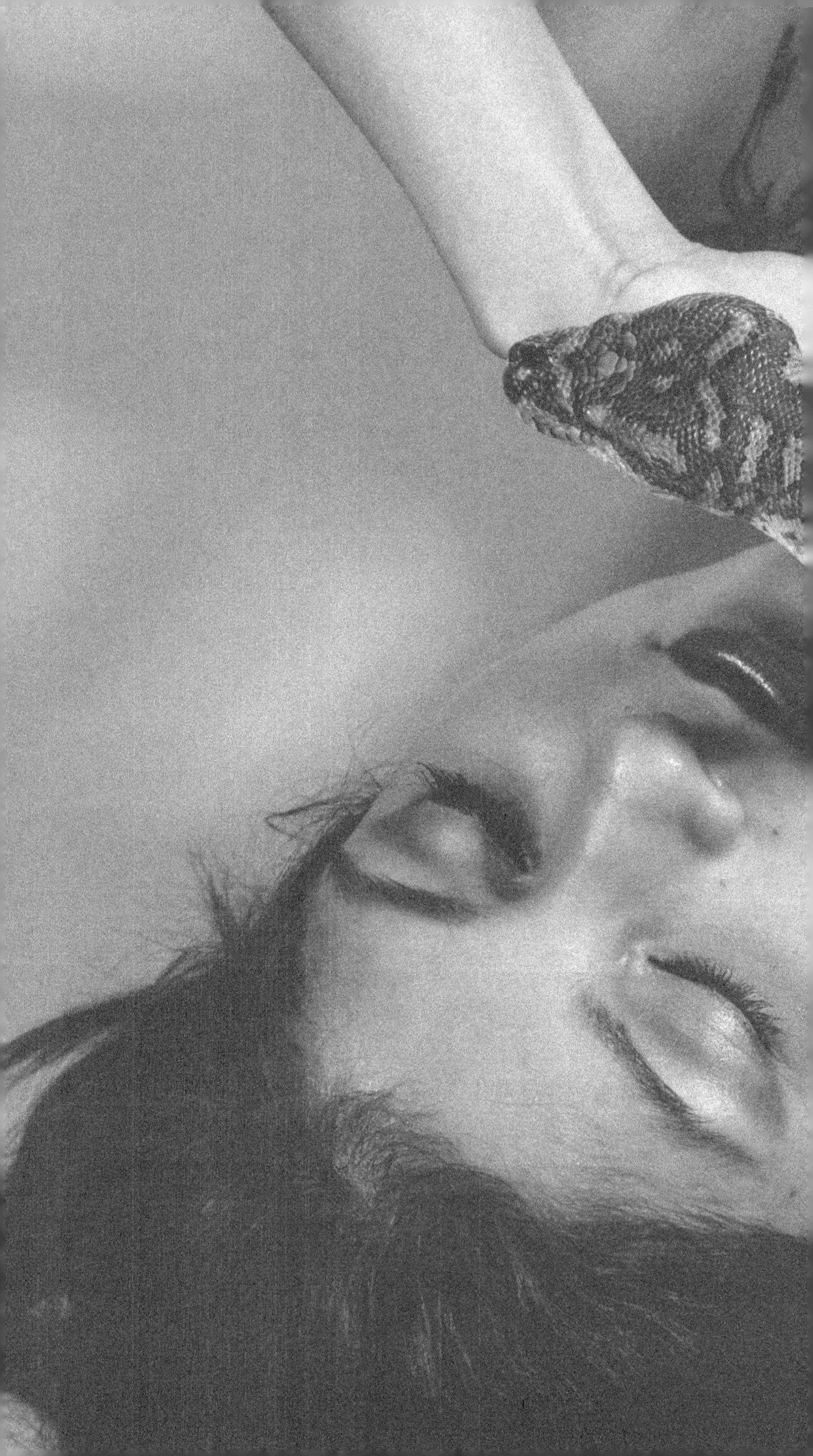

TWENTY-THREE

*When The Harbinger magic was created, it caused
the host to go mad.
She had no balance to counteract the darkness.
This is why we created the balance within her
mate.
However, the longer she is without that grounding
magic, the easier it will be to lose her entirely to
the darkness.*

– Carmine Family Grimoire

Astrea

Standing outside the small apothecary shop located in a back alley of Gothic Grove, I allow myself one moment of second-guessing before I shake it off, straighten up, and walk in. The bell above the door tinkles and the scent of herbs hits my nose, followed by the tingle of magic over my skin. It itches immediately. If I were less powerful, that magic would have dropped me to the ground. Unfortunately for this witch, I am very powerful. Letting out a low chuckle, I bid my snakes forward, and Onyx and Buttercup drop off me, their smokey bodies becoming solid.

"It's funny that you think that type of magic would stop someone like me." My magic weaves between and over my fingers as I walk, a sensual caress, the black lightning sending flashes throughout the shop. I move my gaze slowly around the space, until I catch a small shift in the air. *Gotcha.* I give a tiny nod, and Buttercup shoots out, wrapping her massive iridescent body around the glamoured witch.

She lets out a screech and her magic drops, so I can see her pathetic form thrashing against the snake. I move over and bend down to her level. Enjoying the fear I see in her eyes as they lock with my own.

"Mm, that was very naughty to try to avoid me like that. And to think I was originally just going to ask questions."

The fear on her face morphs into fury. "I know who you are. You would never show mercy like that. Harbinger." The name is spat like a curse in my direction.

The idea of being a curse upon the witches and vampires of Gothic Grove is intoxication. It makes me smile. "Maybe. But now, not only will you never know, but I will make this so much more painful than it ever needed to be."

"You're no better than *she* was!" the witch shrieks.

Lashing out with my hand, I grip her neck, nails piercing into her flesh. "You and your coven made me this way. You let Kallen take my mate—you worked with her. But you're wrong." I squeeze her hard, cutting off her air. Her body begins to spasm. "I am far worse than she ever was."

She sneers at me as I release my hold on her neck. "You

have no idea what's coming. You'll beg for mercy in the end." The conviction in her words are strong but mine is stronger.

I smile wickedly. "I don't think *you* have any idea what's coming." I let the rage in me shine through my eyes, the desperation I feel, and I can see the moment she realizes exactly what it means that I'm here for her.

It takes fifteen minutes before the witch breaks. Another ten minutes before she is begging for her life. And another forty-five minutes before I'm walking out covered in her blood, with the answer I have been looking for.

<hr>

I had assumed panic would be crawling through my chest seeing the front of this place again, but all I feel is the numbness that has settled into my core. The witch told me all I needed to know in one name: Alexi. Alexi knows where Kallen is keeping Ciaran. And so, instead of going back to our safehouse, I came here. The place where it all began. I'm still wearing her blood when I tilt my head and take in the massive gates that block the road from the prison.

The building itself is a concrete monstrosity, once grand and elegant time has not been kind. Moss grows up and around the edges, cracks have formed around the building that even from this distance I can pick out. The fountain that stands in the center of the round driveway looks stagnant; algae having grown over the water left in it. A crow is perched atop the fountain portion. The cry echoing from its beak echoing across the desolate front yard.

The guard booth holds two vampires, their eyes going wide as they take in the bloody mess that adorns my body.

They don't survive me blowing the gate wide open.

Onyx and Buttercup move off my body and flank me as I walk up to the front door. My power cracks into the building breaking the door open.

"*Alexi,*" I call out in a singsong voice. I know I sound slightly unhinged, and the blood on my face makes me look like a warrior of old. "We need to have a little talk." Stepping over the rubble, I peek in to see chaos. People running around, bodies of those that didn't make it before the front came down scattered haphazardly. It feels good to watch them panic after years of them doing *nothing* to help those of us trapped here.

"Find him. Kill anyone else." My snakes take off in both directions, and the screams that echo fill me with such joy, I let out an unhinged laugh. A few brave vampires attempt to stop me, jumping forward, but if my magic doesn't stop them, my blades take them. By the time I'm into the upper levels of the prison, there isn't a portion of me that doesn't have blood on it, and I fucking love it.

I'm carving into a vampire when Shadow appears at my side. "Astrea . . ." he says in warning.

I shoot him a look. "What?"

He looks like he is going to say something, but he is interrupted by Onyx's massive body coming down the hall toward us, and curled in his tail is Alexi Helvig.

Shadow

When Ava told me Astrea was taking down the prison, I didn't believe her. Then I stepped into that apothecary and saw what she had left behind of the witch, and I knew she was over the edge. The shop had been left in ruins, the witch in literal pieces around the floor. And on the windows, painted in blood, a message:

"I will come for you all. You wanted the Harbinger. You have her now."

She has a look in her eyes that worries me. Covered in blood, she's given into her magic fully, allowing it to control her and push her. I know the look well. It's what I look like when I've given my beast control. She smiles ruthlessly as the snake, Onyx, drops the vampire at her feet. The other snake, Buttercup, moves up behind us, blocking any rescue attempt his people may try. Not that anyone seems to be trying.

"Well, hello there, Alexi. My, how the tables have turned, haven't they?" she says, her voice sounding chipper.

"You bitch," he sneers. "You are going to pay for this."

She lets out a laugh. "That is one of the more ridiculous things you've said. And you've said a lot of ridiculous things in your life." She sits down in front of him, wiping one of the blades across her blood-splattered pants, like we have all the time in the world. "You are going to help me."

"Like hell I will, *witch*," he spits. He goes to move, but that black snake lets out a low hiss.

"Mm. You don't seem to understand you have no choice." Quicker than I can track, she lashes out with her blade and stabs it through his leg, nailing him to the ground and allowing the snake to move away from him. He lets out a long howl. But Astrea pays him no mind. "Did you know, when your son helped me get out of this place, I asked one thing? Just one little thing." She leans closer to him. "That I would get to kill you, to rip you to shreds for everything you did to me. Now, let's try this again. You are going to tell me where Kallen took Ciaran."

"Why would I help you? You'll kill me anyway," he says through gritted teeth.

She stands, slowly dragging her hand up with her. Her

magic pulls at Alexi, his body following the path of her hand. His screams echo through the halls as his leg pulls against that ancient blade driven through him into the ground. The black smoke swirls over her hand and through her fingers as it flows out to him. "You are correct. But let me give you a taste of how you'll die if you don't help me." Black veins begin to spread over him, and the inhumane sounds that come from his mouth make even my stomach sour.

"Astrea . . ." I say, a warning in my voice again.

She glares at me over her shoulder before rolling her eyes and releasing Alexi from the spell she had on him. Those black veins receding, he gasps for breath, urine now streaming down his legs.

She crinkles her nose at the sight. "I'm disappointed in you," she says as she spins the other blade around in her hand. "You spent years torturing me and yet I do one small piece of cursed magic and you're pissing yourself. Tsk tsk." She slashes out, her blade arching across his face, the flesh splitting from below his left eye down to his mouth. "Now, I asked you a question. Where are Kallen and Ciaran?"

Alexi glares at her. Astrea taps her foot impatiently. "Well? I'm waiting." Her magic zaps him one more time, causing him to scream out before she pulls it back.

Panting Alexi slumps forward, "He's at my house. A few miles out of the city. She's got him there. Now, please —" But his pleas are cut off as those veins reappear, and fresh screams explode out of him, echoing into the ruins.

(Haunting- Halsey)

She turns to look at me. "Let's go."

Alexi continues to scream, begging her to end him, as her magic slowly works through his body. Both snakes follow us, and as we move, the building continues to come down around us. Everywhere she steps, ruin is left in her wake, and I realize this is what the Harbinger magic is. Death. Ruin. Destruction in its purest form.

By the time we are back outside and I'm opening a portal to the safehouse, the prison is nothing but a smoldering pile of bricks and bodies. It takes me a moment to realize that the grove of trees in the back has gone up in flames as well.

"I burned our prisons down. Don't let them win by keeping one in your mind," she says as she steps through the portal.

Astrea

(Carry on Wayward Son- Neoni)

Part of me firmly believed that when I exorcized that building my trauma would pack itself away into a neat little coffin at the back of my mind and the ghosts would stop haunting me. But as I step through the open portal I realize that was a foolish hope.

Ava and Drago call out to me as I move into the house. But I don't stop walking until I'm in the bathroom. I don't look in the mirror as I strip myself out of the bloody clothing. My hands are shaking as I try to unbutton the jeans. Seconds. I only have seconds before this all crumbles around me. I can hear voices, but Buttercup has remained outside the door to keep them out. Onyx lays himself out across the floor next to the shower, his tongue poking out every so often to taste the air around us.

I'm barely holding myself together as I turn on the hot water, my hands now trembling so badly I can hardly turn the faucet on. But as soon as it hits my skin, I let go. All the emotions I've held in flow out of me as I sink down onto the floor, sobbing. My chest heaves as I gasp for breath—it's *all* finally breaking apart around me. The parts of me that are falling and shattering against the tile of the bathroom floor have never before been allowed to crumble. Because that damn building still held me in a prison, just not a physical one anymore.

First, it's the little girl in me desperate for love from her family who tumbles out onto the wet tile. Her tears feel like warm summer days sitting with my sisters. They smell like my mother's perfume lingering in my doorway after she's told me I need to lose weight. They sound like my father's absence from every family event. I hold her tightly, whispering how sorry I am that she never got the family she deserved. Telling her it was never her fault.

Next it's the teen in me I allow to fall apart. These tears feel both terrified and enraged. They smell like my childhood home burning. They feel like my stomach aching from the emptiness of trying to avoid eating. They sound like my mother's voice saying I'll never be good enough. My fists clench, nails digging into my palms. I want to burn and rage. I scream for her, a terrible, gut-wrenching sound that echoes in the small bathroom. One that is laced with my power that was held under lock and key for so long.

The adult in me who grieves for the year lost to being tortured falls after. And those tears have a visceral feeling attached. My skin crawls as they stream down my face. My stomach turns and I lurch forward, dry heaving on the cold tile floor. I can smell my own fear in these tears. My deep, aching despair and the desire to die. I've kept her locked away for so long in that box with the nightmares, she's broken and battered. She deserved so much better than what she's been allowed. I can't keep the broken sobs quiet, the sounds echoing around the bathroom.

And finally, the last part of me that breaks apart is the

one that grieves because my mate is missing. The part I've avoided since I watched him walk away. The feeling of my heart physically breaking is so painful, I wonder if my chest is actually cracking in two. I wonder if this pain can kill me, because it certainly feels like dying. I beg for Ciaran to come home, his name a broken prayer on my cracked lips. Eventually, it is only his name coming from me as I rock back and forth, trying to hold myself together with my arms.

I finally allow myself to feel it all in that burning-hot shower as the blood of my enemies washes down the drain. Allow myself time to break apart so when I go to find my mate nothing will hold me back.

Shadow

As Astrea disappears through the portal, I catch the looks of shock on Ava's and Drago's faces at the other end as they take in her gore-covered body. I close the shimmering portal before they can say anything to me. Close it knowing, praying, this might be the time that they stop looking for me. Stop trying to save me. The irony isn't lost on me that I tried to escape my father so he couldn't mold me into this, only to be thrown into a place that created a villain anyway, that used me as he would have regardless.

The Eufori is in my mouth before I can register the taste. My hands shake as I take drag after drag of the drug, the red smoke curling out of my nostrils like dragon fire. Astrea didn't free me; I was free from the physical prison long ago. This place hasn't held power over me in years. The only way I'll be truly free is to be free of the mental prisons, and unfortunately, my quest for that freedom continues to be interrupted.

Regardless, the need to see my physical cage ruined drives me. My feet carry me through the rubble of the prison. Astrea's magic still lingers, that black lightning moving over the carcasses of vampires. Anyone alive fled as soon as they realized I hadn't followed her into that portal. They all remember me, remember what I am.

I walk back toward that burnt grove, the trees still smoldering. They have the appearance of corpses as I make my way through them. Just to the back is the metal structure I spent so long in. The aviary that broke me apart and remade me into this. The air is still around me as I take in the smoking remains of the metal structure. Astrea's magic, having twisted the iron bars into grotesque shapes, the glass blown out across the land like confetti, did a spectacular job of destroying the cage that held me for so long. But her magic can't destroy the cage I've created in myself, can't crack it open wide enough to release me from my self-imposed prison.

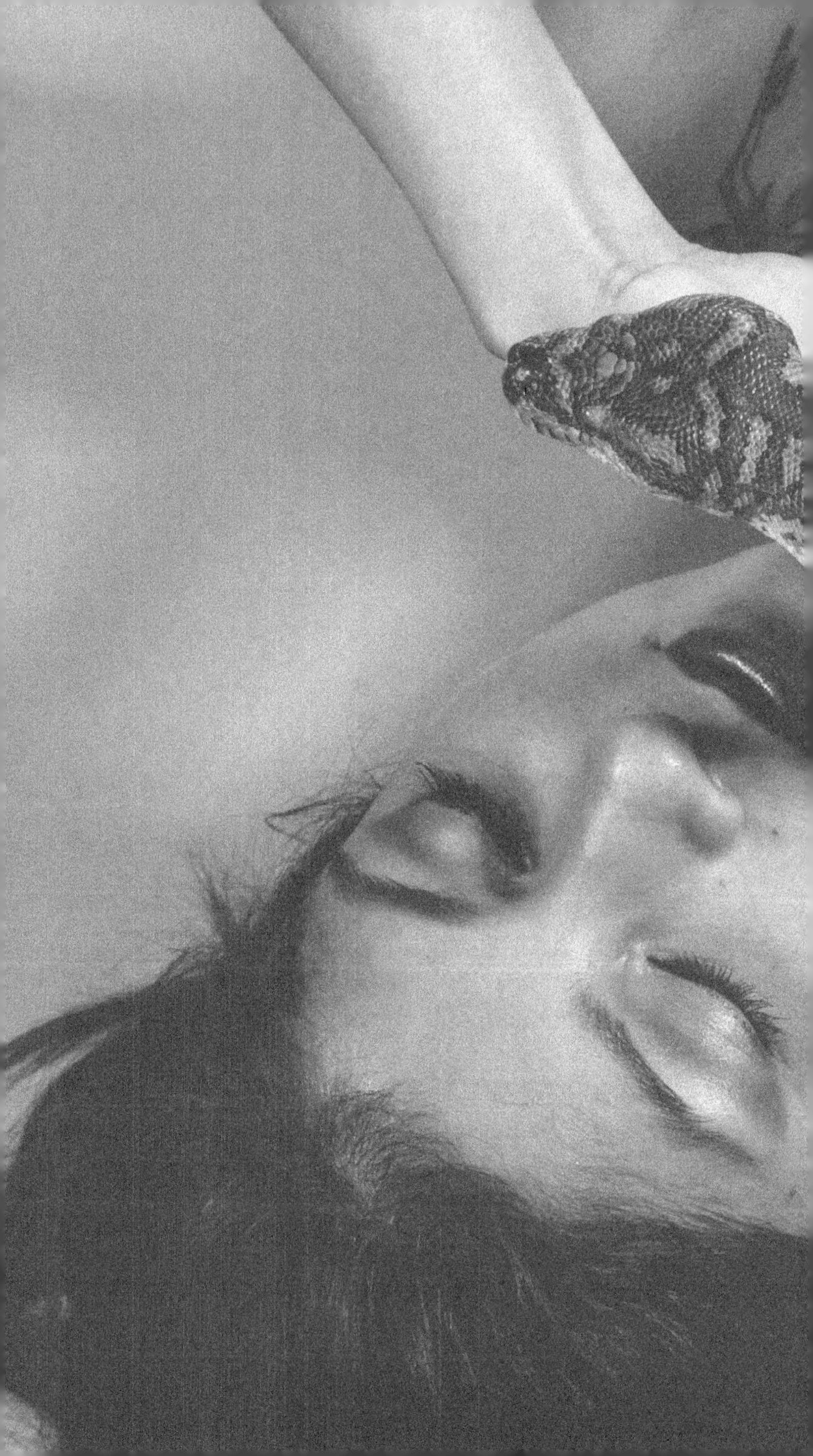

TWENTY-FOUR

The loss of a mate will drive you to a place beyond madness.

– Kallen

Astrea

Hours have passed by the time I get out. Pulling myself to my feet, I find a towel to dry off with, wrap myself in it, and pad into the room I've been using to search for new clothing. Eventually, I discover one of Ciaran's sweatshirts, his scent still strong. My eyes fill with tears again. "Fuck." I growl, scrubbing them away, I pull it over my naked chest before grabbing shorts.

When I walk out of the room, I'm met with silence. But a comfortable silence, the type that indicates you aren't alone but there also isn't any pressure to fill it. I let out a long breath as I discover Ava in the living room, Samhain perched on the back of the velvet couch behind her, and

Poppy curled up on her lap. Taking a long, hard look at her, I can see her exhaustion. She's almost shrunken in on herself, a hollowed-out look I know all too well.

"Where is everyone?" I ask as I sit on the floor across from her spot on the couch. The carpet feels soft under my seat.

Her silver eyes shift from the stormy sky out the window to my face. "Drago went looking for Shadow."

I frown. "He didn't follow me?" She simply shakes her head. Lightning crackles outside, lighting up the inside of the room, before the distant sound of thunder rattles against the windows. "Do you want to talk about it?" I ask hesitantly.

She rolls her eyes. "Do *you* want to talk about it?"

Shrugging, I say, "There isn't anything to talk about. I needed answers, and I got them. What good is this magic if I don't use it?"

Her silver eyes flicker, but she doesn't say anything. Instead, she goes back to looking at the dark sky outside. "It was Shadow and Ciaran who rescued me, did you know?" Her voice is quiet.

"No, they didn't tell me anything about your rescue."

She smiles. "They are very protective of me." She stretches up her shirt, shifting and exposing a long, jagged scar across her alabaster skin. The vicious-looking mark spreads across her whole stomach and disappears up into her shirt. "Alexi liked me . . . a lot. I was a favorite among his vampires. Shadow found me. And eventually he brought me to Drago. When he pulled me out, I was not well, to say the least, for many reasons. So, when I tell you, Astrea, that I truly understand your need for revenge, you can know it's the truth. But if you let it continue to devour you like this?

There will be nothing left of you by the time we get Ciaran back."

I don't allow myself to say there is already nothing left inside me. Because part of me believes Ava already sees that. And this warning is simply lip service she is paying to a friend. Standing she sets Poppy down onto the couch. My familiar curling up into a puffed up ball of red fur. "Shadow told us what Alexi said. Word around my club is that Kallen is hosting a masquerade ball for All Hallows' Eve at his mansion."

(Machine- Neoni)

I pause. The realization hits me that I have no idea what day it is, let alone month. It feels like an eternity since Ciaran pulled me out of Jody's while also somehow feeling like just yesterday.

Ava smiles at me. "That would be tonight." She walks over to the kitchen, and I hear the gentle clinking of glass. She comes back in with two shot glasses and hands one to me. "Let's get ready to get your mate back, Astrea."

Standing in front of the full-length mirror in Ava's room, I can't fully comprehend what I'm looking at, or who I'm looking at. The floor-length black dress clings to my body like a glove. The slit going from hip to the floor allows lace with intricate beading to peek out against my ivory skin. That same lace and beading covers the bodice, which is held up by two thin straps. The train of the dress flows out behind me in an inky black pattern. The mask she gave me is whirls of gold and black, and it makes my green eyes pop like two bright emerald flames. She painted my eyelids in a fox eye and my lips a deep red. The contrast between how I looked a few hours ago and now is jarring.

My hair is pulled half-up into a braided crown, the rest cascading down my back in thick curls. Circled atop my braid is Buttercup, nestled against my hair in her small size, and around my neck circles Onyx.

Ava walks up behind me and catches my eyes, "are you sure you want to do this?"

Standing straighter in the mirror I give her a curt nod, unable to pull the words from my mouth that if I don't do this I will go mad with grief.

I feel like Medusa reincarnate. And I am ready to seek retribution.

(I am not a woman, I'm a god- Halsey)

Ava and I exit out of the town car, umbrellas pulled up overhead to shield us from the rainfall. We didn't wait for Shadow and Drago to return, despite Ava's insistence that we do; I refused, and she wasn't about to leave me alone.

Eyes shift to us as we gather our dresses in hand to ascend the steep stone staircase leading to the front door. I can't blame them for the looks, we're quite the pair. She chose a sleek white gown, going for a "goddess of spring" theme. The backless piece hugs her small frame, while her hair rests in a loose braid with white flowers woven throughout, and her mask is an intricate piece of white lace. Atop her head is a golden diadem that sparkles even in the dim light. She holds herself like royalty, her back straight and little to no emotion on her face. When a man rushes forward to escort us up the steps the look she gives him is nothing short of ice cold. Wisely the man bows to her and motions us up the stairs.

The mansion Kallen is residing in, Alexi's old home, is set off a roundabout driveway with a giant fountain in the middle. The home itself is architecturally a gothic style laid with brick on its face. The arched windows are bright with activity. The large staircase leading up to the front door is lined with a red carpet, and our feet barely make a sound as we ascend. We are met by two guards standing on either side of an intricately carved black door. The carvings themselves are whorls of gold set deep into the paint. If one didn't know better, they might think they were purely for decoration, but upon a more careful inspection, one would see them for what they are. Spell work. Alexi warded his house at one point. Now, however, they are broken. Jagged lines cutting through the spell.

I know Ava sees them as well, but we say nothing and step over the threshold. The foyer is flanked by two staircases that lead to the upper levels. Heavy oriental rugs lay on the cool floor, and golden sconces decorate the walls. In the distance I can hear music playing, an instrumental melody that sounds haunting. Another man rushes forward and takes our wet umbrellas from us, squirreling them away god knows where. Ava catches my eyes and shrugs before turning her attention forward again.

A portly gentleman wearing a black and white tuxedo step forward towards us, "If you'll follow me, my lady." We are ushered through the hall into the ballroom. Not one to miss an opportunity to be dramatic, Kallen has outdone herself. The ballroom is decorated with pumpkins lining the walls, the candles within their carved faces casting eerie shadows across the dance floor. Bats flutter across the ceiling, and low-hanging, flickering black candles sit above the heads of the dancers. Aerial entertainers are performing from ribbons wrapped around their bodies, and shimmering women stand to the side dancing with flames moving over their bodies. And presiding over all of it is Kallen atop a golden throne.

"We don't make a move until we see him," Ava reminds me as she watches my eyes zero in on Kallen. She wears a red dress, and atop her head, two devil horns stick out of a crown of black flowers. Her long white hair is pin-straight down her back. Her green eyes survey the crowd as she raises a goblet to her mouth, taking a long drink. People are dancing and laughing all around, either unaware or uncaring of the individual presiding over them. My blood boils at the thought of my sister's body being used as it has been.

(Gods and Monsters- Lana Del Ray)

I feel Ava tug on my hand. "We need to look around. Split up. We'll do a lap and meet here. Try to blend in. Please." I roll my eyes and nod. She frowns for a moment, her head whipping to the right, eyes wide before she blinks and looks back at me.

"What was that?"

She frowns, shaking her head. "I thought I saw someone. . ." She trails off before taking a deep, steadying breath. "Lets do this."

I give her a slight nod and watch her tiny form disappear off to the right, then I allow my body to move to the left. I grab a flute of champagne off the tray of a server going by and slowly move about the crowd of revelers, sipping the bubbly liquid and letting the sweet flavor explode across my tongue.

I feel a hand grab my wrist at the same time I hear the slurred words of a male, "Hey, baby, want to dance?"

Turning around casually I glance down at his fingers where they grip my wrist. "Remove your hand." Disgust rolling through me at the audacity of this man.

He yanks me closer. "Come on, I just want a dance." His rancid breath dances across my cheek. Onyx moves up off my collar bone, emitting a warning hiss, but the drunken man doesn't seem to realize it's a real snake looking at him.

"If you don't step away from me I will force you to," I say quietly.

The man looks at me in confusion for a moment before his eyes harden with anger. "Stop being a fucking bitch," he sneers and squeezes my wrist as hard as he can. I shrug, and Onyx lashes out, striking the man's face before returning to my neck just as quickly. The man drops my wrist, clutching his bleeding face in horror.

I allow myself to crowd his space, leaning down to his ear. "You know my issue with men? You all think you are owed something. You take and take and take. You might ask if we want to dance, but when we say no and you lash out, it's clear it wasn't a question. It was something you felt you were owed." I don't dare let my magic out, but I can feel it pushing against my skin. The feral rage it drives in me is hot in my body. Instead, I pull him in for a hug, easily seen as a lovers' embrace, and let both snakes bite down hard on him. "Women don't owe you shit. If anything, men owe us. After all, without us, you would be absolutely nothing." I pull away and dissolve back into the crowd before his body slumps to the floor.

"You were supposed to blend in, not kill someone," Ava hisses as she walks up beside me.

I shrug. "I'm tired of letting men do shit like that."

She groans and takes a sip of her own drink. The music pulses around us, the bodies on the dance floor writhing, lost in the sultry sounds of Lana Del Ray. No one pays any mind to the collapsed man.

My eyes shift around, trying to find Ciaran. I tentatively press on that spot that used to hold our bond, but it remains devastatingly empty. Panic is starting to claw at my chest; if he's not here, I'm at a loss on how to find him. I don't know if I'll survive much longer without him.

Kallen

Magic leaves a mark. Once it's touched you, you'll always know it. So, the moment Astrea and her friend walk in, I'm aware. From my perch, I can see her trying to blend in, but women like us don't blend. We weren't made to blend; we were made to rule. I have respect for her, and in a different life, we might have been friends, but without that magic, I cannot get back to my mate. Cannot continue my revenge. Which, unfortunately, makes us enemies.

I take a sip of my champagne and continue to watch her. She's struggling to control the magic, even from here I can see that. My eyes catch on the small girl she's brought along. Her magic isn't of this place, it reeks of Hell. It's simmering under her skin, an unstable amount of it. She's ready to detonate, and magic like that takes no prisoners. She smiles at Astrea and takes another sip of her own drink. Again, in another life, these two could have been close with me. For a moment, that thought leaves me with anger and more rage toward the ones who cursed me and my mate. Who forced me onto this path of revenge.

My mood spoiled, I stand up and exit the room quietly, heading to the back bedroom where Ciaran awaits.

Ciaran

Time has no meaning anymore. I could not tell you

what day it is or time aside from it being night. My body feels broken down from the magic constantly invading my body. Pain is the only thing I know now. Physical and emotional.

Standing in the room Kallen has forced me into. I let my gaze soften until my eyes shut. My mind is dark. I am tired. The relentless scratching on the wall in my mind. The constant fighting. Sometimes, I can feel emotions that aren't mine. The devastation they leave as they rip through me is like a tsunami. I want to give up, to just let that oily black magic take me, but something won't let it. No matter how much I beg to be free, it won't allow me to drift away.

"Ciaran." A voice breaks through the haze in my mind. "Ciaran, you are going to need to wake up, my love."

I want to open my eyes, but I can't. I can only tilt my head into the darkness of my mind, toward where that voice is coming from. *I'm tired.*

"I know you are. But she needs you, Ciaran." I feel warmth spread down that rock wall in my mind. *CRACK.* A small amount of golden light leaks through, so bright I can sense it behind my closed eyes. Another crack echoes through my mind, and that light floods my brain, my body, my soul. All lit up in the darkness.

"My son," I feel hands on either side of my face. "I'm sorry to do this to you." She kisses me on my forehead, and then the real pain begins as those runes etched on my head begin to burn away the dark magic that's invaded my veins.

Astrea

A gasp leaves my mouth and I clutch at my chest in pain, the champagne flute dropping from my hand and shattering across my feet.

"Astrea? What's wrong?" Ava moves into my vision, grabbing my arm to steady me.

"Ciaran," I huff out. "It's the bond. Something is happening."

Pain swims across my body as the bond awakens again. I can *feel* him again. The burning in my veins belongs to his veins. The suffocating feeling in my head belongs in his head. My whole body aches. The music around us is muffled as the pain overtakes my whole being. Tears stream down my face uncontrollably and Ava can barely hold my body weight up as I sink to my knees on the cool marble floor.

Kallen

The music has faded to a dull sound as I move to open the door to the bedroom Ciaran is in.

"Come on, pet, we have a show to put on." But the moment I walk in, I know I've lost him. I can smell his mother's reeking magic throughout the room, and those runes etched on his head are glowing, the protection spell burning off my magic. His eyes may be vacant, but I no longer hold him. Something else does.

Stepping over the threshold of the room, I feel my body freeze, suspended by magic that's not my own. Panic worms its way into my chest as flashbacks of my previous life invade my brain, images of being held against my will flooding me.

A female voice enters the room. "He's alive." And from my right, I see a shade step out of the shadows, ringed in blinding light. Shades, unlike spirits, hold their physical form when haunting this plain. Fury burns through me at the sight of someone from the family that betrayed me.

Kara Carmine.

"What?" I breathe out.

I watch as she moves forward, assessing me. "Your mate. His soul didn't move on. He still lives. We made sure he lived."

The world stops. My breathing goes ragged. "You're lying," I hiss.

She shrugs. "I'm trying to make right what happened all those years ago. But I assure you, he lives."

"You can't make it right! They killed him because we wouldn't allow our power to be used for whatever they deemed necessary," I say harshly.

"You're right. They did that. And it wasn't fair to you or him. But that doesn't make it okay, what you did after."

I let out a long laugh. "It was your ancestors who provided me with that power. They all but gave me permission to become what I am."

She has a sad smile on her face that makes me sick. "We never should have given you that power; without balance, you were never going to survive it. And for that, I am sorry. I know you won't stop hunting Astrea and my son for that magic, but I also know you want your mate so badly, it kills you each day to be without him. So, now you have a choice. Go find your mate or go take that magic back."

My empty chest heaves. *He lives.* I touch that place he used to reside, but I still feel nothing. The gamble I would be taking walking away from my magic on the word of my enemy would be huge. But if he lives, it would be worth it. I never wanted that magic, never wanted anything other than him. I was not made for this world without him. But giving up on the revenge that has kept you warm for so long is like trying to pump poison from your veins with no antidote in sight.

My body shakes with the effort of pushing against the

magic she is using to restrain me, making me want to scream out in frustration. Kara might not be the Carmine who eventually betrayed me, but she is still a Carmine, and I will never fully trust one again. My rage and grief simmer below the surface, and the hold she has on me waivers.

"You know, Kara, I may not be able to hurt you, given you're already dead, but your son is flesh and blood. I could carve him to pieces and make you watch." I push against her magic again, my hand now able to move. I smile viciously and keep pushing the magic out, slowly breaking it down. Kara's face holds alarm but also a sadness that makes me want to throw up. I fucking hate pity. I will never regret what I've become, because what I've become has allowed me to survive.

She moves between me and her son, blocking his body from me. As if she can stop me. "I know you are angry. And I truly cannot imagine what it would be like to lose your mate as you did." She shakes her head. "No one should suffer that way." My other hand becomes free of the spell as she steps toward me, and I let out a feral hiss when her ghostly hand reaches for my forehead. "So let me show you what I've seen." When she presses her two fingers to my forehead, the room disappears, and I'm thrown into her vision.

I feel tears streaming down my face as the small part of me that has been hopelessly empty pulses briefly. And I feel horror push into my soul when I see everything else she's seen of the future. Abruptly, she pulls her hand from me, and the magic she had around me drops. I collapse to my knees panting, my eyes wild as I clutch my chest, my skin still buzzing from the residue of her magic.

I look up at her as she kneels to my level. "Why? Why would they invade now?"

"Because we took something long ago that did not belong to us." She says.

I shake my head, as my whole world is suddenly turned upside down. "So, you'll just let me leave? After everything I've done to your son and Astrea?"

She shrugs again. "You'll find a way to make amends in the end, I have no doubt about that. After all, you know what I've seen. You know what's coming. You and your mate will be needed before the end."

I nod, slowly edging myself toward the window that leads out into the backyard, never taking my eyes off the shade in front of me. As I reach the window, I pause before leaping out. "They will never allow them to be together. Those covens. They may have followed me for now, but they won't forever. They are more powerful and have more control than you know."

She nods, but I shake my head, it's evident she is pacifying me. That despite her post-apocalyptic vision of the future she still believes her son and Astrea will win against the covens. "You don't understand. Something or someone is controlling their leader. They are dangerous. They have a grimoire—they have access to old magic. Magic that I don't think any of us want unleashed."

Her vision goes hazy for a moment before she refocuses on me. "They are tampering with magic that shouldn't have been touched." Her breath shudders. "Thank you. I will pass it along to my son. But why warn us?"

"Because you offered me mercy by telling me my mate is alive. Despite what I did to your son and Astrea, I would never wish what that coven has planned upon anyone. And I don't think you would want what happened to me to happen to them. If you truly are remorseful."

"So, why were you working with them?" Her anger is palpable, laced with confusion.

I shrug. "They were a means to an end. And I had that magic a lot longer than Astrea. Had I gotten it, my first act would have been to kill them all. She's not powerful enough yet, Ciaran isn't powerful enough yet, to take them on." I glance over at him, the runes shining gold. "I imagine he's her balance. That's clever, building it into her mate. I hope it's enough." And before she can ask any more questions, I launch myself out into the night to find my mate.

TWENTY-FIVE

Nothing will ever be more imporant than a mate.
Not magic.
Not revenge.
Anyone who says otherwise is a fool who has
never known that love.

– Kallen

Astrea

The pain in my chest eases and Ava pulls me to my feet again. Now that Kallen is no longer presiding over the room, the air seems to grow anticipatory. Partygoers suddenly standing still, waiting for something. Outside, thunder still rumbles, the electric feel of the storm adding to the tension in the room. A mousy, brown-haired woman walks out into the center of the room and raises her hands above her head, calling attention to herself. I grab Ava's hand and pull her back, deeper into the shadows.

"Shit," I mutter. Ava looks at me in question. "That's

Cordelia Fairmore. She was supposed to be dead." I am still desperately searching the faces in the crowd for Ciaran's. The bond is fully awake and vibrating in my chest now, but I won't relax until I can see him with my own two eyes, not just feel him. All around us, the crowd presses inward toward Cordelia.

"Sisters! Brothers! I thank you for coming tonight. For years, we have stayed in the shadows. For years, we have fought and scraped by. Lived a half-life. One that we built off the ruins of the mistakes of the founding families." Murmurs of agreement ripple throughout the ballroom.

I frown at Ava. "She's part of those same families. Who is she kidding?"

"But no more! We are done living in the gutters, living off scraps they throw at us. We will take this city, and anyone who isn't with us is against us." She stops and surveys the room. At one point, Cordelia was beautiful, but now, she looks sunken in, her body moving in jerky motions that don't seem entirely her own. "We will help pave the way for a new age of magic."

"Something isn't right," Ava murmurs, tilting her head to the side as she studies the witch.

"No shit," I hiss. "She looks like one bad mushroom trip away from being institutionalized."

But Ava shakes her head. "Someone is controlling her." She takes a deep breath, eyes flaring. "That scent is not of this world."

Before I can say anything, Cordelia's voice echoes out across the ballroom. Her dark eyes land on Ava and I standing in the shadows, and a manic smile plasters itself on her face. "And just the witches who will help us. Astrea Mori, come forward, dear. And bring that little friend with you." She snaps her fingers, and from behind, I sense a witch and vampire flank us.

"Shit," I mutter again. Ava and I step forward into the light of the room. "I have no interest in helping you with whatever this is, Cordelia. I'm here for my mate, that's all."

She smiles at us, the gesture not reaching her cold eyes. "Yes. Your mate. I'm pleased we won't have to hunt you both down. Everyone we need is all in the same room. I'm looking forward to seeing how your powers serve us."

The closer we get to her, the more I can smell the stench of decaying flesh wafting from her. Her skin, up close, is a mottled gray and her hair appears to be delicately placed to hide the areas where it's falling out.

"You were not meant to come back, Cordelia." Ava says. "You won't last long like this; you have to know that."

She turns her dead eyes on Ava. "And you, *princess*, someone has been looking very hard for you, my dear. I'll be excited to return you to him." She cackles. I frown, glancing at Ava whose face is cold and unyielding.

Sensing danger, Buttercup and Onyx shift off my body, their movement spawning an audible gasp through the room. No longer masking my magic, I allow it to move across my body. "I don't think we'll be serving you, ever."

(Madness-Ruelle)

The laugh she lets out grates on my nerves, snapping the little patience I have left. My magic shoots out and drops the witch and vampire closest to us, and their lifeless bodies fall to the floor. The old witch growls at me, in the same moment snapping her fingers, and I feel magic falling on us like dust.

It's Ava who moves first, and when her magic unfolds, I take a step backward in utter awe at the raw power. Her whole body is shimmering with it as it drips off her like honey. She's a far cry from the person I've been staying with the past month.

"I'm not sure where you gained the knowledge of that spell, Cordelia, but you won't win this," she says before turning to look at me, her face pale and almost frantic. "I'll keep them at bay—they are trying to trap you. Find Ciaran." She begins to chant, and all around us, I see runes popping up. I don't stay to take it all in; instead, I go to follow that pulsing bond.

Three vampires step out into my path, but Onyx is quick to strike, taking them out while I push forward. Buttercup veers off and keeps everyone off of Ava, which I expected—the snake has an odd attachment to her. I rip the mask off my face and pull out the blades I had camouflaged on my body. I curse the dress now as I'm trying to fight my way through vampire after vampire. The witches seem intent on stopping Ava, but so far, none have been able to touch her. Her magic is too strong, and any that get close, Buttercup devours. Ava's magic is something I've never felt before, and I make a note to ask my friend just what she is hiding.

Skidding to a stop in the chaos, I close my eyes and attempt to search through the bond to find Ciaran's location. Unfortunately, the lack of movement allows more vampires, and now a few witches, to move in behind me. The witches are using magic, trying to whittle away at my own.

"Are you sure you want to do this?" I ask, holding up one hand gloved in smoke and black lightning. None of them say a word, so I just shrug. "Your funeral." My magic unfolds around me, the ground cracking under my feet, dark fissures shooting out towards the bodies in front of me.

Screams are cut short as my magic takes on a life of it's own destroying anyone in it's path.

As the last vampire drops dead at my feet I see a figure step out from the room located behind Kallen's throne. "Ciaran." His name falls off my lips in a desperate plea. He is wearing dark jeans and a white T-shirt, his hair braided back, those runes on his head shining. He pulls the sword from his back as he looks over at the witch standing in the center of the room, before his eyes fall on Ava and then, finally, on me.

Ciaran

My eyes lock onto my mate's emerald ones. I see the relief flash through them before I feel it shoot down our bond. She looks beautiful standing there covered in blood. Her dress hugs her curvy body; somehow, she's managed to fight her way through the ballroom while wearing it.

I jump down off the dais and move over to her, my magic flaring out anytime someone gets close. Vampires and witches alike go up in flames when they hit that barrier. Screams of agony turn into a symphony, and when I'm finally within arms' length, she rushes to me. I bracket her face with my hands and pull her mouth to mine and kiss her deeply. She tastes like home.

"Ciaran," she whimpers into my mouth. The room around us fades away, and for a brief moment, it's just us. Just the feeling of her in my arms. The bond in my chest is humming with peace finally. After weeks of agony the feeling washes through me like a cooling balm.

I pull back and bow my forehead to hers. "Later, *kamerat*. We need to focus." And just like that, the battle comes roaring back in. "We need to get to Ava." She nods, determination spread across her freckled face. But before she pulls from me I see something *else* flash over her, something that is unnerving and worry tugs at my chest.

She moves back away from me, her face now alight with her magic She lets out a deep growl as her eyes snag on the witches and vampires around us. More witches have appeared, and they now seem to be doubling their efforts in the spell they are attempting to cast. Even from this far, I can see Ava is starting to falter; the magic she is pouring out isn't sustainable. Even for someone like her. Astrea and I begin working our way toward her. A never-ending stream of vampires impedes our path, and every now and again, I can feel new magic testing the boundary Ava is holding for us.

My sword cuts through a minion of my fathers, his uniform still on from the prison. His warm blood sprays my face as his head rolls across the floor. Another rushes towards me, meeting the same demise at the end of my blade. My mate moves fluidly, her own blades cutting through another guard. My body is vibrating from the scent of blood and magic around us so I don't notice that Astrea has slowed down next to me, her body now a few steps back.

"Ciaran, we need to hurry. Something is wrong." She is panting just behind me. "This feels too much like when we were at my family home." Her snakes have retreated closer to us, but both are sluggish, their movements mirroring Astrea's. I pull her close, pushing my own magic into her the best I can without draining myself. My mother warned me not to push too hard while our magic is still so untested. But my purpose, according to her, was to ground and sustain Astrea's own magic. So I try to push some towards her, to grant her more strength.

Astrea sends out more of her magic, that glittering black lightning taking down a few witches. But it doesn't stop them from casting, the fallen bodies quickly replaced by others. We continue to fight our way toward Ava, close enough now I see it the moment she burns out. Her eyes snag mine, and she mouths, "Sorry," before they roll back into her head and she drops. The shield she created for us drops with her, and the entire brunt of the magic this new coven is casting hits us both full force.

Astrea

I watch Ava fall in slow motion, the last of her magic winking out in a flash. As her small body crumples on the marble floor, the witches she's been holding back are released and their magic suddenly assaults us. The force of it barreling into my body like a freight train. I grit my teeth against the onslaught of it and press my body against Ciaran. We stand back-to-back, the vampires crowding in on us, each of us utterly spent. Our magic is barely hanging on. My hands are slick with blood and tendrils of my hair have fallen out of the braid and now hang in my face. Those spelled blades drip with blood and glow from the amount of death they have caused this evening, each slain enemy feeding their hunger.

The finality of the situation hits me. "I love you," I say. Nipping at my own magic is the spell the coven is casting. "Without Ava, we don't have a chance, there are too many of them. We are too spent," I say, feeling sweat bead at my brow.

"Don't you say that" Ciaran growls. "We are getting out of this." He throws out a long arc of golden light, disintegrating a vampire who was charging us. But I feel his body sag with it. His magic is too new for him to continue to use it at this pace. The smell of burning flesh is ingrained in the air from our magic. The screams of those vampires and witches echo through the ballroom. But it's still not enough.

The doors to the far left open violently in an explosion of flame, pulling everyone's attention to it. A whimper of relief escapes my lips as I see Drago and Shadow emerge through the dense smoke. Both in dark jeans, Drago has his white button-up shirt rolled up on his forearms, while Shadow wears his leather jacket over a black T-shirt. Flames wreath both of his hands. Behind them, as the smoke clears, I can see more dropped bodies. Witches and vampires alike are dead. Drago's death magic is potent in the air, his own hands blackened by dark veins disappearing under the white shirt.

This is the man people fear, the one who has held the criminal underworld in a vice grip. That even Alexi didn't dare cross.

The room pauses collectively as the two predators stand against the backdrop of the slaughter. Cordelia glares at the two of them, rage contouring her face into something inhuman. Drago looks bored as he cracks his neck, his eyes never leaving hers.

"This isn't your fight." Cordelia hisses. Her voice betrays the fear that is now worming it's way into her.

Drago raises his eyebrow, "anything that happens in this city is my fight. That has never changed, *witch*." He doesn't spare any of us a glance, as if the room isn't full of people waiting to kill us all. "Do you really want to try and go against me?" Shadow, however, sweeps his gaze around the room. I watch as he zeroes in on Ava's crumpled form. Those whiskey-colored eyes suddenly shift to a glowing gold.

Ciaran mutters a curse a second before Shadow unleashes himself in fire so bright, I have to shield my eyes.

When the light dims behind my closed lids, I reopen them and find standing in the remains is a golden dragon. He stretches his massive wings out and shakes his golden-scaled head. Each wing fades from gold to black at the very tips, and his long neck has whirls of black between each scale. His wings brush the ceiling of the ballroom. His claws dig into the ground, causing the foundation to crack under them. He lets out a roar, and the building trembles around us. He's going to bring the whole building down, if not by his size, then by the power he holds.

"Holy shit," I breathe out. I watch, transfixed by him as he lets molten fire pour from his mouth. Like lava from a volcano, its destruction on our enemies is catastrophic. His sole focus is on Ava's crumpled form. We are all but forgotten as the witches move to try and contain him with magic, but Drago is there letting that terrifying power leach life from them. Their bodies fall like husks. Cordelia is screaming in rage, but no one is listening to her now. It's utter chaos as the two move through the room.

The magic holding Ciaran and I drops, and I feel the connection to my power flood back. All around us, vampires flee the dragon and Drago. My magic unfolds and I allow the snakes to ghost from my body. I watch, with a sick satisfaction, as Onyx squeezes a witch so hard, she bursts, the gore covering his ink-black scales. A manic laugh bursts from my lips as the few who remain alive flee from us. I make a move to go after them, blades raised to cut them all down, but Ciaran grabs me.

"Not now. We need to back away slowly." I'm confused by his hushed tones. "Call the snakes back to you. Get them on your body," he whispers as he ever so slowly shifts himself in front of me. And that's when I notice the all-consuming silence that has descended upon the room. No chanting or screaming. No roars. Just silence. The type of silence that descends before a crash of thunder, the kind that leaves you on a knife's edge.

Glancing up, I feel my eyes widen as I see the dragon is now poised over Ava, his lips pulled back in a beastly growl. I don't dare move, don't dare even call the snakes back, despite Ciaran's request. Instead, I send a silent prayer to whatever gods are listening that Shadow doesn't eat us. Or that Buttercup doesn't decide she needs to protect Ava.

Drago calmly shifts between us, hands relaxed at his side, so his body provides a barrier between us and Shadow's dragon. "You've protected her. There are no more threats to her. I need you to give him back now so we can take care of our mate," he says.

The dragon shakes its massive head. "He'll lock us away again." Its voice is so loud and deep, it hurts my ears. My head rings with it. Ciaran crowds me back further, edging us towards the open smoldering remains of the doorway.

"I won't let him keep you away this time." Drago slowly pushes forward, closer to the beast.

It lets out a deep growl. "We need to claim her."

Drago nods his head. "I promise, it'll happen, but not like this. If you don't show him you are nothing to fear, it'll be harder for me to convince him you shouldn't be locked up."

The dragon huffs, smoke billowing from his nostrils. He lowers his massive head toward my friend's prone body, and I stiffen as those teeth near her. Instead of what I fear, I watch in awe as he only nuzzles her before shifting back, and a very naked Shadow drops down unconscious next to Ava.

Silence descends on the room again before I finally look up at Ciaran, "Uh . . . What in the actual fuck was that? No one wanted to tell me we had a motherfucking dragon as a friend?"

———

Drago took Ava and Shadow both back to his home with the assurance he would let us know when they awoke. Ciaran and I made our way back to the safehouse we had been staying in prior. Not having access to Shadow's magic meant we had to drive back, which felt oddly normal. After fighting with magic, seeing your friend shift into a dragon, and watching your magical tattoo snake eat people, driving felt weird. Drago was kind enough to give us his car, which I suppose was better than calling a car service.

That was a week ago. Ciaran and I have spent the week in bed, only getting up to use the bathroom or eat. I would like to say we spent it fucking, but we were both so exhausted, we slept for most of it. Even now, my body still feels run-down, despite the rest we've gotten. But today, I couldn't lie in bed any longer, so instead, I got up, showered, and have been pouring over the grimoire again. We never found my family's book, which makes me nervous, given what the Fairmore witch knew. I have a sneaking suspicion they have it. A nervousness moves up my spine as I think about my grimoire being in the hands of someone else, not just because of the magic but because since the battle I've felt less and less in control of this power. Less like myself. And that scares me.

"Imagine how disappointed I was to wake and not have my mate by my side," Ciaran states behind me. I turn to look at him. His gray sweatpants hang low on his hips, and I bite my lip looking at his shirtless chest. Walking over to me, he plants a kiss on my forehead before grab-bing himself a cup of coffee. "What are you doing, Astrea?"

I take a sip of my own coffee. "We can't just rest forever. We have to find Kallen. And what are we supposed to do about the covens? They won't just let us be, Ciaran. They'll hunt us until they can get this power from us."

He stretches upward, and I can't help my mouth watering a little at the movement. He smirks as if he knows where my mind is at. "I don't think we need to worry about Kallen right now. She found something better than her magic."

Something hot burns through me, an uncontrollable anger rising up, "What's that?" I growl.

He narrows his eyes in concern at the sudden hostility before allowing a smile to move across his face. "Her mate. He lives."

The rage blinks out, leaving me cold. "Wait, what?!"

He shrugs as if he didn't just drop a bomb on me. "His soul is still out there. So, yes, her revenge was important, but her mate was more important."

"How did you figure that out?" I ask, closing the book in front of me, now much more interested in what he has to say.

"My mother. Her shade crossed over—she was the one to help free me. Break whatever hold Kallen had on me. She somehow knew his soul was still here," he says. "They spoke for a while but I was still held by the magic so I'm unclear as to what was said."

I blink at him in utter confusion. "I'm sorry, your dead mother popped in to rescue you, as well as tell our mortal enemy that her mate is still alive? AND she let her go find said mate? You realize how absurd that is?" My anger towards Ciaran's mother grows with each passing moment that she could do something so stupid.

He laughs before moving over to me and wrapping his strong arms around me. I let his scent brush over me, calming me, and throw my arms around his neck. Burrowing my nose into his bare chest.

"Can we talk about the absurdity of this later? I've missed my mate." His voice is low, and it sends shivers down my spine. A low moan escapes me, my body suddenly heating and arousal pools deep within. Sensing what I need, he lifts me up on the countertop, his eyes going red.

"Let me feast." He pulls my leggings off and spreads my legs, his eyes zeroing in on my glistening sex. "Fuck." He spreads my pussy lips open, leaving me feeling vulnerable. "You are so fucking beautiful." He slowly pushes a finger inside me, and I bite my lip to suppress a moan before he adds another.

He bends down and swirls his tongue around my clit, and I throw my head back, letting out a long groan of pleasure. "Yes, just like that," I breathe out, my voice heavy with desire. He continues leisurely licking me and fucking me with his fingers, the pace slow and torturous. "Fucking hell, Ciaran. Please. I need more," I beg as I try to arch my hips into him to gain more friction.

"Tsk, tsk. You know who is in charge here, and right now, Astrea, it's not you." He continues the assault, bringing me to the edge before pulling me back. Sweat drips down my spine and my legs shake. He pulls back and smiles at me. "I think maybe you need some help staying still." I feel it the moment his magic comes out; it intermingles with my own. The golden beams wrap around my arms, keeping my hands bound, unable to touch him. The warmth of it spreads up my body.

He doesn't say anything as he slips his own sweats off, his long cock bobbing out freely.

Pulling me down to the floor, he lifts me up, hovering my entrance above his head before slowly lowering me. Inch by inch, his cock penetrates me. The feeling is so overwhelming, I can barely catch my breath. When I'm fully seated, I open my eyes in time to catch him devouring my body with his gaze.

"Ride me, Astrea. Take your pleasure from me. I want you dripping down my cock. And when we are done, you can clean up the mess you've made on me." Those words alone have me coming undone. I whimper as I shift my hips.

"Release me. Please. Let me touch you." I hold out my bound wrists, encircled by his golden magic.

He grins wickedly. "I don't think I will. I think you need to find it without your hands."

I growl at him, and the snakes take their shadow form and move off my body, one snapping those gold bonds with its jaw while the other moves down and wraps around Ciaran's wrists, dragging them upward. "Mine," I hiss, leaning down and licking up his neck. He groans at the feeling, his eyes rolling back in his head.

"Do you want my blood, little *kamerat?*" he asks, his voice husky as I rock my hips back and forth, and I moan out a yes. "So fucking take it."

It's all the encouragement that I need, and I bite into him savagely. It's not delicate or pretty, my dull teeth ripping at his skin. His spicy blood flowing into my mouth feels like a hit of Eufori. I greedily drink him down, desperate for more as he pumps up into me. My release slams into me in a sudden wave, and my knees scrape against the floor as I keep riding him, desperate to keep the feeling going.

Once the feeling starts to fade, I release his neck from my dull teeth, and my snakes release his hands. He grips my hips hard, and I feel him thrust into me over and over until his hot release paints me. I slouch forward as we finish, my body burning all over.

I allow my eyes to travel up to his face, and he gives me a wickedly devious smile. "Clean me up, mate. You've made such a mess of my cock."

My pussy flutters at the words. "With pleasure." Pulling off him, I move down to his spent cock and take him into my mouth, moaning at the taste of both of us. Once satisfied, I sit back up and smile at him. "I love you, Ciaran."

"I love you, *kamerat*."

"Are you ever going to tell me what that means?" I ask as I curl up on his side.

"It means 'mate.'"

I look up at him in confusion. "But you've always called me that. Even before the spell."

He smiles and kisses me on the forehead. "It's because I always knew."

TWENTY-SIX

Ciaran

We stay wrapped together on the kitchen floor until the sun sets and the room grows dark. The floor is cool against my back, albeit a little hard. Finally stirring, Astrea stands up, stretching out her body. She's silhouetted against the night sky, the moon casting a glow on her. I bite my lip and hold back from launching myself at her. My cock hardens again at the thought. Looking over her shoulder at me, Astrea smirks, hunger flashing in her eyes.

"We need to talk first. As much as it pains me to deny myself more of your pleasure," I say as I also move to stand, grabbing my discarded pants to pull them on. I watch

Astrea pull her clothes back on and move back to her original spot at the counter. "Have you found anything helpful there yet?" I ask, motioning to the old grimoire. I search for my discarded coffee before realizing it's most likely freezing. I dump it out and begin a new cup, the intoxicating aroma blending with the scent of our sex and blood.

She shrugs. "Not really. Just that your magic balances mine out, and once bonded, one can't exist without the other. I get the impression your family made it as a failsafe. On the off chance the power did awaken, the covens wouldn't be able to do what they did to Kallen." She chews on her lip for a moment before continuing. "I think balance is important, this magic feel. . . alive under my skin, uncontrollable even. So I think we need to figure out how to bond our magic not only so it can't be taken but so I can keep control of myself."

I push towards her, gathering her in my arms for a moment. "You won't lose yourself like Kallen did."

"I did though, Ciaran, the things I did when they took you. . ." she trails off. I can't see her face, but I can feel the tension in her body.

"Astrea. I will never judge you for what you did. There are moments in life where we make choices that we would never make in any other time. I know who you are, Astrea. Despite the magic you have, I know you're a good person. We'll figure this out." I pull back and kiss the top of her head before looking in her shimmering green eyes. She offers a tentative smile before pulling back and leaning against the countertop again.

"So, what were the witches doing? If they can't separate us or kill us, what is the purpose?" I ask.

"I think we have bigger players on the board controlling

the pieces than just Cordelia." Drago's voice enters the kitchen just before he walks in from the shadows. While Shadow can portal, Drago uses shadows to move from space to space. Another talent that makes him incredibly powerful. I'm suddenly very thankful I didn't allow us to go for round two. The smirk on his face, however, tells me he can scent what just transpired between us. A feral, unhinged, side of me hates that he can smell her, and it takes everything in my power to tamp down the urge to rip him apart.

"Cordelia has tracked you somehow; you'll need to leave soon," he says. He continues talking, despite the smell and the carnage across my neck left by Astrea's teeth. And ignoring the growl that I unconsciously let out. "She's rallying her coven. They don't want to make the same mistake. They aren't sure if you have Ava or Shadow with you, and they can't risk running into them again. As I'm sure you can imagine, they don't particularly want to face a dragon again. Or Ava."

"What is she?" Astrea asks. Pushing up next to me, grabbing my hand. Drago shakes his head, a refusal to answer anything.

My mate drops it, a huff of annoyance coming out. "Where are we supposed to go?" Astrea asks, her grip on my hand tight. The only indication that she might be uncomfortable.

"I have plenty of safehouses; you can go between those. They are outside of the city, so hopefully less likely to be found," he says. "And if you keep moving, it'll be harder for her to track you. Or whoever is helping her."

I bristle. "We aren't just going to run."

He shoots me a look before pushing his hands into his pants pockets. "Have you figured out how your magic helps each other?"

The silence between the two of us is answer enough. "So, you go, figure it out. Find out how to protect yourselves and leave the covens to us for now."

"I think they have my family grimoire," Astrea says. "It's the only way I can think of that they would have access to this type of magic. Even Ciaran's hints at that. The Fairmores weren't the least powerful, but they certainly didn't have access to what my family did."

Drago nods in agreement. "I'll talk to Ava about that. She has some theories."

I frown. "What are her theories, exactly?"

"I'm not at liberty to share those yet. If they pan out, she'll tell you," he says.

A growl forms low in my throat. "You're putting us at risk by not sharing."

He shakes his head. "No. I'm not. Either way, you need to learn to use your magic. Either way, you need to avoid Cordelia."

"And if someone else is after us as well?" Astrea pips in.

"Avoid being seen." Drago states.

"Fine," I concede. "Astrea and I train. You, Ava, and Shadow figure out what the fuck is going on with Cordelia."

"And we just ignore Kallen?" Astrea asks, venom dripping from her voice.

"Yes," I say. "She's been through enough. Decades of torture being cut off from her mate and believing he's dead? That's punishment enough. She won't search us out again."

Drago nods, but Astrea huffs out a frustrated sigh. "She certainly left us with a mess to deal with."

Pushing forward, Drago moves back toward the shadows he originally stepped out of. "I'll contact you if we find anything." With no goodbye, he vanishes into the dark, the apartment settling like he was never there.

Looking at my mate, I pull her into me before kissing her forehead. "Come on. Let's go figure this shit out so we can come home."

EPILOGUE

Should they bind together, hope is not lost.
We've created a spell.
A failsafe.
One that will still give us what we deserve.

-Mori Family Grimoire

Ava [illegible]

([illegible] M[illegible])

W[illegible] still out there, [illegible]mpting to find Ciaran an[illegible] taken everything in me to remain in this [illegible] friends need [illegible]—they haven't seen what's coming. I have. I know who hunts us, who wants us, and I know the life I've built here is a tinder box ready to spark at any moment. Once it all comes out, the life I've created, the one I've fought so hard for, will burn around me, and I'm worried we won't survive.

A groan next to me pulls my attention, and I look down at my mate thrashing in his sleep. I place my hand across his forehead, smiling sadly at how my touch calms him in a way it never has when he's awake.

"Ava." I whip my head over to the door where Drago stands, his arms folded across his massive body. He jerks his head for me to follow him.

I slowly and quietly stand, slipping myself out of the bed to follow him out. I take in his form, silhouetted by the fireplace, as I enter the living room. He looks exhausted. My hands itch to touch him, to hold him. But we made a deal long ago: if we didn't all agree, we wouldn't be together. Despite the pain we feel. We couldn't do that to Shadow. Not after everything.

"He's not getting better," I say. "The nightmares keep getting worse."

He lets out a long sigh. "We've done all we can for him right now."

"Not all," I say hesitantly. *You and I haven't bonded. Haven't tried to force him awake to claim me as well, to claim us.* I don't say it, but I can tell he knows what I'm thinking.

"We can't do that. Not yet."

I only nod at him before sitting down on the couch.

He continues talking. "I warned Ciaran and Astrea; they've moved to the outskirts of the city. Cordelia's covens found them again."

My stomach bottoms out. The newly formed covens have access to magic that I have only seen in one other place. My home. And that type of magic comes with a heavy price. The spell they were attempting to cast is similar to the spell used on Kallen and her mate, however, this spell keeps the hosts alive so they will have unlimited access to the powers. Ciaran's magic works because of Astrea's. He balances her darkness. One without the other will no longer work. It would mean a life of captivity for both of them. At least until they die from the power drain.

The two of us watch the rain fall over Gothic Grove. Worry gnaws at me, both for my friends and my mates. "Cordelia saw you, Ava. She saw your magic. You'll be her next target."

"I know," I say in defeat. I haven't told him what she said to me, that *someone* was looking for me. "But I couldn't allow anything to happen to Astrea or Ciaran. It was worth the risk."

Another heavy sigh escapes him. "I hope you're right because right now, it certainly doesn't feel worth it. It feels like I have one mate spiraling out of control and my other mate in danger. Neither of which are bonded, might I add, making this all the riskier."

I slowly walk to him and slip my hand into his. His whole body relaxes, and I close my eyes as his scent invades my nostrils. "Nothing will happen, Drago. We'll be okay."

At this moment, I'm thankful he cannot read my mind. Thankful he cannot see what I have, because if he could, he would know the lie I just let fall from my mouth for what it is.

TRANSLATIONS

Kamerate mate (Norwegian)
Rakkani my beloved (Finnish)

Chapter One

Aelius

Immortality is boring and predictable.

Pussy all feels the same.

Ass all looks the same.

And blood is only a means of survival now.

It's fucking boring.

The current pussy I'm in was a find out of boredom. A girl meandering alone through the woods that for a moment I thought could spike my interest in the hunt once again. Unfortunately, she turned into another blood whore the moment she caught sight of me, never even putting up a fight. How fucking typical.

I look down at the female impaled on my cock as she screams into the evening sky, uncaring that a party rages just on the other side of the trees. Judging by the amount of drugs I can taste in her blood she would have fucked me in the middle of the party with little care. Not that I'm one to kink shame.

"You are so fucking good, yes yes yes!" Her shouts get increasingly more annoying. I shove her face harder into the ground hoping it'll shut her up so I can finish but it doesn't seem to help, it actually seems to only spur her on.

Where the fuck was this enthusiasm when I was trying to hunt her?

For a few years now, my twin and I have thrown these parties to provide a break in the monotony of our lives, now that we no longer live with our family. It also gives me a chance to feed the beast within; the one who thirsts to hunt our prey.

It achieved the goal at first; now, however, the parties all feel the same. The hunt no longer appeals to me, despite my twin thinking otherwise, I know he worries about my obsessive tendencies. But truly nothing has held my attention lately; everything feels fucking dull and lifeless.

My hips snap forward as I continue to fuck her, my cock barely rallying now. The wind kicks up slightly and I lift my face to it catching a mouthwatering scent. A scent that shoots through me, instantly hardening my cock. My eyes open wide as I search for the source of the intoxicating aroma, needing to see who it belongs to. A flash of dark hair is all I'm given as I see someone flee the tree line but it's enough to have me rip my cock free of the girl and let my cum splatter across her back. She lets out a squeal in annoyance as she fumbles forward but I simply don't care.

The alluring scent of smoke and nutmeg drifting through the woods, lures me away from the pathetic creature on the dirt floor to this female, who is so clearly out of place. An outsider, watching and waiting. Her eyes wide as she takes in the scene before her. From this distance I can see her fiddle with something in her ear before she frowns and removes a small device, crushing it with her boot l heel when she drops it to the earth.

My mouth waters at the thought of how delectable she would taste, and my cock hardens once more at the idea of how it would feel to slide my fangs into that milky white skin while I pull wanton moans from those full lips she is currently nibbling on.

Stalking my prey, I move forward until I'm just behind her.

She's everything I've wanted. Even having never spoken to her I know she'll fill a void in me.

Already I can feel the obsession taking root. She will be mine by the end of this party.

Mine.

Mine.

Mine.

"What do we have here? A lost little rabbit?"

Deianira

Twilight in Hell is my favorite time. The normally suffocating heat of the day transitions to the comfortably warm air of the evening. The streets are in flux, with the last few people heading home from their day jobs while others are heading out to start their night. People smile and say hello. It's peaceful compared to where I come from. And one of the reasons I decided this is where I needed to live.

Tonight, however, does not feel peaceful.

The normally pleasant night air feels heavy. The humidity presses in around me as I watch the partygoers stumble around the property. The full moon bathes the front yard in an eerie glow, as if she knows the evening's intent. It doesn't help I'm feeling unnaturally settled after having watched the man in the woods fuck that girl so hard. I have never been a voyeur but in that moment the temptation to watch him finish was overwhelming.

"You're taking too long." The voice comes from the small com link I wear in my ear, covered by my dark wig. "People are going to wonder why you are just standing there."

I roll my eyes, "No one is going to notice or care." I grumble as I try to wipe my sweaty palms on the satin leotard I'm wearing. The original costume L picked felt ridiculous and a little bit of a kick to the gut if I'm being honest. A fucking witch.

So instead, in an act of rebellion, I allowed one of the other girls to dress me, which I'm now deeply regretting. The white bunny ears are already squeezing my head too tight in combination with the dark wig. And the stupid puffy tail on my ass feels ridiculous. The squeeze of the built-in corset to the leotard is the only saving grace, giving my small chest a face lift.

Compared to my sisters I was the one that got the least amount of curves. I've always been envious of my younger sisters and the way their bodies are built. Me? I'm a fucking bean pole that needs restrictive clothing to give me any cleavage.

"Deianira, hurry up." The voice says again. For a moment the name confuses me until the wind brushes my hair against the fresh brand on my neck. "This is what happens when you send a techie out."

With the brand came the name. And with the name came this new life and the beginning of the end to my old one. Tonight is one step closer to cutting that life from my soul.

My eyes trace up the old mansion just beyond. The stone building is home to my two targets, or at least it's the dwelling that's public knowledge. The knowledge that I've memorized backward and forward.

Identical twins.

Aelius and Kalani. Previous Heirs to the throne of Divinity, abdicated the throne to their younger sister, Rhea who is currently engaged to the presiding King of Hell's son. The brothers now run the cartel in Divinity, running drugs being their main source of income.

The only difference between the twins, tattoos included, is eye color. Aelius has a deep blue, almost black. Kalani has a light blue with a streak of hazel. Between the two, Kalani is seen as the more stable. Aelius has a history of killing his lovers and leaving their bodies to be found by authorities.

The last Daughter to attempt to infiltrate was never seen again.

I run the facts over in my mind again and again, skipping quickly over the last one. Nothing good has ever come from thinking of one's death. I have no interest in starting now.

"L says not to forget this is a long game, don't get too over eager. Make them want you." The annoyed voice in my ear states.

"I fucking know." I hiss. "I know how to seduce someone."

A quiet laugh is the only response I receive. I growl low and grab the commlink from my ear, cracking it apart under my heel on the forest floor. "Fucker." I mutter. The words did their job though, my nerves were shot before this and now the doubt is seeded. Even if L hand-picked me.

"Why me?" I ask as L heats up the brand.

"Because you won't be tempted by the vampires. You have a history with them." She strokes my face gently. "You know what they are capable of."

"But I'm not trained in the art of seduction like some of the other girls."

L smiles at me, "Which is what will make you perfect."

A fresh breeze picks up blowing hot air down my bare skin and sweeping the memory away. Sweat starts to build up under the wig making my scalp itch. I resist the urge to fidget with it

"What do we have here? A lost little rabbit?" The sultry voice freezes my body even as the sound sends shivers down my spine. My mouth goes dry as one of the twins' steps in front of me. The dark grey eyes seem to stand out against his sun kissed skin, they have a dangerous edge that has my body wanting to flee. And when they shift to red, a madness seems to set in, a madness that seems to bring my own out. As if he too has a creature inside him that's begging to play.

His smile is wicked, none of his fangs showing, and eyes hungry as they trail over my body. My boot still rests on the crushed piece of equipment causing my heart to race.

Get it the fuck together.

I blink once before offering a shy smile, "I was just heading into the party."

He tilts his head, a predator assessing his next meal, before he tucks his hands in his pockets and circles around me. His eyes ghost across my skin and I swear he leans in and breathes me in for a moment. My pussy clenches with a need to be filled by this man and my breasts ache. This feeling foreign and unwanted in this moment.

"All alone?"

"What?" I ask momentarily confused by the question.

He laughs, "You're here all alone?"

My own laugh sounds nervous and wrong as I answer. "Yeah, uh. I'm new here so I figured it would be good to check out."

He offers no response but comes to a stand in front of me one last time. The silence builds between us, uncomfortable and full until he finally steps out of the way and gestures towards the house. "By all means, enjoy yourself little rabbit."

I swallow down my nerves and tuck my hair behind my ear before giving him a quick nod. "See you around." I mutter.

"Yes. Yes, you will." It's a dark promise as it spills out of his lips behind me.

Need the rest of their story? Join my Patreon for access to the novella! Trust me, you won't be disappointed in this, spooky, spicy, prequel.

Thank you for reading Ciaran and Astrea's journey. While their story is far from over for now, they are going to take a rest and focus on harnessing their magic behind the scenes.

Craving more?
Make sure to check out Heavy Is The Crown to see what Ava, Drago and Shadow are up to!
Followed by the unhinged novella that follows Kallen and her mate.

Make sure to head to my website and sign up for my newsletter for discounts, previews, preorders and more!
www.authorjageorge.com

ACKNOWLEDGEMENTS AND THANK YOU

First and foremost, I need to thank you for making the leap of faith, dear reader, and dipping into Gothic Grove. As authors we would not be here without people who immerse themselves in our stories. So from the bottom of my heart I thank you for taking the time to read. Without your reviews, and TikToks, and posts our books wouldn't reach anyone. The bookstagram community as a whole is a lifeline for all indie authors. And honestly a lifeline for me as a reader. I never, ever, would have even thought of engaging in this passion again without some key people in that community.

I have so many people who made this book possible. So I want to start with my family. First to my partner, Thomas, who kept asking me if I was still writing. Who would come into the bedroom saying "lets make some more book content". Who listened to my story out loud so that he could be a part of it. He is the sunshine to my grumpy.

I appreciate you and love you so much, thank you.

And to my little banshee, your refusal to sleep allowed me to write the first half of this book at all hours of the night. And to my eldest, for the love of god when you discover these books no you did not. Because I know you, and I know your soul is like mine and we enjoy the dark and gritty. And never ever let anyone tell you that it's wrong to like the darkness. Also, never stop doing jump scares.

My found family also needs thanks:

Serena, you will never know how much your love and support means to me. And while book three is more your baby book one wouldn't have happened without you. And I hope you enjoyed that little word choice I put in just for you. I will be really disappointed if you didn't find it.

Jakey, I don't even know where to start in thanking you. I can't thank you because words don't actually work. So I'll thank you during hockey season by feeding you.

Sam, you created the most beautiful cover but also you let me share parts of Shadow that no one else saw. You were there in voice memos when I struggled and when I just needed to talk. I will be forever grateful we became friends. Honestly when did that happen? Because I can't remember a time when we weren't friends at this point.

To my alpha readers: Kristin Moore (authorkristin-moore) and Mads (breathelesslitpa).

Kristin, I wouldn't have kept pushing without you. Watching your process was so inspirational and I can never thank you enough. And the never ending chaos messages we sent back and forth will be some of my favorite memories.

Mads, honestly I'm not sure I would have shared this story without your encouragement after you read my very first piece I sent you. The formatting and proofing as well was so helpful and lovely. Oh and lets not forget the beautiful TikTok's you created me.

To my lovely smut collective: Mads, Blake, Kelsey, Kenan and Edie. I credit you all for helping me get real creative with the spice. Honestly you guys kept me laughing in moments when I didn't think this book would make it.

To my beta readers: Jakey, Amanda (brewsbooksand-buttes), Charlotte (powers.of.the.pen), and Hayley. This book would not have made it out the front door without the feedback yall provided.

To my OG editor Paisley. Girl. You did this while having a baby. I can never thank you enough. You are a true gem.

And oddly enough to the following Peloton instructors because you got me out of my head long enough to jump back into the story the way it needed to be: Aditi, Kiera Michelle, Jess King, Adrian Williams and Tunde Oyeneyin.

And last. . . to my character Shadow. He started as a side character, just the best friend of Ciaran. But slowly he morphed into my own healing journey. He allowed me to share parts of myself that had been kept locked away for a very long time. He let me voice fears through him that had only ever lived in my head. I'm excited, and terrified, for you to read about him next.

Loved Gothic Grove? Make sure to go leave a review! It is a vital part of being an indie author.

Make sure to connect with JA on social media:

IG: PNWwritingWitch

TikTok: AuthorJA_George

Join Patreon for exclusive sneak peaks, novellas, art and more!

Discord: https://discord.gg/XTUqUYASqe

ABOUT THE AUTHOR

JA lives in the PNW and thrives in spooky season. She can be found with a cup of coffee and kindle in hand most days while wrangling her tiny gremlin humans. She and her partner also have a direwolf, velvet hippo and savannah cat.

She loves all things dark romance and can't imagine life without books.